YOU'RE
MINE NOW

HANS KOPPEL

Translated by Kari Dickson

sphere

SPHERE

First published in Sweden in 2012 as *Kom Ska vi Tycka om Varandra*
by Telegram Bokförlag AB
First published in 2013 by Sphere
This paperback edition published in 2014 by Sphere

A CIP catalogue record for this book
is available from the British Library.

ISBN 978-0-7515-5118-1

Typeset in Horley Old Style by M Rules
Printed and bound in Great Britain by
Clays Ltd, St Ives plc

Papers used by Sphere are from well-managed forests
and other responsible sources.

MIX
Paper from
responsible sources
FSC
www.fsc.org FSC® C104740

Sphere
An imprint of
Little, Brown Book Group
100 Victoria Embankment
London EC4Y 0DY

An Hachette UK Company
www.hachette.co.uk

www.littlebrown.co.uk

YOU'RE
MINE NOW

1

There's a quarter landing halfway up, where the stairs change angle. Erik has fed one of his ropes round the banister upstairs, and is now standing on the ground floor, holding both ends.

His mother watches him with a wine glass in her hand.

'What are you doing?'

She's drunk and her tone is accusing.

'You can't climb here, the banister won't hold you.'

Erik doesn't answer.

'Did you hear what I said? You're too heavy.'

'I wasn't intending to climb.'

'Take the rope down then. Erik, darling, listen to me for once.'

He ties a loop at one end.

'Take it down immediately.'

Erik looks up and then tests it with his body weight.

'You'll damage the banister.'

His mother puts down her wine glass and comes towards him.

'Do what I tell you,' she snaps, and puts out her hand to take the rope.

Erik grabs her arm and twists it up behind her back.

'Ow, what are you doing? Let me go!'

He puts the loop over his mother's head and pulls her up into the air. She struggles to loosen the noose. When she doesn't manage, she kicks and tries to get her feet on to the balustrade in order to take the weight off her body. Erik holds on to her calves and pulls her down while he holds the rope taut.

'How old was I the first time?' he demands.

His mother can't possibly answer. Her eyes are bulging out of their sockets and her face is swollen and red.

'Fifteen,' he tells her. 'You've been doing this for ten years.'

There's a loud crack. It's difficult to tell if it's her neck or the banister that has given way.

His mother's arms and legs spasm as her body lets go. She hangs freely, swinging silently with no resistance, like a pendulum. Erik holds the rope taut as he goes up the stairs, where he ties the end round the banister. Then he sits down on the sofa and watches TV. When the programme has finished, he calls the police and says that his mother has hanged herself. He finds a knife and cuts her down. He sits down on the floor with her lifeless body in his arms. When the police arrive, he's crying.

2

Anna looked at her daughter, who was sitting at the kitchen table, her nose buried in a book, a half-eaten slice of bread in her hand.

'Please can you get a move on, sweetie? Daddy's giving me a lift to Mölle and I don't want to be late.'

Hedda tore her eyes away from the book and looked over at the clock on the wall.

'But then I'll be too early.'

'No, you won't.'

'Yes, I will.'

'Max ten minutes,' Anna insisted. 'That's not a problem, is it? You can look over your homework again.'

'I've already done that,' Hedda retorted.

'Well, if you want a lift, you'll have to fit in with us. That's the way it is.'

'I'd rather cycle then.'

'Fair enough.'

'Hello, I can't cycle when there's practically no air in my tyres.'

Magnus came out of the bedroom. He was buttoning up a shirt that strained over his belly.

'What's up?' he asked.

Anna shook her head.

'Nothing. But if Hedda wants a lift she's going to have to move it.'

'We're not in so much of a rush. It only takes fifteen minutes.'

'Exactly,' agreed his daughter, who had no idea.

'It takes half an hour, at least,' Anna said.

Magnus pulled his chin in.

'Does it?'

'It certainly does. It's fifteen minutes just to Höganäs.'

Magnus relented. In the mornings, he was the one who

smoothed over the ruffles and backed down. In the evening, it was the other way round. Yet another reason why they worked so well together.

'Okay,' he said, turning to their daughter. 'Poppet, listen to your mother.'

'But . . .'

Hedda gave a theatrical sigh and got down from the table with the slice of bread still in her hand. Ten minutes later they dropped her off outside school.

'See you tomorrow then,' Anna said.

'What? Are you staying there overnight?'

'Just the one night. I'll be home again tomorrow. You and Daddy can do something nice together tonight.'

'Okay. Bye then.'

'I'll phone to say good night.'

Hedda closed the car door and walked towards the main building. They watched her with an amused look, until Magnus slipped into first gear and pulled out.

There wasn't much traffic. Most cars were going in the opposite direction, from the residential areas along the northern shore in towards Helsingborg. Anna changed the radio station and turned to look at the sea that opened out at Christinelund. The view was wasted today. A greyish-white sky, dull brown fields. The colourless Skåne winter in November, a month that seemed to last for ever.

'Is the whole editorial team going?' Magnus asked.

'No, just Trude and Sissela.'

'And how is she?'

'Who? Sissela? Fine. Why?'

'Is she still in love?'

Anna had no idea what he was talking about.

'Didn't she meet someone new?'

'That was actually a year ago. And it's over now.'

'Fancy that,' Magnus said, ironically.

He didn't have much time for his wife's boss, who he thought was disturbingly self-centred.

'So she's single again?' he asked, trying not to sound disparaging.

Anna shook her head.

'No, she got back together with her husband.'

'That was quick.'

'A few slamming doors, but not much more.'

'Jesus,' Magnus sighed.

Anna looked at him.

'What do you mean?'

'Well, she could have kept quiet about it. I mean, if it

was nothing, just a little something. Why upset her husband? All I'm saying is that the one who strays has to deal
with the crap themselves. Why burden the poor sod who's
been betrayed with all that rubbish? It's not fair.'

'No,' Anna hesitated. 'Maybe not.'

'Shameless,' Magnus maintained. 'But then she's the
boss.'

'I think she's just restless, has to have something happening all the time. She creates drama for the sake of it.'

'If you decide to stray, I don't want to know.'

'No risk of that. It all seems so messy.'

Magnus laughed.

'Messy?'

'So complicated and tedious. Yuck, no, not my thing.
And in any case, you smell too good.'

'Well, there you go, a quality as good as any other. I'll
have to update my CV.'

'Oof, there's this new guy in sales,' Anna continued, with
a shiver. 'And his breath smells like a dog. Pure ammonia.
And he always invades your personal space when he talks to
you. Touching noses, almost, I swear. And he's so happy and
nice. All you can do really is smile and keep your distance.'

'You should say something.'

'Right,' Anna said.

They took the new road past Viken and didn't have to slow down until they came to Höganäs, where they passed the old publishing house. The business had been bought out many years ago and the new owner soon realised that you couldn't get the best people to relocate here, so he moved the whole operation to Malmö. Anna wondered whether it still existed.

'The car,' Magnus said, interrupting her thoughts.

Anna gave him a blank look and he shrugged.

'I don't know, maybe it's time to get a new one.'

'Why?'

'This one's driven over eight thousand kilometres. It'll start needing repairs soon. I just think it might be wise.'

'And the roof?' Anna asked.

Magnus moved in his seat.

'There's no rush.'

'There isn't?'

'We patched it up. And it hasn't rained since then.'

'The felting is over twenty years old. Magnus, please don't start.'

'Our car is the oldest one on the street,' he said, and sent her an accusing look.

'So?'

Anna looked at him with raised eyebrows.

'Just saying,' Magnus muttered.

'Saying what? That you think we should forget about the roof so we don't need to be ashamed of a car that's only four years old?'

'That's not what I said.'

'We can't do both.'

'I just said there wasn't any rush. The roof is okay.'

'For the moment.'

'We repaired it last summer,' Magnus reminded her. 'It's not likely to leak again.'

Anna filled her lungs and closed her eyes.

'What?' Magnus said, sheepishly.

'The car is working fine, there's—'

'For the moment.'

'—absolutely no reason to get a new one just to keep up with the neighbours. I'm so sick and tired of all that nonsense.'

Magnus didn't say anything. Anna prayed that he wouldn't, that he'd understand it wasn't worth pushing it. She was hoping for too much.

'It's still working fine because it's relatively new,' he

objected. 'And that's why we can still get a good price for it, if we trade it in. If we wait, it will lose value. So we're losing money by keeping it.'

'How come?'

'What do you mean, how come? That's the way it works. If you want to get anything for anything you trade in. It can't be too old, that's all.'

'Would you just listen to yourself?'

'You don't get it,' Magnus said, and changed gear with force. 'You think it makes financial sense to fix and save. But sometimes it doesn't. Sometimes you actually have to . . .'

'The car is running fine. So please explain to me how we can save money by buying a new one, go on. Convince me that it's smarter to trade in a car that works than to repair the roof over our heads, which, by the way, is over twenty years old.'

Magnus shook his head.

'You're not listening,' he snapped.

'Magnus, I am listening. But I'm not going to let you . . .'

They sat in silence.

'So, how's Trude then?' Magnus tried, as they passed the Krapperup Estate.

'She's fine.'

'She has to be the second most beautiful woman in the world.'

Anna looked at her husband. Never mind that they argued sometimes, it didn't take long before they made it up again.

'Sweetie,' she said, and put her hand between his legs. *The second most beautiful.*

'Darling, not while I'm driving.'

'Okay.'

She studied him, amused.

'Thought you liked it when I touched you.'

'Yes, but there's a time and a place for teenage groping. Now, if I was turn off and stop . . .'

'Absolutely,' Anna said, 'if we had the time.'

She looked out of the window to the side.

'It's strange with Trude, you know,' she mused. 'So beautiful and so smart, and yet she doesn't believe it. I guess it's like they say.'

'What?'

'The wrong people doubt their own abilities. The arrogant rule the world.'

'Yes, maybe it is.'

They sat in silence the rest of the way.

'Nearly half an hour,' Anna confirmed, looking at her watch, when Magnus pulled up outside the hotel.

'Have fun then, darling.'

She leaned forwards and kissed him on the lips.

'You too. Speak to you this evening.'

3

Anna closed the car door and waved her thanks, then walked towards the entrance. Two men were struggling with unwieldy golf bags in the boot of a car. Sissela and Trude were standing by the reception and had just been given their keys.

'See you in ten minutes,' Sissela chirped, then disappeared with an extended *ciao*.

Anna checked in and went up to her room. She had a clear view of the town and the water. She put her blouse for the evening on a hanger, changed her shoes, picked up a notebook and the printout of an article proposal that she'd put together the week before.

'There's coffee in the thermos,' Trude said, when Anna came into the meeting room.

'Thanks, think I'll take a mineral water instead.'

Anna helped herself and sat down at the table.

'Isn't it lovely?' Sissela said, looking out.

'I do like the Grand,' Trude agreed. 'There's never any problems.'

'You know how it all works,' Anna chimed in.

'Considering how many times we've been here, that's not so strange,' Sissela said, and straightened her back. 'So, what do you say? Shall we just get started?'

By half past twelve, the female management troika of *Family Journal* had planned every edition until Easter and could go to lunch with a clear conscience.

Trude routinely inspected the men on offer. If anyone caught her attention she would get up immediately and go over to the sumptuous buffet, where she would spend ages helping herself. All the men in the dining room would stare until their eyes popped out. It was a performance, Trude couldn't help it. It was deeply ingrained in her. All the attention she had received since puberty had done nothing to satisfy her need for confirmation. To the contrary, every longing glance simply dug deeper into her bottomless pit. Pit? It was an abyss, a black hole, a minor continental drift.

Anna couldn't understand it. The only thing that actually prevented Trude from being more unfaithful was her beauty. It frightened men. Only the dregs dared try their hand, the ones who had nothing to lose.

The exception to the rule was Trude's husband. Successful, attractive and a considerate husband as well as a fantastic father. As far as Anna could tell, he left nothing to be desired. And what's more, he was neither grumpy nor felt sorry for himself, unlike most other men.

'And what about the features page?' Sissela asked, when they had retired to the veranda, full and happy. 'How's that early death series doing?'

Sissela was talking about 'And Then the Game Was Over' articles, which were essentially extended obituaries of people who had died too young. Their nearest and dearest were given the opportunity to talk about their loss and grief, following a sudden and unexpected death. The Stockholm-based freelancer Calle Collin, who wrote most of the articles, used just the right combination of sentimentality and positivity, and the readership figures spoke for themselves.

'It's doing well,' Anna said.

'The last two were a bit too old.'

'The people who died, you mean?'

'Yes, and it was cancer in both cases, wasn't it? Cancer is a bit like the flu these days. Are there no other interesting diseases?'

'I'll check with Calle.'

'It doesn't even need to be an illness,' Sissela continued. 'It could be an accident. Or a natural catastrophe. The main thing is that they died young, and preferably under dramatic circumstances.'

'Okay.'

'But the pitch is good, bloody good. He's not interested in doing any celebrity stuff?'

'He wasn't the last time I spoke to him. But I can check again.'

'Good. Do that. And what about our life stories . . . ?'

They finished at four o'clock. Trude went up to her room for a rest, Sissela declared that she intended to have a long soak in a warm bath, and Anna went for a walk.

She followed the street closest to the water, out towards the cliffs, which were being gradually swallowed by the dark. The best houses stood empty after August. There were no cars or people. And yet the odd light shone here and there inside the houses. Anna guessed they were on timers and didn't fool anyone, not least any local kids in search of a drink, who had the decency only to smash up the furniture of stingy townies who hadn't had the sense to leave a couple of bottles in the cupboard. A kind of local tax that outsiders had to pay for the right to roam around in towelling robes in summer, to feel real and greet other similarly clad people from Stockholm with air kisses and falsetto voices.

'Oh, hi! Fancy meeting you here!'

Mölle was a summer place. Could never be anything else. It was too far from Helsingborg. You could buy the same sort of property for about the same price in Hittarp, Domsten and Viken, where the commute into town was less than half an hour, and people lived there all the year round, unlike Mölle.

Anna decided that she'd had enough of an adventure and turned around. The southwest wind that had been on her back felt raw against her face and she pulled her coat in at the collar. By the time she got back to the hotel, she was totally windswept. She switched on the TV for company and stepped into the shower.

4

The waiter spent ages fussily garnishing the fish dish with some expensive drops that were supposed to be sauce. He drew a brief outline of the fish's life, which had apparently been happy right up until its inevitable demise. And, as with all posh restaurants, it neither tasted particularly good nor was particularly filling. When they'd finished eating, Sissela disappeared out for a cigarette and Trude and Anna went to the bar to order Irish coffees. Two middle-aged men in golf gear burst in, drunk and happy. The ever-attentive Trude sent them furtive, doe-eyed glances over the top of her glass, which made them squirm.

What was expected of them? An invitation should never be rejected out of hand. It would be unnatural and self-disqualifying as they were now in close company with a business card burning in their pocket.

The bait was laid and Trude played the innocent.

'Not again,' Anna said.

'What do you mean?'

'You know very well what I mean.'

'Ach.'

Sissela came back, reeking of cigarettes.

'What are you talking about?'

'Trude,' Anna sighed, exasperated. 'She's at it again.'

'But there's no one here,' Sissela said, looking around.

She spotted the men, deep in discussion as to the best strategy.

Trude was too attractive, it made them uncertain. Sissela looked at her colleagues.

'Bagsy the one with the hair,' she said, and waved over the waiter so she could order.

Anna gasped like a fish, Sissela gave a crooked smile.

'I get no attention at home. A glass of red wine, please.'

Sissela put her hand on Anna's shoulder and burst out laughing.

'You should see your face. We're having you on, didn't you realise? Oops, look smart, they're coming over.'

'Hi, can we join you?'

'Absolutely.'

'My name's Sven, and this is Olof.'

'Hello.'

They shook hands and said their names.

'So,' the man ventured. 'Are you here with work?'

'Yes, we're having a scheduling day. We usually come here.'

'Scheduling?'

'We work for *Family Journal*.'

'The magazine?'

Sissela nodded.

'Excellent magazine,' the man said, spontaneously.

Sissela straightened her back.

'Thank you,' she said, as if the magazine were all her own work.

'Just the right mix, lots to read. My mother gets it.'

Sissela deflated. The man noticed and adjusted his tactic.

'I've thought about subscribing myself, but my wife only reads fashion and interior design magazines. It's a shame really, because *Family Journal* beats them all hands down.'

He looked like he genuinely meant what he said.

'Lots of people think it's just for mumsies,' Sissela sighed.

'But you have male readers as well, don't you?'

Sissela shrugged. 'Men flick through it,' she said. 'But generally they're most interested in the crossword. What about yourselves? What do you do? It was Sven, wasn't it?'

He nodded.

'We run an advertising company, a small one. It's just the two of us and another colleague.'

'Any good clients?'

'Yes, actually.'

He mentioned a clothes chain and a travel agency.

'We're here to celebrate our first anniversary, play a little golf, calling it a meeting.'

Sissela laughed.

'Might have guessed that you worked in advertising,' she said. 'It's hard to tell you apart.'

'That's easy enough. I'm Sven, S as in suave, and he's Olof, O as in ordinary.'

'But you're wearing quite an ordinary suit,' Sissela joked.

'You're right, it's not easy.'

Ten minutes later, Anna had discovered that the men weren't as pathetic as drunk men in hotels usually are. They actually listened. One of them was quite funny. But it did follow the usual pattern. Anna and Sissela got most of the attention, Trude stood beside them, unobtainable in her beauty. Men seldom knew how to behave in her presence. But everything changed when the third man turned up.

'Aha, here he is. This is Erik, Erik Månsson, our new star.'

Even Trude was taken aback. Erik, the advertising company's new copywriter, had gone up to his room to try to remove a red-wine stain from his shirt, without much success. So he was now dressed in jeans and a T-shirt, an outfit that accentuated his muscles and showed that, more than anything, he was fit. Trude's beauty had no effect on him: she probably looked like all the women he went out with. And what was more, he was far younger than the others.

Anna sighed to herself. She could image the next couple of hours. Sissela would giggle like a studio audience at jokes that weren't funny, wind her hair round her finger and lick the bottom of her front teeth with tip of her tongue, she would do all she could to spark his interest and then, if she did succeed, against all odds, she would pull out at the last moment like the prick-teaser she was. While Trude wouldn't hesitate for a moment if the opportunity arose.

Anna was wrong. It turned out to be a good evening.

The flirting wore thin after a while and instead wallets and purses were pulled out and photos of children and spouses passed around. Erik, who was single and didn't have any children, rolled his eyes at all this, but they were beyond conference flings, they were mature men enjoying themselves and were good company.

'So you're from Stockholm?' Sissela asked Erik.

'Yes.'

'Which agencies did you work for there?' she continued, knowledgeably.

'None,' Erik replied.

'Oh, so you're completely wet behind the ears?'

'Yep.'

'What did you do before?'

'Served behind the fish counter in a supermarket.'

Sissela threw back her head and laughed.

'Seriously?'

Erik nodded. Sissela couldn't hide the smile playing on her lips.

'I'll bet you smelt good on a Saturday night,' she said, smoothly.

'Haha, I've never heard that one before,' Erik said, wearily, dismissing her as yet another witty Gothenburger.

The atmosphere changed and Anna slipped out to the toilet. When she came out, Erik was standing there, waiting for his turn. There wasn't much room and just as she was about to squeeze past, he kissed her. She barely had time to register it.

'I'm sorry,' he said, and slipped into the toilet.

Anna went back to the others and sat down. The atmosphere was relaxed again. Erik came back and sat down opposite her. A quick questioning look, but otherwise nothing. Sissela went out to smoke, and the older men decided to keep her company. Social smokers, cigarillos, to be on the safe side. Trude had to go to the ladies' room. Anna was left on her own with Erik. He looked at her.

'I'm in room eighteen,' he said. 'You're welcome later, if you'd like company.'

'I'm married,' Anna replied. 'I've got a ten-year-old daughter.'

'I know,' Erik said. 'You showed us the pictures.'

The smokers came back. Erik stood up.

'Well, I'm think I'm going to go to bed.'

Trude came back from the toilet. She had fixed her make-up, fluffed up her hair, tightened her bra and, just to be sure, opened another button on her shirt.

'Where's Erik?'

Maybe it was the feeling of being the chosen one, the power had gone to her head. Anna wasn't used to that kind of attention. Or maybe a reaction to the fact that her colleagues always said she was so proper. Or perhaps it was pure lust, a momentary aberration.

'God, you're so lame,' Sissela said, when Anna got up to leave a quarter of an hour later.

Neither she nor Trude would ever have guessed.

Anna went up to her room, brushed her teeth and stared at herself in the mirror.

'Go to bed,' she said to herself.

She took out her phone. Magnus had called. She looked at the clock – quarter past eleven – and phoned him. He answered, half asleep.

'Sorry, did I wake you?'

'No problem.'

'We were sitting in the bar,' Anna told him. 'Met some golfers. They bought us a drink.'

'That's nice.'

'Is Hedda asleep?'

'What do you think?'

'Sorry I didn't ring earlier.'

'Darling, I was asleep.'

'Okay, okay. Sorry. Just wanted to call and say I love you.'

'And me you. Sleep well. See you tomorrow.'

'Yes.'

She hung up and took the charger out of her bag. The telephone buzzed when she plugged it in. A summer snap of her husband and daughter flashed up before the screen went dark and the phone switched to idle mode.

Anna looked around. The room was like any other hotel room. Bed, wall-mounted TV, a desk where no one sat on the chair, which was only used as a dumping ground for clothes. On the table, a faux leather file of information about WiFi and breakfast times, and some local tourist brochures. A small bathroom with an extra roll of toilet paper, and a full soap container on the wall.

He tasted like strawberries. Or something. Early teenage lipgloss. Maybe she was imagining it, making the association because he was so much younger, a kind of cerebral red light. She wasn't damn well going to do anything she'd regret later. She wasn't even drunk, certainly not enough for it to be used in her defence.

She breathed into her hand and sniffed, picked up the

key and went to room eighteen. She glanced quickly in both directions and knocked on the door. He opened it.

'I thought you weren't going to come,' he said.

His voice made it sound like a nice surprise. He stepped to one side and held open the door. Anna went in, she didn't want to stand in the corridor and risk anyone seeing her.

'Well, I just wanted to say that I'm not coming,' she said.

'Okay.'

'I don't do things like this, I'm happily married. We have a daughter. But I've told you already.'

'Would you like something to drink? Wine?'

'No thank you. I'm going to go. I am.'

Erik looked at her, nodded.

'Okay.'

He didn't say anything else, didn't try to get her to stay. Anna was restless, shifted the weight on her feet, looked around. The room was identical to her own.

'Can I just ask something?' she finally blurted out.

'Of course.'

'Why did you kiss me?'

'Because I wanted to.'

'So you think it's okay just to kiss anyone you feel like?'

'And because I thought you wanted it too.'

Anna nodded, tried to fill her lungs with air. Her breathing was uneven, almost agitated. Erik took a step towards her.

'No obligations.'

She turned her head, looked down at the floor, felt his hand on her hip.

5

He snored on the in-breath, which meant he was asleep. Which meant that Anna could get up and slip out. She had put one hand on the mattress to push herself up when his arm landed over her stomach.

A strange man's arm lay across Anna's stomach. Proof of her waywardness. She had been unfaithful to her husband, slept with someone else. What had been unthinkable only five hours ago, something she could never have dreamed of, was now an inescapable fact. She looked at the arm. Like the rest of his body, it was taut and muscular.

The sex. God, the sex was powerful and naked, and not least, natural. Physical encounters with a stranger often amounted to nothing more than awkward fumblings, flavoured with reassurances and misunderstandings and incompetence and pretending to be interested. At least, that was how Anna remembered her teenage years. Good sex was something you had to work on. It required intimacy and security and trust. It had never occurred to her before that two bodies could be a perfect fit, like pieces of a puzzle.

She carefully lifted Erik's arm and got out of bed. It was still dark. Anna looked around the room for her pants and found them at the foot of the bed. Her blouse had been thrown on the floor, as had her bra. She could roll her tights up in a ball in her hand, but she didn't want to go out into the corridor without her bra on. God help her if she ran into anyone, if Sissela was out there. The sun wouldn't even be up before the rest of the world knew then. Trude would be bad enough, but Sissela was something else.

Anna bent down to pick up her bra and heard a click behind her. She turned around. Erik was lying in bed with his hand stretched out, pointing a mobile phone at her. He smiled.

'Did you take a picture?' Anna asked.

She walked towards him and reached for the phone in his hand. He snatched it away, obviously amused by the possibility of a fight.

'Give it to me.'

'You have to let me have a memory to keep,' he said, and ducked away from her hands.

'Don't you believe it. Can I have the phone?'

'No, it's mine.'

'Stop messing around. Give it to me.'

Erik laughed when she wrestled with him, but in the end he gave up and handed her the phone. She opened the album and studied the picture.

'Ugh, is that what I look like?'

'What do you mean, ugh? You're a hot milf.'

'Hot? More like fat. There, gone. Would've been fun if that went live, wouldn't it?'

'Then I'd have had something to wank to.'

'Wank? How old did you say you were?'

'Fourteen.'

'As old as that?'

He put out his hand and stroked her arm, let the back of his fingers glide down over her soft skin, the curve of her breast. She closed her eyes.

'I have to go,' she said.

He gave an understanding nod.

'Are you okay?'

'Yes. Absolutely. It was . . .'

Anna tried to find the right word and felt her eyes fill with emotion and guilt. Erik sat up, lifted the hair that had fallen over her face and pulled her to him. She held her arms up in front of her in a half-hearted attempt to fend off any more intimacy.

'Wait,' he said, and disappeared into the bathroom.

He came back with some tissues and a glass of water. Anna blew her nose and drank the water.

'Sorry,' she said, with an embarrassed laugh.

'Don't apologise.'

'I've never . . .'

She was about to start crying again, but managed to stop herself.

'So,' she said, and patted him on the knee, 'I should go.'

Erik nodded.

'Have to.'

'What time is it?'

They both turned and looked at the blue digits on the radio-clock. Nearly five. Erik looked at her.

'I've got an idea,' he said.

*

'Is this your car?'

'No, I've got something smaller. Somewhere in town. This is Olof's.'

'And you've got the keys?'

'They had some beers down at the clubhouse, so I drove back.'

'You don't drink at all?'

'Rarely. I work out quite a lot.'

'You can tell.'

'I guess the right response is thank you.'

Anna nodded to herself.

'Small car, big . . .' she said, surprised at herself.

'What kind of car do you have?' Erik asked.

'Volvo.'

They drove past the unmanned ranger's hut towards the cliffs. Erik put the headlamps on full beam and started up the steep, narrow road. He stopped at the viewpoint and they looked out over the town. The damp air smudged the glare of the streetlights and made everything look like a dark bluey-grey watercolour painted on wet paper.

'I love Kullaberg,' he said, and drove on through the bare beech woods. 'I come here as often as I can.'

They passed the golf course and carried on up towards

the lighthouse, from where the beam swept majestically over the white morning mist. Erik turned off the engine and opened the door.

'Come,' he said, and got out.

He took her by the hand and led her over towards the cliffs.

'Careful. It's steep here.'

He stopped by the edge. The beam from the lighthouse swept over them rhythmically, the sea lay like a carpet below, frightening and full of promise. She breathed deeply, listened to the space between the waves that crashed against the rock at regular intervals, glimpsed the white foam against the black water.

'One wrong foot here and it's the end,' Erik said. 'We're standing on an overhanging headland. When you go climbing here, you hang upside down like a spider.'

'You go climbing?'

'As often as I can.'

'Let's hope the granite holds then,' Anna said. 'Always some Dane or another who falls down and gets killed.'

'Is there?'

'Every year,' Anna said. 'And in return, there's always some drunken Swede who falls off the rollercoaster at

Bakken. I think it's an agreement, a kind of annual death exchange.'

Erik laughed.

'You're funny,' he said. 'Hold on, I'm going to scream now.'

'Okay.'

'Thought it might be best to warn you in case you got a fright and fell.'

'I'll try to stay on my feet.'

'Ready?'

'Ready.'

'I'm serious, I scream loud.'

He screamed, a primal roar into the night. His voice echoed both high and low and Anna didn't hear her own laughter until he stopped.

'What?' he said.

'Nothing.'

Anna dried her eyes.

'You sound like a teenager at a rock concert.'

'Come on then, your turn.'

'No, no, no, I'm far too reserved.'

'Come on, it's feels so good.'

'Not my thing, not my thing at all.'

'How do you know, when you haven't even tried?'

'Okay, what should I shout?'

'Just scream. Let's change places, you have to stand right on the edge with only the sea in front of you.'

'I don't dare.'

'Come on. It's not dangerous. I'm not thinking of pushing you over.'

They swapped places.

'Scream.'

'Aaah.'

'You can do better than that. Scream properly. Scream out all your shit, all your disappointments, everything that hasn't happened, everything that's gone against you. The pleasure, the cherry on the cake that you're scared you'll lose.'

Anna screamed.

'A good warm-up. Now again.'

She screamed. Screamed from the pit of her stomach, pressed everything up and out of her mouth, over the water. When there was nothing left, when she had emptied it all, she filled her lungs with fresh, salty air, gasping as if she'd been for a long run, and then realised she was crying. Crying with relief, joy and renewal. Because it felt good and because it was the complete opposite of the controlled person that she normally was.

He took her hand. They walked back down to the car, where they kissed each other openly and wordlessly as she rode him in the driver's seat until they came.

6

'A bloody good thing that the hunk went to bed,' Sissela said, tapping the top of her breakfast egg with a spoon.

Anna pretended not to understand.

'Who?'

'That guy yesterday, the body.'

'How do you mean?'

'Otherwise Trude would be sitting here full of regrets.'

'You think so?'

Sissela snorted.

'Couldn't you tell? She was obscenely horny.'

'Was she? I didn't notice.'

Sissela peeled the shell off with her fingers.

'She should watch herself.'

'What do you mean?'

'I mean, hello, how old do you think he was? Twenty-five?'

'He was thirty at least.'

'Well, and Trude's fifty-two. What was his name again?'

'Can't remember.'

Anna took a sip of juice and swallowed the lump in her throat.

'Erik,' Sissela exclaimed, waving her index finger in the air. 'Trude could be his mother. Not a word, here she comes.'

They watched their colleague coming towards them with heavy steps. Sissela found it hard to conceal her eagerness.

'Good morning, sunshine,' she trilled. 'Did you sleep well?'

Trude glared at her.

'Where's the coffee?'

She looked around, spotted the coffee machine and went to get a mug.

'So,' Sissela said, once she'd sat down. 'I'm guessing that

you're really glad now that you stayed until the bar closed and forced down that last glass.'

'It's not that bad,' Trude replied, stretching. 'I slept really well.'

'Just said to Anna that it's a good thing the hunk went to bed early.'

'Why?'

Trude was well aware that what Sissela said as a joke to her face was presented as something else behind her back.

'You know.'

'No,' Trude insisted. 'Tell me.'

Sissela gave a nervous giggle.

'I'm just having you on.'

Trude could hit back and Anna loved her for it. It didn't happen often, but it was there, that last line of defence. If Trude had sat there full of remorse, Sissela would have exploited her weakness with false compassion, but now she was just hung-over and so wouldn't put up with being treated like that.

'So,' Anna said, to lighten the mood. 'What time did you eventually get to bed?'

'I was in bed just before two,' Trude replied.

'So was I,' said Sissela, careful to fit in now. 'We went up at the same time. You went to bed between ten and eleven, didn't you?'

She looked at Anna, who squirmed.

'They seemed really nice, those advertising guys,' she said.

Trude nodded in agreement.

'Very nice.'

'Nice is one thing,' Sissela quipped. 'But you wouldn't really want to grind with a red-cheeked Viagra man. You'd have to keep your eyes firmly shut. The hunk, on the other hand . . . '

She turned to Anna, and changed the subject.

'We talked business with them. Thought they could send in a pitch for our next campaign. If they managed to sell subscriptions, I might be able to give the boy a magazine or two.'

Trude pulled a face, Sissela couldn't understand why.

'What?'

'Good morning.'

Erik was standing behind Sissela, fresh-faced and youthful in comparison.

'Did you all sleep well?' he asked, taking time to look at each of them.

'Absolutely,' Trude said. 'And you?'

Erik shook his head.

'Not much,' he replied.

Anna took a sip of coffee. She couldn't bring herself to look at him.

'No?' Sissela exclaimed.

'I never sleep well in hotels,' he said. 'The pillows are too big, and there's too much noise.'

'You should have stayed up longer,' Trude teased. 'And learned from those of us with more experience and poorer judgement how to drink yourself to sleep.'

'Next time,' Erik smiled. 'Though I have say, I feel pretty refreshed and rested all the same.'

Anna knew he was looking at her: she could feel it with every nerve in her body.

'Where are your friends?' Sissela asked.

'They're on their way.'

'Are you playing golf again today?'

'A conference is a conference. And you?'

'We'll be working.'

'That's an alternative. Will you be in the bar again this evening?'

'No, we're leaving this afternoon,' Anna said.

Erik looked at her and nodded.

'Well, it was nice meeting you. Hope to see you again some time.'

He moved over to the buffet. Sissela followed him with hungry eyes.

'Me too, pool boy,' she said. 'Me too.'

7

A six-month schedule and five-week printing procedure kept any anxious followers of fashion at bay. *Family Journal* was a prehistoric dinosaur in the digital information age. A kind, monster herbivore not to be swayed by the soon-forgotten dramas of everyday life. The general tone of the magazine was that of a wise, loving grandmother comforting her grown-up daughter who was worried about her teenage children: everything will be all right in the end, just wait and see.

By lunch they were done with the end of the school year, midsummer, the holiday edition and the crayfish season special. They had done what they set out to do and were ready to check out and order a taxi back to the office.

'That went fast,' Sissela concluded, from the passenger seat.

Trude agreed.

'It certainly did.'

'It was fun with Olof and Sven,' Sissela said, turning round. 'Anna, a shame that you went to bed so early.'

'I was tired.'

'Advertising people are nice,' Trude said. 'Those over forty, at least. The young hotshots can be a bit stressful.'

'He can stress me out any time,' Sissela said, and then became acutely aware of the driver next to her.

She laughed, embarrassed, and tried to cover it.

'Internal joke.'

The taxi driver nodded and forced a smile.

'Why did he go to bed so early?' Sissela mused.

'I guess we were too old,' Trude said.

For a moment, Anna wondered whether they were having a go at her. If they'd been standing in the corridor outside the room and heard everything.

'Sober, moralistic youth,' Sissela snorted. 'A non-fucking generation.'

She put a hand on the driver's shoulder.

'You'll have to excuse us, we've just had a planning meeting.'

'I'm used to it, nothing I haven't heard before,' he said, but did squirm a bit in his seat.

'We're all bark and no bite,' Sissela assured him.

Anna looked out at the passing landscape. Everything lay fallow, the opposite of what she felt inside. The second time up by the cliffs had been even better, if that was possible. Raw, uninhibited, frantic. Anna felt an almost physical hunger for his body. She wanted to remember every moment.

She imagined herself in an old people's home. A nurse talking down to her in an artificial, friendly, loud voice: *Good night then, Mrs Stenberg. Let's hope that Mrs Stenberg gets a good night's sleep.*

Anna would put her hand under the covers and dig out Mölle 2012 from her mental archive. What was done was done, and she didn't want to regret it or feel ashamed.

'So, were they nice then?' Magnus asked, once they'd finished dinner and Hedda had left the table in favour of the television.

'Who?'

'The golfers?'

Anna felt her cheeks burning.

'You said that they bought you all drinks,' Magnus continued. 'When you phoned yesterday. Have you forgotten that you called?'

'No, no, I'm with you now. Yes, they were very nice. They run an advertising agency. It was a good evening. I didn't mean to wake you.'

'No problem. What was the agency called?'

'Oh, I can't remember. They were called Sven and Olof, or something like that. Older boys, closer to sixty.'

'*Jurassic Park* in their business.'

'I guess it is. There was a young guy with them too, but he went to bed early.'

'Ah, the youth of today,' Magnus said, and got up. 'Don't know what's the matter with them.'

He started to clear the table, scraped and rinsed the plates and stacked them in the dishwasher.

'So there were no scandals?' he added, blithely.

Anna pulled the newspaper over towards her and pretended to have seen something.

'Not that I know of.'

'Has Trude grown up then?'

'I'm not sure about that, but she behaved herself. They were actually really nice, the men. Talked a lot about their wives.'

'Oh, you want to watch out then.'

'What do you mean?'

'It's another way of saying I want a fuck unless you're going to be silly and fall in love and go mad and stalk me.'

'How do you know that?'

Anna gave her husband an accusing look. He shrugged in amusement.

'God, that's elementary conference sex etiquette.'

'Ugh, listen to yourself.'

Magnus grinned, pleased with the reaction.

'More wine?'

'Yes, please.'

8

No. No, no, no.

What had she done? How could she do that and risk everything?

Anna lay in bed staring up at the ceiling. The glow from the streetlights slipped in through a gap in the curtains, making shadows that danced in the heat from the radiator.

Her heart was pounding, her thoughts bounced off the inside of her skull. The alcohol was working its way out of her body and amplified her anguish, her stomach was cold and bathed in sweat. She had slept with someone else, been unfaithful to her husband, the only man she had ever loved unconditionally, the father of her daughter. For what? It wasn't the sex. Sex was sex and wasn't such a big deal. Everyone knew that. Self-confirmation? Hardly, she wasn't like Trude. Why on earth had she jumped into bed with someone else? A young pup at that. To prove that she was alive? That she didn't say no to life, that she was liberated and independent? To show that she was more than just Hedda's mum, more than a suburban wife with a career, a well-tended garden, a beautiful home and a vibrant social life?

Anna couldn't understand it. It wasn't like her. She didn't do stupid things, she was stable and secure and ordinary. Exactly that, ordinary. No saint, but ordinary. And now that she'd done something stupid, she felt an overwhelming need to confess, take full responsibility, atone for her sins and start afresh. Never again. The first, last and only time.

I did wrong, let me walk with my eyes to the ground and slowly win back your trust, dear husband.

She couldn't. Only inconsiderate people spilled their hearts. She still remembered the day her father had come home and told them he'd met a woman at work. Anna's mother had thrown him out the same day. A few months later her father was abandoned by his new love. He never met anyone else and died only a few years after he retired. Anna was convinced that the real cause of his death was loneliness.

She got out of bed and went to the bathroom, peed quietly and drank some water from the tap.

What had she been thinking in the taxi on the way home? She'd seen it as a benefit. A moment to be remembered and celebrated, something that was her own. Hers and the pup's.

He wasn't actually that young. If it had been the other way round, if she had been younger, no one would have reacted.

Anna took a deep breath, released the air through rounded lips. She went back to the bedroom and crept in under the duvet. Magnus might well be awake, but she didn't want to ask and risk waking him. They seldom talked at night, both happy in their own silence. They were comfortable in most situations. Magnus' lower lip only started to quiver when he was threatened with violence. Like most middle-class men, his authority was fragile and the protective coating of ironic jargon was thin.

Someone they knew had lost his job a couple of years ago. He was humbled overnight and started to talk about other values in life, spewed up philosophical clichés. He managed to make an utter twit of himself before finding a new white-collar job with the help of some friends and returning to the stupid conservative ramblings that had previously been his trademark.

Anna had done the right thing. She had been made an offer and accepted it. It was a moment of madness, a film she could replay in her mind later when boredom set in. And in any case, what was done was done, she couldn't rewind and delete.

And so what? She wasn't exactly the first person in the history of the world to make a mistake. What was important now was not to be tempted by the false sense of relief that a confession might give. She would have to keep it to herself. Full stop. She turned over on to her side and pulled the duvet up towards her mouth. The motorbike position, comfortable and safe. Her husband sighed like a sleepless martyr of the night. Her secret, no one else's. And if she felt compelled to open her heart she could talk to her mother.

Anna closed her eyes and was just on the verge of falling asleep when a noise outside made her jump. Something tapped against the window. A timid nail knocking against the glass. She nudged Magnus.

'What?' he said, drunken with sleep.

Anna turned on the bedside lamp and Magnus blinked his tired eyes.

'What are you doing?'

'It sounds like there's someone outside the window.'

For some reason, Anna whispered.

'It's just the wind.'

'Shhh . . .'

They listened attentively. Nothing.

'I'm certain,' Anna said.

'Maybe a bird then,' Magnus suggested.

'In the middle of the night?'

'Or a branch or something.'

'Please . . .'

Magnus heaved a deep sigh and push himself up off the bed. He went over to the window and opened the curtains.

'Nothing,' he confirmed and pulled them shut again.

He crossed back to the bed with dragging footsteps and got back in.

'Happy?'

Anna nodded and turned off the light. She stretched out her hand and stroked his chest.

'My hero,' she said.

9

Where are all the men?

It was a question that sixty-seven-year-old Kathrine Hansson and her friends often asked. Men of their age seldom seemed to travel any great distance, they didn't go to the theatre or other cultural events, and only occasionally appeared at evening classes.

The sad truth, Kathrine guessed, was that men of her age sat at home in front of the telly and made negative remarks about the young people they were forced to watch.

It was a terrible waste of time. Why were men so self-destructive? Had they given up? Adopted the attitude to life that nothing really mattered as they were going to die soon anyway? It was like never making your bed as you were going to sleep in it again soon enough.

Kathrine Hansson went into the library and glanced quickly around the reading room. She counted no fewer than seven men there, and no women.

Of course. Grumpy old men always had to be up to date with what was happening. Not to be rapped on the knuckles and lose face in some pedantic word duel with another man. Kathrine was reminded of her own father, who, in his autumn years, sat in front of the news on television with such concentration that you might be forgiven for thinking that world peace depended on his total attention.

The need to always be informed. Kathrine couldn't for the life of her understand it. Once a month she got a newsletter from a self-appointed intellectual with a career behind him, who was, incidentally, married to the managing editor of the magazine where her daughter worked. In his letter, the man gave his view on world events and finished off with recommendations for good restaurants and fine wines. In all seriousness.

Women blogged, mainly about the joys of their personal life. Men wrote newsletters, commented on world politics.

Why? Did they seriously believe that the world was screaming out for their comprehensive analyses?

Kathrine wanted to sit down with the men, soak up their
presence, try to understand. But what was her alibi? She had
already read the paper and didn't want to just sit there and
pretend.

She went into the fiction section and looked for something good to borrow. She didn't find anything and went
back out into the reading room, wandered slowly along the
shelves of newspapers. Someone sombrely turned the page.
Otherwise there was silence.

Kathrine studied the men furtively. Of the seven, three
were acceptable, one was definitely more than that. He had
the slightly apish ugly-good looks that Kathrine had always
fallen for.

She took a paper, something from Småland, and sat
down in the chair next to him. He automatically moved,
made a noise that might or might not have been to show his
irritation at not being able to spread the pages any more.

'What are you reading?' Kathrine asked, when she thought
she had sat in silence and turned the pages long enough.

The man gave her a blank look, uncertain whether it was
him she was talking to or not.

'Is there anything interesting?' she continued, with a friendly smile. 'In the newspaper, I mean.'

'Why?' he barked, aggressively.

Kathrine felt herself shrink.

'Sorry, I didn't mean to disturb you.'

Kathrine stood up swiftly, hurried along the wall of shelves, put back the paper she'd been reading, possibly in the wrong place, and left as quickly as she could.

10

'Anna Stenberg.'

'Hi, Anna, it's Erik Månsson from Mölle. Am I calling at bad time?'

Anna looked around. Trude was in a meeting with the journalists, Sissela was over at layout making some last-minute changes.

'No, no, not at all.'

'Well, I thought I'd just ask if it would be possible to come and see you?'

Anna swallowed nervously. Fragmented images from the night at the hotel last week whirred through her mind.

'Well, I'm not really sure whether that would be a good idea . . .'

'Not like that,' Erik interrupted. 'About work. I don't know whether your colleagues mentioned it to you, but apparently we've been given the go-ahead to make a pitch for your subscription campaign.'

'Yes,' Anna said. 'They did mention it. But to be perfectly honest, I'm not sure that I'm the right person. Perhaps you should . . .'

'Work is work,' Erik cut in. 'A quick coffee in town. No nonsense.'

'When were you thinking of?'

'Whenever suits you. Preferably as soon as possible.'

'Okay.'

Anna stood silent with the phone pressed to her ear.

'Are you still there?' Erik asked.

'I'm still here.'

'Well, what do you say? When would be a good time?'

'Why me?' Anna asked.

'You're the features editor and we want to focus on the reading material.'

'I don't mean that. I mean the other thing.'

'I'll tell you when we meet,' Erik said.

Anna noticed that Sissela had finished with the layout and was approaching the desk.

'Can I call you back?'

'Of course,' Erik said. 'Do.'

Anna put the phone down and looked guiltily at Sissela, then pointed to the receiver.

'The advertising guys.'

'Okay. Which one? Sven or Olof?'

'The young one.'

'The beach boy?' Sissela said. 'What did he want?'

'The campaign. To ask some questions.'

Sissela nodded slowly.

'Okay.'

'He wanted to meet me,' Anna said.

'How nice. Have fun.'

'I didn't think it was serious.'

'What? The campaign?'

Anna nodded. Sissela shrugged.

'Anyone who wants to can put in a bid. But it's on spec. I've got no intention of forking out if it's not worth it.'

Kathrine was riddled with angst. Picking up pensioners at the library? And what's more, being rebuffed.

She wandered restlessly around the flat before ending up by the window. She stared blankly into space. The fact that even her best intentions were dismissed as an unworthy annoyance was soul-destroying.

Kathrine started to worry about the next time she went to the library. What if the apeman was there? Kathrine could just imagine them meeting in the door. They both moved to the side, but the same side, and several times, so the whole thing became awkward, protracted and unbearable.

The potential humiliation made Kathrine smile. In a moment she was chuckling to herself, almost laughing out loud. That was the advantage of getting older. She had already done so many stupid things that one more wouldn't make a difference. The pain passed quicker, as there were far better things to use your energy on.

A newsletter, for example. Perhaps she should start one where she commented on world events with absolute confidence, drew her own conclusions and bored people. Not such a bad idea. But it was far simpler to pick up the phone and tell Ditte about her fiasco at the library. Certainly more entertaining. She thought that she might also tell her daughter, Anna. Even though, generally, children weren't so amused to hear that their parents might have dreams and hopes of a more amorous nature.

Kathrine went to get the phone.

11

Erik put two mugs of tea on the table, then sat down.

He smiled. Anna looked around. She didn't feel comfortable. To sit in a café with a man who was too young and too good-looking was to tempt fate in such a small town. And Helsingborg would never be anything else, no matter how big it grew. The social constraints were more sophisticated than anything George Orwell could make up. At the same time she felt proud to have been intimate with the young man on the other side of the table. All wandering eyes stopped at him, did a double take and then rested there. Erik Månsson had chosen her, if only for one night. And it had been fantastic.

'Nice to see you again,' he said, and smiled.

Anna looked at him, answered his smile.

'Likewise.'

Erik tried the tea.

'Are you nervous?' he asked.

'No,' Anna said. 'Or yes, a little.'

She pointed at the table.

'Are you not going to write anything?'

Erik didn't understand.

'Shouldn't you at least have a notebook or something?'

'You're right,' he said, and dug a spiral-bound notebook and pen out of his bag, which was still strapped diagonally across his chest.

She glanced around again. No other guests within earshot.

'What happened last time . . .' she started.

Erik's head jerked up. 'Yes?'

'That was a one-off.'

Erik nodded.

'Totally,' he said.

'It won't happen again.'

'No.'

'I just want that to be absolutely clear if we're going to work together. Okay? No nonsense.'

'Of course.'

He nodded and picked up the pen, pressed the nib against the paper. Anna took a deep breath.

'Just sitting here makes me feel uneasy,' she said. 'As if I have to project my voice so that no one misunderstands.'

Erik put down the pen.

'If it would be easier for you, we can go back to my place.'

Anna turned her head, looked at him from the side. Was he joking?

'I live straight across the street,' he said, earnestly, pointing in the direction with his thumb. 'To the right of the big brown building. Number sixty.'

'Are you seriously suggesting that I go home with you?'

She laughed, and he shrugged.

'I've got tea as well. Might even be able to rustle up some biscuits.'

'And you think that's a good idea?'

'Biscuits? Maybe not in bed, given all the crumbs, but otherwise, I love biscuits.'

'You think it will be easier to talk in your flat?'

'It won't be any harder. You're not comfortable here.'

'It's not that bad.'

'You keep looking over your shoulder. I'd even go as far as to say it's a bit suspect. And we don't have to jump into bed. I can in fact control myself.'

He was right. Her behaviour was erratic. Better that no one saw them.

'Just talk? No nonsense.'

Erik nodded.

'Absolutely.'

Anna studied him.

'What's the code?' she asked, in the end.

Erik didn't get it.

'I'm not going in with you. I'll come a couple of minutes later.'

'One six three two, top floor. It says 'Månsson' on the door. Give me five minutes to tidy up.'

He stood up.

'And I can't promise,' he said, 'that I've got any biscuits. I may have run out.'

Anna stared up at the ceiling and gave a deep, contented sigh. Erik lay beside her, breathing heavily.

'Sweet Jesus,' she said.

'What?'

She shook her head.

'This. I don't get it.'

'Water.'

He got up and walked naked out into the kitchen. She turned her head and followed him with her eyes. He came back with two glasses, his package hanging free.

'That must be the biggest I've ever seen,' she said.

'"Little consolation in a poor home,"' he sang the popular song to her, and handed her one of the glasses.

Anna sat up and drank it down in great gulps.

'Good,' she said, out of breath, and looked around.

Her opinion of him had changed having seen his flat, now that the tension had been released and she could view it with a clear eye. It wasn't very homely. There was hardly any furniture and, judging by the mess, not much storage space. There were more films than books on the shelves and the bed was a mattress on the floor. An ironing board stood permanently by the nearest socket in the wall and his shirts were on hangers on the cupboard door.

'I thought you said you were going to tidy up?'

'I'm sorry, it was worse than I thought. I've only been living here a few months and haven't got everything sorted yet.'

'Where did you live before?'

'Stockholm, I thought I told you.'

'Yes, but where in Stockholm?'

'Huddinge, to the south of the city. The first thing people ask about down here. I barely have a chance to open my mouth before someone asks where I'm from, in an accusing voice. I normally say Huddinge. Most people have no idea where it is, so, unlike Stockholm, it doesn't have negative connotations.'

'Do you have any connections here?'

'None. Other than work.'

'So you just moved down here?'

'My mother died, and I thought, What the hell.'

'Oh, how awful. She can't have been very old.'

'No.'

'What did she die of?'

'She committed suicide. Hanged herself from the banister.'

Anna pulled her chin in.

'What? Are you serious?'

Erik took a deep breath.

'Nearly two years ago now. I found her.'

'I'm sorry,' Anna said, and reached a hand out to him. 'That must have been terrible.'

Erik looked at his glass.

'How noble I am,' he said. 'A glass of fortifying mineral-rich tap water.'

He looked at her and broke into a big grin.

'You do realise that I'm having you on?'

'What do you mean?'

'She's alive.'

Anna got up abruptly.

'How the hell can you say something like that?'

'It was a joke.'

'Well, it wasn't a very funny one.'

'Oh, come on. I didn't mean any harm.'

Anna went to the toilet.

'Do you have a towel I can borrow?'

Anna ran the water until the temperature was right, got into the bath and pulled the curtain. She pressed the shower head to her chest and said to herself that it had been a mistake. Lying about his mother in that way. Not matter how seductive he might be, she did not want a relationship with someone who made such tasteless jokes.

She smelt the soap. It wasn't the same as at home, but at least it was neutral. Magnus' sense of smell was not particularly well developed, thankfully.

She washed herself quickly, and dried herself, then wrapped the towel around her body. She went out into the room, past Erik and over to the bed. She pulled on her pants before turning her back and taking off the towel. She could feel that he was looking at her.

'What?' she said as she did up her bra.

'You're so sexy.'

Anna snorted.

'But you are,' he assured her.

'Very good. Worth about five kronor.'

She pulled her blouse over her head and looked around to check that she hadn't forgotten anything.

'It's not going to work,' she said.

'What do you mean?'

Anna filled her lungs with patience, went over to Erik and patted him on the chest.

'It was . . .'

She looked for the words but couldn't find them.

'You know what I'm trying to say. Good, fantastic in every way, but it was the last time. Okay?'

She stroked his cheek and gave a fleeting smile, feeling that she was pushing the boundaries of what was acceptable. She was the one who made the rules and he had to play by them.

'Thank you,' she said. 'Or, something like that. Sorry, that doesn't sound right either.'

The seconds of silence were uncomfortable.

'I have to go,' she said, and as if to make it clearer, pointed to the front door.

She lowered her head and looked at him, a kind of appeal.

'Are you okay?'

His nod was barely noticeable and his smile was faint.

'Good,' Anna said, as if to convince herself. 'I'll go then.'

12

'So, no other sensations?'

'No, a bit thin on the ground.'

Magnus sighed and looked out over the empty street.

'Bangla, the town that never sleeps.'

'Bangla,' Anna repeated. 'I don't know anyone else who says that.'

She was looking through the morning papers. The second reading was always quieter and less demanding. In the morning she whipped through the pages, but in the evening she turned each one as if she were looking at an antique bible.

'It was a friend of my dad,' Magnus said. 'He called the houses Arab boxes because they had flat roofs, and there must have been a famine in Bangladesh at the time or something like that.'

She looked at him.

'And they got Bangladeshi confused with Arabic?'

'People weren't so sensitive then. Here, or elsewhere.'

Anna sighed.

'The question is whether we're actually so much more enlightened today?'

Magnus stood behind his wife and put his hands on her shoulders.

'Oh yes,' she said, and dropped her arms down from the table.

Magnus started to massage, Anna shut her eyes.

'That's so good, if only you knew.'

'The pain in your shoulders is just transferred into my thumbs,' Magnus grumbled.

'It's worth it,' Anna said, and hung her head forwards so he could get to it properly.

Magnus rubbed dutifully for a couple of minutes before he drummed his fingers against her shoulders, without warning, which marked the end of the pleasure.

'Thank you,' Anna said.

'You're welcome.'

Magnus opened the fridge and took out a beer, opened it and drank straight from the can.

'Have we got some nuts or anything like that?'

'You ate them all.'

'Did I?'

Anna turned to the TV page.

'Is there anything good on?'

Anna glanced down the listings.

'Nothing at all.'

'When's Hedda coming back?'

'I guess the film will finish around eight, half-eight. What's the time now?'

'Half past seven.'

Magnus looked at Anna until she turned round.

'Why, are you wanting some?' she asked.

He shrugged.

'Might as well take the opportunity.'

Ten minutes later they were both satisfied. They lay next to each other on the bed. Anna reached out and took Magnus' hand.

'That was lovely,' she said.

'You were eager.'

'Aren't I always eager?'

'You were very eager.'

'Good. Or are you complaining?'

'Absolutely not.'

'It's been a while,' Anna said. 'So good that you took the initiative.'

She patted his hand, got up and went to the bathroom. By the time she'd finished in the shower, he was dressed and the bed was made.

'Maybe it's just me being ridiculous,' she said, when they had settled down in front of the television and the vacuous programmes had switched her brain into a kind of transcendental rest mode.

Magnus turned, looked questioningly at her.

'The car,' she said. 'We can always do the sums.'

13

'How did it go yesterday?' Sissela asked, in a loud voice across the office.

Anna had just come out of the lift and pretended she had no idea what Sissela was talking about. She walked briskly over to her desk, didn't want to share it with the open floor.

'What?' she said, once she'd got there and put her bag down, she could feel that Sissela was still looking at her.

'Your meeting,' Sissela continued, in the same official voice.

'My what?'

'Your meeting. With the lunchbox. The playboy.'

'Who? Oh, right. You're terrible, do you know that?'

'Very curious, possibly. What did he want to know?'

'Nothing in particular, really. More what we were think-ing, target group, that sort of thing.'

Anna sat down and turned on the computer. She opened her email and looked through the inbox. Photographers, freelancers, internal mail and press releases – a constant stream of anxious questions, hopeful proposals and unnec-essary information that never ran dry.

Anna remembered a colleague who had once come back from a longish holiday to three hundred and twenty-eight emails. Invigorated by the salt water and sun-tight skin, she had taken a deep breath and deleted them all. Over the next two weeks, she kept waiting for angry faces, averted eyes and irritated reminders from neglected email contacts. Absolutely nothing happened. Emails had been invented to keep an open line of retreat and to comfort the anonymous. Every ping meant they existed, even if they meant nothing.

'So there was no humping, then?' Sissela asked.

Anna kept her eyes on the screen, double-clicked on one of the emails and pretended to read.

'Absolutely, of course there was. I've come straight from

there. You could wring out the sheet. Don't know whether it was the sweat or the fountain orgasms.'

'Fountain orgasm is just another way of saying incontinent,' Trude interrupted, putting a cup of coffee down on her desk. 'What are you talking about?'

'I was just telling Sissela about my wild twenty-four hours with the sex god,' Anna said.

'Righty-ho,' Trude said.

She sat down and started to go through a knitting pattern. Trude could happily proofread all kinds of specialised texts. Anna couldn't understand how she did it. Her own experience on the handicraft front stretched as far as an oven cloth in class five.

'You didn't ask if he wanted a threesome?'

'He said he'd think about it,' Anna replied.

'Hello, I want to be in on it,' Sissela squealed.

Anna nodded, earnestly.

'I'll ask him.'

'Yes!'

Sissela raised her hands above her head like a five-year-old before she realised the joke was over, and she held out her hand to Anna.

'Have you got the list?'

Anna handed her the schedule for the current edition. The jobs had to be recorded and ticked off to show that they were finished with editing and layout. The crossed squares marked where the adverts were to go.

'What kind of death do we have this week?'

She was referring to the feature series about people who had died young.

'The tsunami.'

'Son? Daughter?'

'Husband.'

'How old?'

'When he died, you mean? Forty-five.'

'And the wife survived?'

'She wasn't there,' Anna said.

'A man on his own in Thailand?' Trude said. 'Isn't that a bit suspect?'

'He was there for work. Pilot.'

'Highlight that, so no one starts to wonder,' Sissela said.

'Already done,' Anna said.

'Good. Pilot ... I like that. Have we got any pictures of him in uniform?'

'Of course. What do you take me for? But I think they

had to isolate him, as it was a group photo from some catalogue or other.'

'So was he good-looking then?' Trude asked.

'Yep.'

'Probably gay,' Sissela sighed. 'Surrounded by willing stewards who know how to keep their mouths open and nod at the same time.'

Anna shook her head.

'God, if anyone could hear us,' she said. 'What would they think?'

'Mamma mia,' Sissela said, and rolled her eyes.

Anna went through her emails, glanced at the text and answered in as few words as possible: thank you, good, we'll sort it, deal with that next week, call when you have a moment. She forwarded two press releases to the relevant editors, and added: something for you? Interested?

Nearly all the bold posts were gone when her phone rang.

'Anna.'

'It's me,' said Erik.

She spun her chair halfway round, away from her colleagues' prying eyes and ears, and felt her cheeks flush.

'Hi.'

She tried hard to sound normal, which only had the opposite effect.

'Are you sitting in a bad place?'

Anna felt for the volume button on the side of the receiver.

'Yes,' she said and stretched to pick a pen up from the desk.

Something to hold, whatever. There was an uncomfortable silence at the other end.

'We have to talk,' Erik said. 'Can I call you later?'

'I'll call you back.'

She tried to sound formal this time, but still sounded unnatural.

'Promise?' he said. 'As soon as you can.'

'Yes, I'll call you later.'

Erik hung up.

'Good, let's say that then,' Anna concluded for no one other than those sitting at the next desk.

She pretended to end the call that had already ended and put the phone down on desk, display-side down. Her throat was dry when she swallowed, she lifted up some papers, looked for something to read, fiddled with her mouse. Sissela was sitting looking at her computer, but Anna could feel her curiosity and knew that she wouldn't get away with it.

'Right, cup of coffee,' she said abruptly, and stood up. 'Anyone else?'

She turned quickly to Sissela, who slowly shook her head.

'I've got one,' Trude said, who was so deep into her knitting pattern that she was unaware of the drama that was going on behind her.

Anna didn't want to leave the phone on her desk, but couldn't take it with her out into the kitchen either. Everything was registered and demanded an explanation. Often with a playful smile so it was impossible to object to the invasion of privacy.

She left her mobile phone where it was and hurried out to get some coffee. The dishwasher was as always nearly full of dirty cups and every decent-sized cup was miscoloured. Anna chose a smaller cup and overfilled it. She tried to take some sips but the freshly made coffee was too hot, so she had to balance the full cup in front of her as she walked. She was a few metres from her desk when her phone started to ring again.

'I'll get it,' she called, but Sissela, ever willing, had already stretched over to her desk and looked at the display.

'Magnus,' she said, disappointed and handed her the phone.

'Thank you.'

Anna took the phone and answered. Her husband announced to her the good news that the couple had been granted an audience with the car dealer himself that very afternoon. If she could be ready by a certain time, Magnus would pick her up outside work. Anna tried very hard not to deflate his excitement and promised to be there.

She put the mobile phone down again, felt calmer. The everyday conversation had taken the edge off the previous call. She tasted the coffee and started to open the readers' letters, a pile that was steadily decreasing. Contrary to popular belief, subscribers to the *Family Journal* were comfortable using computers and more and more frequently emailed in their opinions and suggestions. Anna's impression was that women were generally far less technically challenged than men, particularly those over a certain age. She thought about her own family. Her father had never even learned to turn on a computer, whereas her mother was forever online and on Facebook, and not long ago had started to use Twitter. Kathrine's two followers, Anna and Hedda, received regular updates about what she had been to see at the cinema, what she was reading, what she was having for dinner.

An email pinged into her inbox. It was from Erik and didn't have a subject. Anna double-clicked.

Call as soon as you can. Important.

Did he have nothing better to do? She'd said she would call. He would just have to be patient. What was so important that it couldn't wait a few minutes . . . ?

He had an STD. Young people got STDs. He wasn't that young really, but still single and very definitely sexually active, given how easy it all seemed to be for him and how good he was at the handiwork. He'd just been up to the clinic and done some tests and his blood showed . . .

Dot dot dot.

Anna pushed the thought from her mind. The occupational hazard of working for a magazine that dedicated far too many pages every week to everyday dramas. She deleted Erik's mail, picked up her phone and went out into the corridor.

'Hi,' he said, in his best bed voice.

'What is it that's so important?'

'I just wanted to know how you are.'

'Fine,' Anna said.

'Are you sure?'

She looked around. No one was nearby.

'Aren't you at work?' she asked.

'Yes, yes. The others haven't come in yet. Thought it was best to call when I can.'

'Was that the rush then?' Anna said.

'Yes, nothing else. And I didn't dare to mail you. Your colleague, she seems ... How shall I put it without sounding rude? Naturally curious?'

Anna burst out laughing.

'You can say that. She likes to know what's going on. And sits opposite me, if you were wondering why I sounded a bit stressed when you called.'

'I got that impression.'

'When can I see you again?' Erik asked.

'What do you mean?' Anna said. 'We're not going to meet again.'

'Okay.'

He sounded hurt. Anna took a deep breath.

'Look, we'd just get ourselves in a mess.'

'I understand.'

'Don't get me wrong, Erik.'

Anna regretted saying his name. It sounded patronising

and arrogant, like an adult to a child. She didn't want to remind herself of the age difference.

'What's there to get wrong?' he said. 'You got what you wanted, and now you're scared.'

'I'm not scared.'

'You're not? Well, what is it then? Because I certainly can't remember meeting anyone who I've clicked with like this. Ever.'

'Erik, I'm older than you.'

'So what?' Erik retorted. 'If it works, it works. And you can't say that it doesn't work.'

'I've got a husband and daughter.'

'So why did you jump into bed with me?'

Anna was standing at the end of the corridor beside a weeping fig that was as big as she was. The office was out of hearing, but she still felt uneasy. A private conversation was a secret conversation and would inevitably lead to speculation.

'Sex,' she whispered. 'I was attracted to you.'

'And now you don't want to know me any more?'

Anna sighed.

'I don't think I thought about what was at risk,' she said. 'It really hit me yesterday. I can't carry on, it's just not going to work.'

'So that's it? Wham-bam, thank you, ma'am? You've had your fun, something to gossip with your friends about over a glass of wine. Proof of how liberated and modern you are. A strong woman who just takes what she wants, making up for centuries of oppression.'

'Now you're well off the mark.'

'Am I?'

'Yes, I think you are. It was you who made the pass, the pleasure was absolutely mutual and I would never say a word about what happened to anyone. I'm no kiss-and-tell.'

'Ooh, girly talk.'

'Erik, I have to work.'

'Wait, wait.'

She gave a loud sigh.

'What?'

'Can I mail you?'

'What?'

'Email. I've still got some questions I need answered. About the magazine. There wasn't much shop talk yesterday, if you remember.'

'Yes, you can email me,' Anna said.

'No risk that your colleagues will read it?'

'I don't think so.'

'Anna . . .'

'What?'

'Maybe it was just a bit of fun for you, but it really meant something to me.'

'Erik, believe me, you've got even greater experiences ahead. And if it's any comfort, it was quite something for me too. You're a fantastic lover, you are, but we're at different stages of life. It would be silly to drag it out.'

He said nothing. Anna felt uncertain.

'Are you still there?' she said.

'One last thing,' he said. 'Could I ask you for a favour?'

'What?'

'Can you promise you'll give me a chance? Professionally, that is. That you won't just dismiss my proposal because you don't want anything to do with me?'

'Of course. The decision's not mine to make, but I would never do that.'

'Good, because this job is important for the agency and even more important for me.'

'I promise.'

'Well, I'll email some questions over then.'

'Do that.'

'Kiss.'

'What?'

'*Tchüss*, it's German for bye.'

'Right.'

Anna closed the conversation and went back to her desk.

'Love problems?' Sissela asked.

'Yes, no. It was Hedda. She said, he said, but I didn't mean it, and now he thinks . . . '

'Not easy being a girl.'

Anna couldn't tell whether Sissela had swallowed her lie, but it was done now, so she'd have to weather it.

'Yes,' she agreed, 'but something we all have to go through. And it doesn't help to smooth the way.'

She was full of self-loathing. Using her daughter as an alibi for screwing around.

An email pinged into her inbox and Anna jumped on it. Just a freelance photographer who wanted to remind her of his existence. Anna replied:

Hi, good to hear from you. Promise to keep you in mind.
Speak soon. Anna.

Her reply left the computer with a swoosh. One of the well-known sounds in a modern editorial office, just as familiar as that of a mobile phone vibrating on a desk, or a newly awoken printer whirring rhythmically as it spits out page after page and the quick click of nails on keyboards.

Her computer pinged again. It was from Erik:

> As I said, there are some job-related questions that I need answers to. My colleagues are convinced that you need a PR campaign that targets men, but I'm not convinced that it's the right way to go. I doubt that we could ever attract that many men and am concerned that we might just end up alienating women instead. Your naturally curious colleague said that she wanted people to realise that Family Journal was more than just recipes and housekeeping. I got the impression that she was irritated that the magazine didn't have the same status as a fashion magazine. I don't think that you should compete with them, it's a totally different kind of magazine, another target group. But you could relatively easily glam up the photos in Family Journal without upsetting your readers. I've got a few ideas that I'd like to run by you.
>
> Erik
>
> PS. I understand that we're in different situations and

that there can never be anything between us, but I would still like to meet you again. If nothing else just to clear the air after last time.

Do you want to? Can you?

Anna felt her tense shoulders soften. He wasn't a stupid boy. His analysis of Sissela was perfect, his objection to his colleagues' campaign idea was smart and his apology was sincere. She had nothing to fear. More than her own desire to go round to his flat and ask him to take her again.

No, she wasn't going to do that. She mustn't. Or maybe . . . ?

The big question was what he saw in her. No matter how flattering his interest was, she still had to face facts. Something wasn't right. Anna pressed REPLY. The white page made her hesitate.

Hi Erik, thanks for your email. I have to say that . . .

No. Delete.

Erik, the pleasure was very definitely mutual . . .

Not pleasure. What sort of a word was that? Start again.

Erik. Thank you.

Thank you for what? That could be misunderstood. Gone.

Sorry if I was a bit short on the phone. I think you're on the right track with regard to the campaign. Can't meet you right now. Let's speak in a couple of weeks. Anna.

Swoosh.

Anna swallowed. She clicked on Sent and read her own email again. Was there anything that could be misinterpreted? Had she been too dismissive? Not enough?

She deleted her answer and read his email again.

I understand that we're in different situations and that there can never be anything between us . . .

Had he given up? She had been convinced that there was only one possible solution and that was to put a stop to it immediately, dismiss him with no pardon. Now she wasn't so sure. Should she deny herself the best sex she'd ever had? What was the alternative? Uninspiring two-minute panting for the rest of her life?

. . . but I would still like to meet you again.

Why?

If nothing else just to clear the air after last time.

So he wanted them to sit down and talk? She would sit there and talk about her family and all the years she'd invested and Hedda, or what?

Do you want to? Can you?

Yes. She wanted to. There was no doubt about. One more time at least. Create yet another memory to amuse herself with in the nursing home.

14

There was something easy about the way Magnus drove. He was in control of the situation, confident and unthreatened inside the metal shell. In the car, he was free to comment on his surroundings without fear of reprisal, in the car he could shake his fist at those who drove too slowly and make soothing gestures to those who were irritated. In the car, Magnus was part of the flow, with no obligations other than to stay on the right side of the road and stop at red lights. Magnus was never as free as when he was confined in a car. Anna recognised how ironic the situation was.

The car showroom was on the Berga industrial estate

and the dealer came towards them with outstretched arms and a smile on his lips.

'Hello. Welcome. Coffee?'

'No thank you.'

'Shall we go into my office?'

He ushered them in, offered them a chair each and then took his place opposite. Anna thought it looked like a doctor's waiting room. The dealer made a great fuss turning off his mobile phone. He was busy man, a slave to the electronic shackles of modern life and was tired of people demanding his attention all the time, time which he would far rather dedicate to Magnus and Anna.

'So, are we wanting to up the ante?'

Magnus looked at Anna before replying.

'Yes, it's about time. Our current car is four years old, after all, and it's just as well to trade it in when you can still get something for it.'

'Absolutely, absolutely. Smart move. A lot of people make the mistake of waiting too long. Which is often more expensive. So, what are you looking for? What do you need? Any children?'

'A daughter. And she rides.'

'So are we talking tow-bar and horsebox?'

'No, no, not for a few years. She rides ponies. What I meant was that it can get a bit muddy when it's raining outside.'

It took a few seconds before it dawned on Anna that he was talking about the barely hundred-metre dirt track to the stables. The dealer was even quicker and happy to oblige.

'Ah, a four-wheel-drive,' he said.

Three minutes later, Anna had stopped listening to the endless tirade of abbreviations and performance statistics that were bandied between the two men. It was a foreign language that didn't interest her.

'Right, we're talking an XC60 if I'm right,' the dealer concluded and tapped the pen he'd been playing with during the conversation on the desk.

'I think that sounds like the wisest choice,' Magnus agreed.

'Without a doubt. Shall we take a look at her?'

The dealer smiled fleeting at Anna, to include her in what was going on: time to choose the colour, dear. Your turn. They went out into the showroom. He opened the door to the driver's seat of some shiny model and Magnus got in. The dealer rested his arm idly on the car door.

'The buttons for the seat are down to the right.'

Magnus adjusted the seat slowly back.

'The back also has several positions for comfort, which is good when you're driving long distances.'

'What does it do?' Anna asked.

'Zero point eight, zero point nine, somewhere in that region.'

'Isn't that a lot?'

The dealer shrugged.

'There are cars that take less fuel, of course. But not at this level. We're talking two hundred horsepower, after all. If you were to go for diesel . . . '

'That's not where the money is,' Magnus said, as if to make it clear to Anna that she shouldn't interfere with things she didn't understand.

He got out.

'Get in, darling.'

Anna sat down behind the wheel. Magnus helped her to move the seat forwards. The smell of new cars was overwhelming. Did they use some kind of special spray?

'How does it feel?' the dealer asked.

'Very luxurious. Big.'

'It's a totally different kind of car, sure enough. A new generation, if you like. Not least when it comes to safety. Airbags behind and in front and at the sides.'

Anna got out, the dealer dumped down on the seat and opened the bonnet. Magnus clasped his hands behind his back and nodded sagely while the dealer pointed to various components in the engine and shared some more abbreviations and terms with him. He finished by closing the bonnet with a manly resolve.

'You won't find anything better today. I drive one myself and would never dream of going back. But you should do a test drive.'

Anna looked at her husband and decided that he was every car dealer's wet dream.

'The red one out there to the right,' the dealer said, and handed over the keys.

Magnus took them with reverence.

'Do you want my licence or anything else?'

The dealer closed his eyes and shook his head. No need. He trusted them.

'Is it okay if we take a whirl out on the motorway?' Magnus asked.

He had already accepted the hierarchy of the car salesroom, where the dealer was king and the customer his grateful servant.

'I wouldn't give you the car for less.'

He did, he winked: Anna saw it.

'A true salesman,' she said, as they passed Väla shopping centre.

'You think so?'

'Oh yes.'

'I like him,' Magnus said. 'He says it like it is, isn't trying to sell anything.'

Anna looked at her husband. Was he being ironic? No. She didn't get it. How could a clever man be so stupid?

'Can you feel the pull?' he said, and accelerated.

'Oi, watch your speed.'

'Something else under the bonnet, that's all I'm saying.'

Like a child at Christmas.

Twenty minutes later they were back in the car dealer's office, discussing the price and additional features. The dealer donned a pair of glasses to give him the serious look and was writing down different quotes on a pad that he then turned round for his audience to see. Different deluxe deals worth x were being offered for no more than y, which meant a saving of x thousand, plus he would throw in four winter tyres with alloy rims, because he was feeling generous.

'We'd also like to know what we'd get for trading in our old car,' Anna said.

The dealer nodded.

'Is it a zero point eight?'

'Two point five T,' Magnus corrected.

'Mileage?'

'Eight thousand k.'

'Service?'

'Yes, yes, of course.'

'No catches?'

'Nothing, goes like a dream.'

The dealer sat down at the computer and tapped away.

'Is that carprices.com?' Magnus asked, with interest.

'No, it's an intranet page,' the dealer told him, thereby underlining the difference between amateurs and professionals.

He read what came up and pulled a face.

'Well, I actually shouldn't offer you more than . . .'

He shook his head.

' . . . a hundred and ten thousand, but let's say I add another five. I can't go any higher. We have to give a guarantee, and well, I just can't go any higher.'

'It said a hundred and fifty thousand on carprices.com,' Magnus objected. 'From a dealer, that is. If I sell it myself

I could ask for between a hundred and twenty-five and a hundred and forty.'

The dealer pulled his chin in, a sceptical pose.

'That's sound pretty optimistic to me. We have to go over the car and give it a service, plus we obviously have to take a bit for our services. After all, it's how we make a living. But yes, sure, it might be best for you to sell it yourself. Put an advert in for the top price, but be prepared to drop by a few thousand. Give her a polish and take some pictures.'

Magnus gave Anna a questioning look.

'Worth a try,' she said.

He squirmed.

'Trying to sell involves a lot of work.'

'We can do something nice with the money we save,' Anna said, and turned to face the dealer. 'When we did the calculations at home we said no less than one hundred and twenty-five thousand. We didn't think that we would need to go lower.'

'The difference is only ten thousand,' Magnus pleaded. 'Max fifteen. Plus we'll be saved the bother. And what will we do if we sell the car and then something happens? Not that it would,' he added for the benefit of the dealer, 'it runs like clockwork.'

'I think we should go home and sleep on it,' Anna suggested. 'We still need to pay two hundred and eighty-five. How much would a new roof cost, a hundred?'

She sounded annoyed; she was annoyed. She didn't want to discuss their finances in front of a stranger. But the dealer didn't seem bothered.

'Who holds the purse strings then?' he joked.

The air went out of Magnus, as he knew what was coming. Anna turned to the dealer.

'What did you say?' she asked.

'It was just a joke,' the dealer assured her, his cockiness gone.

'Strange,' Anna said, 'considering it wasn't funny at all.'

'I'm sorry. No harm meant.'

Anna got up.

'We're going home to sleep on it. You'll hear from us tomorrow. And I suggest that you go through your calculations again to make sure that you can't tweak the price a little bit more, at both ends.'

She held out her hand. The dealer was quick to his feet.

Anna walked out, Magnus apologised with a quick

handshake and some gesturing: no worries, I'll call tomorrow. She can be difficult, but who'd want to be married to a sheep?

'What?'

Anna's face was closed and she was staring straight ahead. Magnus looked at her more than the road.

'Thought you were a bit harsh.'

'Did you?'

'Yes, I mean, after all, he wasn't being mean or cocky on purpose.'

'He was just being a pompous horse trader. Sitting there, making it sound like he was doing us a favour.'

'Well, wasn't he?'

'And that stupid last-minute stuff – I'll throw in four alloy rims as well. Like some bloody TV auction.'

'So, we're not going to buy a car then?'

'We are going to buy a car. You phone him tomorrow and get him to give you five more for ours. Either we'll accept that or we'll put in an ad and try to sell it ourselves.'

'But then we'll sell first and buy after?'

'Isn't that what you normally do?'

Magnus shook his head.

'I don't understand why you're so angry.'

'Don't you? Maybe because I don't see the point in shelling out three hundred thousand for a car that's neither bigger nor better than the one we've got, just because it's newer and a lot more expensive.'

'Okay,' Magnus snapped.

His tone of voice was argumentative. He wasn't going to put up with any more shit.

'You were the one who suggested that we should sit down and do the calculations. You were the one who said – now, what was it you said? Life is short and death is eternal?'

He glared at her.

'And you accuse him of being clichéd?'

Anna didn't answer. Magnus shook his head again.

'Sometimes you're so bloody unbelievably pigheaded.'

'Pigheaded?'

'Whatever. You get an idea into your head about something and when it doesn't turn out that way, you get mad.'

'I'm mad because we'll have to bow and fawn and humbly beg to remortgage our house for a toad of a car that won't even smell new in two weeks and what's more, will be dirty, and we'll be all uptight about getting the first scratch and won't be able to relax until it's there, at which point you'll start dreaming about another new car.'

She looked out over a field.

'Pigheaded,' she said, and laughed.

Magnus laughed too. And a few seconds later they were both howling with laughter.

'Okay,' Magnus said, as they turned into their street. 'I'll call tomorrow. If he gives us another five thousand, I'll accept. If not, we'll put in an ad. You okay with that?'

'I promise not to be pigheaded.'

15

Sven, or was it Olof, was standing at the end of an oval table. The other one was sitting beside him, as was Erik. All three dressed like advertising men, that's to say, casual but proper. Their proposal was attached to black panels that were covered with plastic, which had been stuck to the edge of the cardboard. The purpose was not so much to protect the sketches, but rather to make the proposal look more exclusive and important than it actually was. The atmosphere was intense, as it always is when advertising people are showing their wares. Anna presumed that their great earnestness was meant to disguise their candyfloss profession.

It had been to the men's advantage that they'd met them in the bar at the Grand in Mölle, because now they came across as the kind of self-inflated idiots that Anna was more than happy to avoid in daily life. There were disadvantages to being surrounded by mainly female colleagues, but at least she didn't have to deal with male self-importance.

'We haven't targeted the already converted,' droned Sven-or-Olof, 'but rather those with preconceived ideas about the contents of *Family Journal*. We want to open their eyes, make them realise that the magazine is more than just knitting, crocheting and baking. We want men to snatch the magazine from their wives' hands.'

Sissela was leaning forwards. She nodded, in the way she showed her agreement when the magazine management were giving a report. The one that said, yes, I'm a woman but a successful one who knows how to appreciate professional men.

Anna's telephone pinged. She gave an apologetic look to those round the table and opened the text message.

You are totally irresistible when you're sitting this close.
I want to take you here on the table. Now.

Anna looked up, avoided Erik's amused expression.

'So we've designed a campaign that will appeal to the family man as well as women,' Sven-or-Olof continued.

He held up a panel and pulled back the plastic as if he were unveiling a piece of great art. A number of isolated quotes from the most recent edition had been positioned to dramatic effect over various magazine headlines. The pulse of provincial news.

'We thought direct mail to highlight the reading material. Features, biographies, weekly crime features.'

Sissela whipped round and looked at Anna, who was responsible for the material. Anna realised that her cheeks were flushed and she felt distinctly uncomfortable.

Sissela ventured a careful objection that perhaps men would never subscribe to *Family Journal*. This was welcomed by frenetic nodding from the marketing representative, who thought it was an expensive proposal that the publishing house could do better themselves at half the cost.

Sven and Olof weren't so stupid that they didn't nod humbly at the same time as giving assurances in their smoothest voices that they had naturally given this some thought. Even though the campaign was not targeted at the converted, but rather at new readers, it would still have a reinforcing affect on their ordinary readership.

In brief, the proposal they had presented was not quite as catastrophic as the time a bigger advertising agency had, on their own initiative, redesigned the magazine logo and mocked up a front cover that had nothing to do with the magazine's contents, but equally contained nothing to get excited about.

'As we said, this is just an outline and we hope that we can work closely with the editorial team to develop it further. Our proposal is that Erik . . . '

There was something smooth and easy about the way Sven-or-Olof held out his hand towards his younger colleague, as if he were only too aware that recruiting their attractive prodigy to a sector where young blood was the greatest asset had been a huge bonus.

' . . . familiarises himself with the magazine's content a bit more.'

Sissela nodded eagerly. She was more than happy to assist.

'That sounds sensible.'

'And as our proposal is based on highlighting the reading material, it's perhaps best that you do that, Anna, as you're the features editor?'

She straightened her back and nodded tentatively.

'Um, yes, yes, of course.'

'If you could guide Erik through your thinking about the magazine's content.'

Sissela cleared her throat.

'I think that sounds like a good idea. And as managing editor I might be able to add a few thoughts and opinions.'

'Of course. That would be fantastic. If you have the time and opportunity.'

'I'll just have to make the time. But I'm assuming that the taximeter won't start ticking until we've made our decision.'

Sven-or-Olof put on a humble face that he'd probably picked up from the first *Godfather* film.

'I'm sure we'll come to an agreement.'

'Good, we'll discuss this and get back to you as soon as possible.'

Sissela stood up, thereby marking the end of the meeting.

16

They were almost indecent. No, not almost, they were indecent. She who was normally so quiet when she made love, almost silent since they'd had Hedda, had been as loud as a porn star.

Now she was ashamed. Before and after were different worlds.

Erik pressed himself against her, purred, made himself small on purpose. She wanted to get up and leave. False conventions forced her to lie there and feel her pulse beating against her temples.

'Nice,' he said, with a lisp.

Anna felt her body stiffen. Was he talking baby language? No way, that would be too much to bear. She couldn't have a sexual relationship with a man who used baby talk.

'Wasn't it?' he added, removing any doubt.

She smiled in reply. He was a better lover than her husband, far better. But that didn't matter when he lisped in the belief that it was charming.

She tapped him on the chest.

'Towel?'

'In the cupboard.'

'Thanks.'

He was lisping. Who on earth had got him to believe that it was anything other than a complete turnoff? Anyway, it was a good thing. She'd have no problem resisting the temptation in the future. Anna opened her mouth under the water as she soaped herself. Suddenly the bathroom door opened and the shower curtain was pulled to one side.

Anna blinked the water out of her eyes and saw Erik holding out his mobile phone towards her.

'What the hell are you doing?'

She reached for the towel.

'Out!'

She pointed the shower at him, he dodged out the way, laughing. She closed the door again, rinsed off the soap and dried herself thoroughly. She wrapped the towel around her body and went out.

'That wasn't funny.'

Erik was sitting by the kitchen table in his boxers, his mobile phone connected to his open laptop.

'What are doing?!'

Anna rushed forwards and snatched away the phone.

'Were you thinking of posting those pictures?'

Erik sighed.

'I just went on to the internet and I surf on my phone. Why would I want to post those pictures?'

'How dare you photograph me naked!'

'You're beautiful. I just wanted something to remind me.'

'Well, I don't want you to take pictures of me, either naked or dressed. Understood?'

She looked alternately at Erik and the phone screen.

'You did that in Mölle too. Are you are pervert, or something?'

'It was a joke. So that you'd get as hysterical as you did in Mölle.'

'Did I get hysterical?'

'Yes.'

'You don't know what hysterical is. Do you realise what you're doing? Do you know how bloody invasive that is?'

Erik went over to the sink and filled a glass of water. He gulped it down.

'You were filming me,' Anna said, and held up the phone to him as evidence.

She was almost shaking when she tapped her finger on the screen and deleted the file. 'I was just mucking around,' Erik said, hurt.

Anna went over to him, handed back the phone and picked up his laptop. She checked his history and looked through his files. He stood beside her, watching.

'Lucky for you,' she said, once she'd confirmed that nothing had been downloaded on to the computer.

Erik shook his head.

'You don't have a very high opinion of me, do you?'

Anna controlled herself.

'You can't just barge in and film me in the shower. Don't you get that?'

Erik tightened his lips.

'It was a joke, okay? I didn't mean anything by it. I'm

sorry if I upset you. But it's not exactly like we don't know each other.'

'It is, in fact,' Anna said. 'That's exactly what it is. We don't know each other at all. And I have to go now.'

She went into the sitting room, gathered up her clothes and threw the towel at him.

The water spilled from his glass as he caught it.

'How can you say that after everything we've done?'

'Everything we've done? We've slept together, had sex. That's nothing, that's . . . '

She made a gesture with her hands to show that what-ever it was had now gone up in smoke. Erik stared at her.

'What?' Anna said.

'Doesn't this mean anything to you? Do you really think that I just jump into bed with anyone?'

'Stop. You're young, you're not in a steady relationship, you look the way you do and as far as I've understood, earn pretty well too. I assume you take whatever opportunities come your way. And if you don't, I suggest you change that and do it while you can. We are over. It was you who kissed me, not the other way round. You asked me to your room.'

'And you came. You weren't exactly hard to persuade.'

Anna shook her head.

'Whatever, here and now, it's over. I have a daughter, a husband, a family. And I don't intend to risk that for something that isn't real.'

'Isn't real?'

'We've slept together a few times. Don't make it bigger than it is.'

'So you think it's okay for you to fuck around when you feel like it? A bit of a change to spice up a tired sex life at home. A flat stomach, as opposed to Magnus' belly.'

Anna froze.

'How do you know what my husband is called?'

'Ever heard of the internet?'

Anna pulled on her pants and put on her bra with brisk, agitated movements. Erik observed her, slightly superior.

'I was going to check how old you were,' he said. 'On birthday.se. It said that you shared your address with Magnus.'

Anna glared at him.

'That feels really creepy, you know.'

She pulled her blouse on over her head like a sweater. They hadn't taken the time to undo the buttons when they ripped off each other's clothes. She turned her trousers the right way round and put them on, bent down for her socks, put them on standing as the mattress was low and she didn't want to sit down. She had no intention of staying a second longer than she needed to.

'So you know where we live?' she said, and went past him, out into the hall.

'I wasn't exactly looking for the information.'

'Erik,' she said, as she stepped into her shoes. 'It was exciting, an adventure. Don't make this harder than it is.'

She took her jacket down from the hook, looked at him.

'Promise.'

He was standing poker straight, almost shaking. Anna nodded at the glass in his hand.

'Careful you don't spill it.'

He looked down, held his arm out and crushed the glass with his hand. It broke and the water splashed on to the floor. Anna looked at his hand and then up at him. He stood there holding his bleeding hand out in front of him, without taking his eyes from her.

'Jesus, are you all right?'

She took a step towards him, caught his wrist and led him quickly into the kitchen. She held his hand under the cold water and pulled out two shards that had got caught in his skin, inspected the cut, which filled with blood as soon as his hand left the running water.

'What happened?'

Erik looked at her without answering, watched her concern and care with fascination. Didn't pay any attention to his bleeding hand.

'You'll need to get a doctor to look at that, you'll need stitches. Did you do that on purpose?'

He didn't answer.

'You need to go to hospital.'

'It's not that deep.'

'Have you got any bandages?'

'I don't know.'

She looked around the room, spotted a tea towel, opened it up and saw that it was dirty.

'There's clean ones in the cupboard.'

Anna got one out, rinsed his hand under the cold water again. The blood flow wasn't as intense any more. She squeezed together the edges of the wound.

'Maybe it's not so deep after all. Keep your hand under the water. Have you got any disinfectant?'

He shook his head.

'Alcohol?'

'No.'

'All right,' she said, and turned off the tap.

She dried his hand with kitchen roll and tied the tea towel tight around the wound. She sat him down by the kitchen table.

'We haven't talked about work,' Erik said.

'No, and I don't think it's a good idea that we do.'

'What do you mean?'

'I don't think we should work together.'

'You mean you and me?'

Anna didn't answer.

'What am I supposed to do then?' Erik asked. 'I have to get this contract. I'm new, I don't think you understand how important it is. Who am I going to talk to then?'

Anna inspected her hands, which were red with his blood. She went over to the sink and washed them.

'Email me your questions. I'll answer. Let's keep it simple. Okay?'

She looked at him, shook her head with concern.

'You have to be careful,' she said. 'Don't do things like that. Do you realise that you frightened me?'

He nodded. She stroked his arm.

'I have to go.'

Anna couldn't hide the fact that she was in a rush to get out. She hurried down the stairs and Erik stood in the doorway and listened to her footsteps disappear. He went back into the flat, stood by the window, saw her come out of the door and run across the street.

She didn't even turn round.

Erik went over to the bookshelves and picked up the T-shirt that looked like it had been thrown there by accident, and turned off the web camera that it had been hiding. He got his laptop, stopped the recording and pressed PLAY.

17

'You don't need to come and collect me,' Kathrine said. 'I'll catch the bus.'

'No, Mum, I'll pick you up,' Anna said, squeezing the phone between her shoulder and her ear, as both hands were busy putting the shopping away in the fridge. 'I need to swing by Väla anyway.'

'Well, do that first then,' her mother said. 'I don't want to set a foot in there.'

Anna almost laughed.

'Mum, when are you going to reconcile yourself with Väla?'

'Never.'

'You'll have to at some point. Everyone goes there. I just need to pop into the off-licence and buy a bottle of wine.'

'Can't you do that on Drottninggatan?'

'There's never anywhere to park.'

'I'll sit in the car.'

'Okay. I'll pick you up first then.'

Anna put down the phone and discovered that her daughter had been listening to the conversation.

'I'll come with you to get Granny.'

'No, sweetheart. Not this time.'

'But I want to go to Väla.'

'We're not going to Väla.'

'But you said you were.'

'Granny didn't want to, so I changed my plan. I'm going to another off-licence. You and I can go to Väla tomorrow afternoon. I'm in a bit of a rush right now.'

Hedda let out a disappointed sigh, but accepted her fate. Anna put on her jacket and started to walk towards the car. She tapped on the bathroom window, which was ajar so the steam could get out.

'Just going to collect Mum,' she called.

'Okay,' Magnus answered, from the shower.

Anna got into the car and reversed out. She drove slowly through the residential streets, lifting her finger from the wheel to greet people she knew, she passed the shop where she went almost daily and always bumped into acquaintances. A shop where you could openly look in your neighbours' shopping trolley, out of curiosity and in search of inspiration. Mince? Yes, why not? It was a long time since they'd had meatballs. Rustic and seasonal. Some gherkins to go with it. Have we got vinegar?

Kathrine was waiting outside her entrance on Kopparmöllegatan. She got into the car and gave Anna a kiss on the cheek.

'Hello.'

'Don't understand what you've got against Väla.'

Kathrine shivered.

'Ugh,' she said. 'There are only four truly democratic things in life: pollution, bad weather, traffic jams and Väla shopping centre. A mecca for ugly people. I refuse. Väla has strangled the city centre, we'll end up just like the United States. Massive parking lots, ugly and obese.'

'Yes, Mother,' Anna said, amused.

She steered her way out of the street and down into the centre. She parked in a loading bay and turned on the radio to keep her mother company. When she returned, hiphop was blaring out of the loudspeakers.

Anna looked at her.

'You're just doing that to provoke me.'

Kathrine nodded her head in time to the bass a couple of times before turning it off.

'Okay,' she said. 'Tell me.'

'Tell you what?' Anna exclaimed.

'What's on your mind.'

Anna pulled in her chin and smiled sheepishly.

'I don't understand.'

'You insist on collecting me. Hedda's not here. You want to talk. What is it?'

Anna turned and looked straight ahead. Kathrine put a hand on her arm.

'I like Magnus,' she said. 'I really do. But you are my daughter.'

Ten minutes later Anna had told her an airbrushed version, omitted Erik's lie about his mother, filming on his mobile phone and the broken glass. She had told her mother about the kiss outside the toilet, the subsequent rendezvous in his room, the trip up to Kullaberg and the two encounters in his flat.

'I thought it was something serious,' her mother concluded.

'What do you mean?'

'I'd got it into my head that were you were going to get divorced.'

'Why would we get divorced?'

Kathrine shrugged.

'People do. Suburbia sucks the life out of lots of people. You can guarantee that when a loved-up young couple move in next door, whoosh, the time machine takes you back to when you were young and life was easy, childless and uncomplicated. Your little adventure sounds wonderful. Apart from the fact he's obviously a bit loopy. I mean, primal screams out to sea – there are limits.'

'So you don't think I should say anything to Magnus?'

'Under no circumstances. What he doesn't know won't hurt him. Do you think you're the first woman in history to stray? Just be happy it was such a positive experience.'

'He wants us to carry on meeting,' Anna said.

'Do you?'

Anna paused for a while.

'No,' she said. 'I don't.'

'You sound hesitant.'

'No, not really.'

Kathrine gave an approving nod.

'Sounds sensible,' she said. 'Be glad for what happened. No point in taking it any further.'

'And yet . . .'

'Yes?'

'Well, purely . . .'

'Sexually?' Kathrine prompted.

Anna nodded. Her mother laughed and patted her on the knee.

'What did you say his name was?'

'Erik Månsson.'

Kathrine turned to look at the road.

'Not easy to google,' she said.

18

The friends who had invited them to dinner were as sweet and kind as they were hopeless at cooking. The meat, which for some unknown reason had to be barbecued outdoors, despite the weather and time of year, was put on before the lighter fuel had burned off and so was torched on either side for a couple of minutes.

'Take out the potatoes, the meat's done,' the husband shouted.

'But I don't know if they're ready.'

'They must be. Surely half an hour is enough.'

Two minutes later they were sitting at the table with a

piece of cooling meat that was still red in the middle in front of them and a baked potato that no fork in the world could get into.

'Delicious, isn't it? Help yourself.'

There was no salt and pepper on the table, the only thing that could help with the taste was some bought Béarnaise sauce. The couple praised each other's cooking and were oblivious to the fact that neither of their guests joined in the chorus. Both Anna and Magnus tried to find something positive to say, but had to concentrate to avoid looking at each other, so they didn't lose it and start to laugh, because then they wouldn't be able to stop. Which ended up being the case anyway, when Anna had to cough up a piece of meat that she couldn't chew into swallowable pieces.

When Anna and Magnus left their friends just before midnight, they had barely rounded the corner before they collapsed and had to support each other home. They both really liked their genuine, warm-hearted friends, there was nothing to dislike about them.

Kathrine was pleased to see the pair of them so relaxed, but when Anna tried to recount the evening's culinary highlights, she laughed so much that the story was broken into unrecognisable snatches.

'You're so horrible,' Kathrine said.

'I know, but I can't help it. You couldn't eat it.'

'But if they're so bad at making food, why don't you ask them here instead?'

'We tried. But they really wanted . . .'

Another howl of laughter interrupted her and she only managed to breathe in gulps.

'Are you drunk?' Kathrine wondered.

'No, unfortunately.'

More laughter and doubling up.

'Delicious, isn't it?' she mimicked, and dried the tears from her eyes.

'Poor people,' Kathrine said. 'Imagine if they knew what you were saying.'

'Won't you have a glass of wine?' Magnus asked.

'Just the one glass?' she teased, and looked at the clock. 'Actually, half a glass. I thought I'd catch the last bus home.'

'You can stay here, if you like,' Anna offered.

'Thank you, that's kind. But it's always good to wake up in your own bed.'

Magnus came back with a bottle and some glasses.

'I think it's a bit strange that they praise each other,' Kathrine said.

'Yes,' Anna replied, 'but that's the whole thing. It's so charming, their guileless delight.'

She fanned her face in her hand.

'Oof, I feel so mean.'

'But you had a nice time?' Kathrine asked. 'Apart from the food.'

'Oh yes,' Magnus said, with undisguised enthusiasm. 'There was a dessert as well.'

'Ice cream,' Anna howled. 'It's always ice cream. Every time.'

'With a fruit salad,' Magnus added. 'From a tin!'

Kathrine shook her head.

'I hope you didn't show your contempt while you were there,' she said. 'You actually sound quite nasty. I'm no great star in the kitchen either. What do you say when you've been to me for dinner?'

'Mum, you're in a totally different league. Not even the same solar system.'

'You make really good food,' Magnus assured her.

'No, I don't,' Kathrine said. 'I make food, but it's seldom very good. Cheers.'

They raised their glasses.

'When does the bus go?'

'Half past,' Anna said. 'Take a taxi. We can pay for it.'

'Taxi? When I can take the bus? What a silly idea. And in any case, it's fun. Always some tipsy teenagers who get up to give me a seat. And then I can sit there and listen to them talk about their dramas. All their feelings on the outside. It energises me just to hear them.'

'You're joking?'

'Not at all. Today's teenagers are very well brought up. Anyone who says otherwise is just frightened, but doesn't know what of.'

'Okay, as you like,' Anna said. 'But I'll come to the bus stop with you.'

The air was cool and moist, the wind was soughing in the treetops along Landborgen. Anna and Kathrine walked arm in arm. Anna hoped that it was a tradition that would be passed on to the next generation.

'Was everything okay with Hedda?' she asked.

'Just fine. She fell asleep in front of the television, so I carried her to bed. She's such a lovely girl. You've done well by her.'

'I don't know that we've done anything really. She came ready-made.'

'I think you can take some of the credit. Is she still riding?'

'Twice a week. She thinks it's fun.'

Kathrine nodded.

'That's the main thing,' she said.

They walked in silence, side by side.

'And you're having fun too,' she added. 'You and Magnus.'

'Yes,' Anna confirmed. 'We can laugh together.'

'That's important. That and the sack, and then you can solve most things.'

'We're okay on that front too. What happened, it was just ... Did you ever do something stupid?'

'Yes.'

'Do tell.'

'No, no, never. Strictly off limits.'

They walked past Hedda's school, which stood deserted in the dark.

'Empty schools are spooky,' Anna said. 'You can hear the echoes of all the break-time voices.'

'The nights are okay. Sunny summer days are worse.'

'What do you mean?'

Kathrine shrugged.

'You always seem to see some poor lonely soul on the

swings or the climbing frame, someone with no friends who should really be on the beach. Someone who wants the holidays to end and the automatic social life of school to start again. Children left to look after themselves.'

'Perhaps,' Anna agreed.

They sat in the bus shelter. When the bus appeared over the crest of the hill like a lit-up ferry, they got up. Kathrine gave her daughter a hug.

'Take care,' she said. 'And for God's sake, don't confess to Magnus. That would be a greater offence than the original one. People share their rubbish whenever they feel like it these days. It's not good, not for anyone. If you need to talk, call me, promise.'

Anna nodded. Kathrine stroked her cheek.

'Good, darling,' she said, and got on to the bus.

Anna stood and watched as her mother made her way down the aisle of the bus, which was full of drunk teenagers ready to party. Just like a fish in water, she thought to herself and raised her hand and waved as the bus accelerated in towards town.

Then her heart flipped.

Erik Månsson was standing on the other side of the road.

19

'Damn,' he said, and crossed the road.

He looked at Anna, who couldn't make a sound.

'When's the next one?'

She stared at him.

'What are you doing here?'

'What? Oh, I've been to see a friend. When's the next bus?'

Anna didn't answer. Erik walked past her into the shelter and ran his finger down the timetable that was hanging there. She looked at him uneasily, tried to find a logical explanation why the man she had slept with suddenly appeared only a block from her house just after midnight.

'It was the last one, wasn't it?' he said, shaking his head.

'What are you doing here?'

Erik looked at her as if she were stupid.

'I just said. I was at a friend's. Why? Can't I come here? Do you own this part of town?'

'What's his name?'

'Who? My friend? What makes you think it's a he?'

Erik gave a self-confident laugh.

'Are you following me?' Anna asked.

'Am I what?'

'You heard,' Anna said.

He seemed to be more amused than anything else.

'Why on earth would I follow you? I've been to visit a friend.'

'Who?'

'Why? Don't you believe me? He's called Johan, he lives in one of the white-brick buildings down there. Johan Andersson.'

'Johan Andersson.'

'An old friend, married, two kids. Why? What are you doing here?'

'I live here. You know that. You've checked my address.'

'I mean, what are you doing out here in the middle of the night without a dog or anything?'

'I was keeping my mum company while she waited for the bus.'

'Well, she caught it then,' Erik sighed. 'Lucky for her.'

'How old are the children?'

'Which children?'

'Your friend's. You said he had two children.'

'How old? Three and five.'

'Called?'

'Saga and Max. Why?'

He laughed again and shook his head.

'You really think I've come here to do what – to spy on you? Don't you think you might be exaggerating your own importance just a little?'

Anna didn't answer.

'Come on,' Erik said. 'You're making me nervous. Exactly what would I get out of it?'

'Which one's oldest?'

'Which what's oldest?'

'Of the children. Mats or Saga?'

'Mats? His name's Max. Who would call their kid Mats

137

these days?' Erik gave a weary sigh and said: 'She is. The girl's the oldest.'

'Saga?'

He gave an irritated single nod.

'Satisfied?'

Anna relaxed a bit and changed tack.

'Sorry,' she said.

'No worries.'

Erik looked away. Anna reached out and gave him a friendly prod on the shoulder.

'I didn't mean to offend you, but I've got a family. I love my husband.'

He nodded, with gritted teeth.

'It's different for you,' she added.

He looked at her.

'What do you know about that?' he said, almost aggressively, and walked off.

Anna hurried to catch up with him, stopped in front of him and blocked his path.

'I'm sorry,' she said. 'I really didn't mean to hurt you.'

He turned his face away like a child who's been treated unfairly.

'Erik . . . please. It was silly of me. I'm sorry.'

He looked at her.

'Do you know how it feels? You're making all kinds of accusations. Why would I follow you? Tell me. Why the fuck would I follow you?'

Anna looked at the ground.

'Sorry,' she said. 'It was just such a surprise to see you. I never intended to jump to conclusions.'

'No, you just did it naturally.'

He took a deep breath.

'Now, if you'll excuse me,' he said. 'I have to walk back into town. It's going to take an hour and I'm tired.'

He walked past her. Anna stood there. What she wanted to say was stuck in her throat.

'You took your time.'

Magnus was in his underpants, with his toothbrush in his mouth.

'The bus was late,' Anna said.

Her husband spat the toothpaste out into the sink.

'Was starting to wonder if something had happened.'

Which is why you're getting ready to go to bed, Anna thought.

'Actually tried to ring,' he added, in an accusing tone.

'I didn't have my phone with me.'

'No, so I heard.'

He dried his mouth on a towel, smiled at Anna.

'Have to say, your mother is very cool.'

'Yes, can't say I don't agree.'

'If you're like that when you get old, I won't complain.'

Anna smiled and squeezed out some toothpaste. She looked at herself in the mirror as she brushed her teeth. She knew what she looked like inside out, but was blind to how she looked from the outside. Like so many women, she saw only her flaws, her shortcomings, the ultimate abnormalities. She wondered whether Magnus reacted to the skin by her ears, if he concentrated on the crow's feet around her eyes, the deepening furrows from her nose down to her mouth. Probably not to any great extent.

Anna had talked to Trude and Sissela about the moment when they'd first discovered that they were women. For all of them, it was when men had started to comment on their appearance, and for Anna, it was a boy in high school. He had passed her in the corridor and spontaneously exclaimed, *Nice tits!* as he passed. As if it were the most natural thing in the world to comment on a stranger's appearance.

Anna looked at them in the mirror and thought to

herself that he hadn't been wrong. In fact, overall, there wasn't much to complain about.

Erik went to his car, which was parked a block away, and drove home. He hadn't planned anything, had just thought of observing from a distance. When Anna left the house to walk to the bus stop with her mum, an opportunity opened up.

He didn't know what he'd expected. If he'd expected anything at all. He had, of course, hoped that she would be pleased to see him, hadn't imagined otherwise.

Instead she chose to confront him. What was he doing there? Who had he been to see? What were the children called?

He'd managed to pull it off, but her reaction was appalling.

He found a parking place by Norra Hamnen, walked back to the flat and turned on the computer. He knew the video clip off by heart, but still couldn't get enough of it.

She was theatrical. Women were. It was as if they got their ideals from films. An uncontrollable passion that took over them, an animal instinct that freed them from responsibility and obliterated their guilt. Preferably up against a wall.

Intertwined and half-naked, they appeared in the picture. Kissing and passion, a quick exploration of each other's bodies, both flattered by mutual desire. The deep sigh of satisfaction when he penetrated her.

Her vulgar torrent of words, how she begged him to go deeper and take her harder, her face that distorted when she came.

It had the same effect every time.

Erik unbuttoned his jeans.

20

Anna looked at her husband with amusement.

'Shall I show you what you're sitting on?'

'Very funny.'

Magnus pulled more of the lead towards him. He had washed the outside of the car, rinsed the rubber mats and was now going to vacuum the inside. All so they could take good pictures that showed the car at its best.

'It's all about turning the buyer on,' he explained. 'The first impression is what counts.'

Sweden's worst car buyer was now an expert in selling and knew how it should be done. The professional dealer they had visited earlier in the week hadn't wanted to give them a better offer, which had annoyed both Magnus and Anna so much that they decided to try an alternative make to the car that was almost obligatory for Swedish families.

'You don't have to put your bum in the same seat all your life,' he continued. 'It's the customer who decides.'

Magnus was lured by the prestige of a German make, Anna by the prospect of something cheaper. But no matter what, the first thing on their list was to sell their existing car.

'You're good,' Anna said, and left her husband to his work.

Half an hour later she was standing in the kitchen with Anna, watching Magnus set up his rarely used camera equipment, which included a tripod and remote control.

'Is he taking pictures?' Hedda asked.

'No, he's creating images,' Anna replied, unable to hold back a laugh.

Hedda didn't understand what was so funny, but was happy just to be part of it.

'Wait,' Anna said, and went out into the hall and dug out a beret from among all the hats. 'Go out to Daddy and say that he has to put this on.'

Hedda went out and handed him the beret. She pointed

towards Anna, who was in the kitchen filming it all on her mobile phone. When Magnus realised that unexpectedly he was entertaining his family with his artistic ambitions, he donned the beret and played along, moved the tripod centimetre this way, a centimetre that – unable to decide which was best.

Two hours later they were sitting in their newly spruced car on the way to Väla. The advert had been posted on the internet and Magnus checked his phone at regular intervals to make sure that he hadn't missed any calls from prospective buyers.

'It's never looked so good,' Anna said, when they'd parked. 'Maybe we should just keep it.'

Magnus looked at her. His entire existence was now focused on upgrading the car. His wife's words made the ground under him shudder on the Richter Scale.

'Just joking,' she said, and took his arm.

The heaving shopping centre was like a cancerous tumour, packed full of hypnotised shopping zombies. Anna nudged Magnus in the ribs and nodded at their daughter, who was walking a few steps in front of them. She looked like a born-again Bible belt American in Jesus country. Hedda's wide-eyed fascination with the people and what was on offer made both Anna and Magnus quiver with delight. They both realised they had to enjoy it while it lasted. Soon enough Hedda would be embarrassed to be seen with them, like all teenagers.

She turned to them.

'Mum, your phone's ringing. Can't you hear it?

Anna fished her phone out of her bag.

'Hello.'

'Hi, it's me.'

Erik's voice. Anna's mood swung from easy and happy to troubled and nervous within a fraction of a second. Her windpipe constricted and her cheeks reddened. She stopped, trying to keep her distance from Magnus. But he stopped too, looked at her, wondered who it was on the phone.

'No, I'm afraid you've got the wrong number,' Anna forced herself to say.

'Call me,' Erik said.

'Not at all.'

She hung up.

'Wrong number,' she said, and put her phone back in her bag.

She could barely swallow, looked around to find something to comment on, something insignificant and everyday, whatever. She was ready to confess, whether it was wanted or not. She couldn't hide her feelings from the man she loved and had shared her life with for fifteen years, it wasn't possible.

'Right,' was Magnus' response. 'Where are we going?'

'I want to go to the pet shop,' Hedda cried.

'I have to pop into H&M,' Anna said. 'Need to buy some tights.'

'Okay,' Magnus replied. 'I'll go to the pet shop with Hedda and we'll meet outside the coffee place.'

Anna smiled at him with love.

'You really don't want to be here any longer than necessary,' she said.

Magnus shrugged.

'Just thought it would be more efficient.'

'Okay, see you there.'

They parted. After a hundred metres, Anna turned to make sure her husband and daughter were far enough away. She got out her phone and called.

'Hi.'

His voice was soft and affectionate, intimate, as if they shared a world together.

'I'm with Magnus and my daughter at Väla,' Anna snapped, and looked around.

'Oh, sorry.'

'You can't call me, certainly not on a Sunday. Don't you understand that?'

'What do you mean?'

'What do you mean, "what do you mean"?'

'Why can't I call you?

'Because I'm married and I have a child.'

'You don't know why I'm calling you. Maybe I want some help with the advertising campaign.'

'Erik . . . '

'I miss you.'

Anna didn't answer.

'I want to see you again,' he continued. 'And not just for work, I want to see you again, like when we were at my place.'

His speech was slurred.

'Are you drunk?'

'I'm not drunk.'

'Have you been drinking?'

'Not much, just a couple of beers.'

'Erik, listen to me. Don't ring me again. Promise me that.'

'Can I text you?'

'No.'

'Anna . . .'

She pressed DISCONNECT and considered turning to silent mode. But then realised that Magnus might try to get hold of her. She couldn't turn off the sound before they'd met up again.

Getting drunk on a Sunday was something that only upper-class people did, and he certainly wasn't one of them. A couple of beers . . . So that was why he'd stayed sober at Mölle with his bosses. He had a problem with alcohol. The thought hadn't even occurred to her earlier. That made things even more complicated, meant that she could never be certain, that any time he might . . .

A new signal, the same number.

'I said that you can't phone me.'

'Just one thing. I assumed you were on your own now as you called me.'

'What?' Anna demanded.

'I like you.'

'Erik.'

'Wait, wait. Let me finish. I . . .'

He was silent.

'You what? Come on, say what you've got to say.'

'Can't you come over?'

'No, under no circumstances. Put the phone down now and don't you dare call me again.'

She hung up and turned off the sound. It would just have to stay on silent. The man was dangerous.

21

Anna put her bag down on her desk and went out into the kitchen. Her hand was shaking as she poured the coffee. She went back to her place, pretended not to notice Sissela's scrutinising eyes.

'Hung-over?'

'Not at all. I slept badly, lay awake practically all night.'

'Why's that?'

'Don't know.'

'Oh, it's horrible,' Sissela commiserated, and then automatically turned the conversation to her. 'I went through a period like that about six months ago, just about drove me mad. It's a vicious circle. Did you try tensing your body? I mean, tense every muscle and then hold it for a few seconds before relaxing. It usually works.'

'Sissela.'

She held up her hand.

'Sorry, just trying to be helpful.'

Anna sat down at her computer, put her bag on the floor beside her and went through the pile of features she'd printed out. She always edited on paper first, then made the corrections in the original document. She printed it out again and made some more small corrections, a third printout, and so on. Editing was an endless job, there wasn't a text in the world that couldn't be better formulated, tighter. Obviously it wasn't prize-winning literature and Anna normally stopped when she started to reinstate previous changes and she had gone the full cycle.

The articles on the table were more or less ready, and only the captions had to be honed.

Trude made her entrance, radiant and beautiful as always. Anna was often struck by her beauty on Mondays in particular. It was as if she had forgotten what her colleague looked like over the weekend, or suppressed it. By Wednesday she'd got used to it again, and when they left the office on Friday she no longer noticed, only to be reminded again after the weekend.

'Watch out for Anna,' Sissela told her. 'She hasn't slept well.'

'Oh, why's that?' Trude asked.

Anna waved the question away.

'Nothing in particular, just couldn't sleep.'

'Didn't you have any pills?'

'I don't like pills, they totally zonk me out.'

'And exactly how bright-eyed are you when you haven't slept?'

Anna sipped her coffee and opened a file on the computer. She clicked on the caption as she read the headline, and tried to think of something better. Quote boxes generally started with 'I', 'Now' or 'My', which got a bit tedious when you flicked through the magazine. Like everything was just a regurgitation of something that had been said before.

'I masturbate,' Trude said. 'Usually works.'

'But then you just get turned on,' Sissela countered.

'Just a quickie. You come, big yawn and zonk. Out for the count.'

Anna wasn't listening. She was sitting with her right

hand on the pile of papers, the top page down to the left, pretending to look through the letters, which had now mutated into black spots.

She was scared. Scared of what lay ahead. Of it all coming out, the showdown. What would happen? How would it affect her marriage? Would Magnus stay? If not, how would they sort out all the practical issues? Their lifestyle was based on two salaries and there wasn't much left over for any extras. She couldn't bear the thought of an every-alternate-week life with Hedda. She couldn't imagine a day without her daughter. Anna almost wished that Magnus would do the same thing so that she didn't need to feel guilty. But that wouldn't happen. Her husband wasn't a ladies' man. His sexual appetite wasn't so great that it couldn't easily be satisfied within social conventions. O happy martyr with good on your side.

'I'll have to try that next time,' Sissela said. 'I normally tense my body. You know, the kind of relaxation exercises we did in gym at school.'

Anna put her hand into her bag and checked her phone without taking it out. No text messages and no missed calls. At least Erik hadn't tried to contact her again after that crazy conversation yesterday.

What if he was mad? Why had he picked her? It had been magical, it wasn't that. But it was pretend, a random meeting, a parenthesis, something that happened outside ordinary, everyday life. Couldn't he just be happy with that?

He had turned up at Laröd. Appeared from behind the bus like something out of a horror movie. He'd been sober then. Why would he take the bus if he hadn't been drinking? What was it his friend was called? Something very ordinary. Andersson. Johan Andersson.

She went on to find.se, typed in the name and 'Helsingborg'. Got more than twelve hits, but no Hittarp or Laröd. She felt her pulse rise, but then thought that maybe the phone was listed under his wife's name. She tried with just Andersson, but was none the wiser. Over two thousand hits. She didn't have time to trawl through them all. And she didn't know if they were married, and even if they were, it didn't mean that the wife had taken his name.

'Enough,' she said out loud, to stop herself from looking any more.

'Enough what?' Sissela asked.

Anna waved her hand.

'Nothing. I'm just thinking out loud.'

She looked down at her captions again, pretended to read.

'How are the advertising boys getting on?' Trude asked.

Anna looked up, but realised the question was directed at Sissela.

'How do you mean?'

'With their campaign? Did they do anything?'

'Oh, right, yes, thanks for reminding me. I was going to leave a message. No, it didn't really amount to much. What do you think?'

Trude shrugged. Sissela turned to Anna.

'And you?'

'I don't know.'

Sissela pulled a face.

'I don't know?' she parroted. 'Come on, say what you think.'

'Well, it wasn't a complete catastrophe,' Anna tried.

'But?'

'I think they're on the wrong track.'

'Good,' Sissela concluded. 'We all agree.'

Lack of sleep reminded her of being hung-over. A short fuse and irritation that could at any moment tip over into giggling delight. With a bit of food in her stomach, Anna felt euphoric. Sissela used the lunch break to bitch about her husband.

'I don't know what it is,' she said. 'He just rings me on the work phone for no reason to check that I'm here. Goes into details and over things again and again.'

'When you've had an argument?' Trude asked.

'No, no, what we're going to eat for dinner and who said what when. And lots of things that have happened recently that need to be analysed and relived and it's just not interesting.'

'He's keeping tabs on you?'

'No, not really, he's more like a dog in a small kitchen, always in the way. You can't turn round without finding him standing there with begging eyes.'

'Maybe he's just restless,' Anna said.

'Do you know how much he does? Wine and food . . . '

'The good life?'

'Yes, and walking and the great outdoors.'

'Sven Hedin style?'

'Exactly. But not one of the experiences he talks about so much can even begin to match the intensity of his rage when someone points out that I earn more.'

'Oh, you're being horrible.'

'On Saturday, when the guests had left, guess what he did.'

Sissela was interrupted by her phone. She held up her mobile, to show that it was the devil they'd just been talking about on the other end. She pressed ANSWER.

'I'm sitting here eating.'

She rocked her head back and forth, indicated her lack of interest with her free hand.

'Okay, I'll call you later.'

She finished the conversation and then checked that she really had hung up.

'Where was I? Yes, that was it.'

Sissela told in great detail how a successful dinner party on Saturday had put her husband in the mood. When it was time to go to bed, he had appeared with a tub of chocolate sauce.

Anna laughed and disliked herself for doing it. She didn't know how she'd be able to look Sissela's husband in the eye next time they met. Without thinking about chocolate sauce and misconceived amorous advances.

The relaxed atmosphere around the table threatened to distance them from the rest of the editorial team. Not only were they sitting slightly apart from everyone else, they were also having fun and very obviously at the cost of someone who wasn't there.

They were still laughing when they got out of the lift at the editorial office and walked side by side down the corridor. Anna wasn't quite comfortable with the role as one of the cool girls. Only someone who was outside the group would imagine that it was something to aspire to.

One of the layout girls was walking towards them. She looked at Anna.

'You've got a visitor,' she said.

'Have I?'

'I gave him some coffee,' the layout girl said, and pointed towards the kitchen.

'Him?' Sissela chirped with delight and headed her troops into the kitchen. 'Oh, hello! Nice to see you again. Everything okay?'

She shook Erik Månsson's hand, warmly, with both hands. He turned to Anna, tried to avoid Sissela's attention by saying a quick hello to Trude as well.

'I hope there hasn't been a misunderstanding here,' Sissela said, taking command again.

Erik didn't follow.

'That you're starting to ask for payment, I mean. I don't want to see any invoices on my desk.'

'No risk, you don't need to worry about that.'

'Good, glad we agree.'

Sissela turned to Anna.

'Well, we'll leave you in peace then. Don't want to disturb the creative process, do we?'

Sissela left them in a good mood. Anna pointed.

'Let's sit down in the meeting room.'

She walked in front of him over to the glass box where Erik and his older colleagues had presented their slightly sad subscription campaign the week before. She held the door open, let Erik through, then went in and closed the door behind her. Erik was carrying a tablet instead of a briefcase. He put it down on the table and looked at Anna.

'Sit down,' she said, indicating one of the chairs.

Erik settled and glanced out at the editorial office on the other side of the glass. Anna had her back to the open-plan office.

'They can see us, but can't hear what we saying,' Anna said with authority. 'Everything we say has to be said calmly and quietly, no agitated waving of the arms. Understood?'

Erik nodded.

'We're two adults talking in a normal voice,' she continued. 'You're here to discuss various proposals for the campaign that we both know is not going to happen.'

Erik turned his head to the side and looked at her in amusement. Then he looked past her out into the office. Anna felt uncertain.

'What are you looking at?'

'Nothing,' Erik said, without moving his eyes.

Anna turned round and saw that no one outside the glass box was paying them the slightest bit of attention. She looked at Erik, who was smiling. He'd taken control without any effort whatsoever. Anna didn't understand how that was possible. It was her workplace, her territory. She straightened up, changed position and took a deep breath.

'You phoned me when you were drunk,' she accused. 'On a Sunday, when I was at Väla with my family.'

'Have you never been drunk?' Erik asked.

'In the middle of the day on a Sunday?' Anna asked, with contempt. 'I don't think so.' Erik didn't seem bothered.

'I was over in Denmark,' he said. 'Had a couple of beers, felt lonely.'

Anna stared at him, tried to force him to look away. Erik

had no problem meeting her gaze. She lost and was forced to shake her head so she could carry on.

'What are you playing at?' she asked.

'I'm sorry, I don't understand.'

'You turn up just a block away from my house in the middle of the night, you call on a Sunday when I'm with my family, come here when nothing has been arranged. What is it you want?'

'I thought you said we were going to talk with normal voices.'

Anna forced herself to breathe deeply three times.

'What do you want?' she said. 'Please tell me.'

'To start with, I want to know what you meant when you said that there won't be a campaign.'

'I mean, what do you want from me?' Anna interrupted.

'What do I want from you?' Erik repeated. 'Why?'

'Don't you understand that there can never be anything between us?'

Erik struggled to keep a straight face. Anna felt her temper rising.

'What are you doing here? What do you want?'

'Well, I partly wanted to talk about the campaign and I partly wanted to see you.'

'I don't want to see you,' Anna said, unemotional and clear. 'I'm not interested.'

'Since when?'

'What do you mean?'

Erik sat up.

'What's changed?' he asked. 'You wanted to last week. Why not now?'

'I've got a family.'

'You've had one all along.'

'Erik, it was in the heat of the moment.'

He looked at her.

'That sounds good,' he said. 'The heat of the moment. But there were more moments, weren't there?'

Anna clasped her hands on the table and leaned forwards.

'Erik, listen to me.'

She looked him straight in the eye.

'There can never be anything between you and me. I am not interested. Do you understand what I'm saying? What happened happened. And until yesterday, I thought it was something positive, a memory that I could enjoy with real pleasure and warmth. Now, I don't know any more. I'm begging you, let's just stop it here. Let it be what it was, and both get on with our lives.'

Erik stared at her with a blank expression.

'Now, can you please open your tablet and pretend to show me a proposal,' she added.

'What?'

'Open your iPad and pretend to show me what you've come up with.'

'What did I do wrong?' Erik asked.

'What do you mean?' Anna replied.

'Why don't you want to see me again?'

'I'm married, Erik. I love my husband, we have a daughter. I live a normal family life. You and I met once at a hotel. Plus the few times in your flat.'

'So it means nothing?'

He swallowed and looked upset.

'Erik, it won't work. You know that too. Please say that you understand.'

He looked down at his hands.

'Thank you,' Anna said. 'Now open your iPad. If you've got nothing to show me, you can pretend to point.'

He pulled his tablet over and turned it on. Then he looked up.

'I can't pretend,' he said.

'No, perhaps that was silly of me. Maybe it's best if you just go.'

Anna got up and held out her hand. Erik stood up and took it hesitantly.

'Good luck,' Anna said. 'With whatever you do. You've got all the opportunities in the world, don't you believe anything else.'

Erik looked at her defiantly, picked up his iPad, left the room and walked over to the lift. Anna took a deep breath, held it in and then went back to her desk.

'Well?' Sissela said.

'No,' she replied. 'They're on the wrong track. You might as well call and tell them.'

'Shame about the big boy.'

'Yes, maybe.'

22

Sven hesitated. Twenty hours or twenty-five. They had grumbled last time, but it was dangerous to drop your prices. Clients believed that they got what they paid for, and no one wants to take the cheapest.

How many hours had he done? It was impossible to say. Actively at his computer and on the phone, maybe seven. On the other hand, you couldn't time the creative process. Sven remembered an author who had been asked how long it took to write a book. The author had given his age as the answer. Pretentious and stupid, but true all the same.

The bigger agencies never had any problems. They set

a price. If the shoe didn't fit, thank you very much. It was the customer who stood with his cap in his hand there. And when the marketing managers went over budget, they never opposed the consequences. They simply bought themselves out, paid a high price so they didn't have to choose.

The little agency often came up with identical solutions, but had far greater difficulties in selling their ideas. When the small agency presented their proposals, the client started to squirm and came out with the most ridiculous objections.

'Well, I took your adverts home and showed them to my daughter. She thought . . . '

Imagine if an auditor was treated in the same way.

'Yes, yes, that's okay, but my daughter thought it looked nicer with more figures on the next line.'

And not only did the clients question Sven's work, he was even assailed privately too. He'd been at a fiftieth birthday party recently and ended up sitting opposite some left-wing person who regurgitated seventies nonsense all night. Life was easy for those who could afford to stick to their ideals, there was no question about it.

Sven wrote twenty-three hours. He calculated the hourly rate and wrote in the total on the right.

Twenty-three, uneven numbers. Sounded reliable and

good. He printed out the invoice and wrote the client's address on an envelope. The telephone rang and he answered.

'Hi, Sissela here.'

Sven didn't make the connection.

'From *Family Journal*.'

'Oh, hello, hello. How's things?'

'Good, thank you. And you?'

Sven told her about the daily trials and tribulations of an advertising man in a light and social manner. Small talk was something everyone in his business had mastered.

'Sorry to have kept you waiting,' Sissela said.

Sven leaned back in his chair and scratched his neck with his free hand.

'Not at all, it's always a process.'

'Yes, however, having given it considerable thought, we have decided not to go ahead with the campaign right now.'

'I'm sorry to hear that.'

'I talked to the marketing department recently and we agreed that we should wait until the spring and then go for a more traditional subscription drive. We don't really believe that we can get men interested.'

'You don't? Personally, I've always found the magazine a very interesting read.'

'Men read their wives' magazines and give them sub-scriptions as a present,' Sissela said. 'But they wouldn't subscribe themselves. Unless it was for tax reasons, that they could subscribe through the company or something like that.'

'I understand,' Sven said. 'It's possible we did go a bit off-piste in our enthusiasm for your product. Could we perhaps submit a new proposal?'

'From what I understand, that's what Erik has just done. Yes, he was here just now and spoke to Anna. And she wasn't particularly impressed. No, I think we'll just leave it for the moment. But thank you so much for all your hard work, and of course, it was delightful to meet you at Mölle. Maybe we'll get in touch again on another occasion.'

I am not interested.

Erik slapped his hand against the dashboard. Who did she think she was? She was old and ordinary, he was young and attractive. He had made her scream. Erik found it hard to believe that her husband managed to do that.

'Very hard,' he said out loud to himself.

I love my husband, we have a daughter.

'You love your husband?' Erik said. 'Is that why you

jump into bed with anyone? Because you love your husband?'

What happened happened.

'Yes, it was convenient. No guilt, a victim of circumstances.'

Erik turned the key and pulled out into the road.

*Until yesterday, I thought it was something positive, a
memory that I could enjoy with real pleasure and warmth. Now,
I don't know any more.*

'No, because it has to be on your terms, when you feel
like it. Well, I've got news for you, Anna Stenberg. You
don't rule the world.'

Erik drove back to work, looked at himself calmly in the
mirror as he took the lift up. He had no intention of showing any of his inner chaos to Sven and Olof. He went into
the office and was met with an accusing smile. Erik looked
at them.

'What?'

'I was just speaking to Sissela at *Family Journal*,' Sven
said.

Erik went over to his desk, tried to look busy.

'Right.'

'And they've said no to the campaign.'

'That's a shame.'

Erik studied them. Unsuccessful advertising men, but a necessary springboard for him to the career that was without doubt waiting just around the corner. Within a couple of years, Sven and Olof would be telling anecdotes about how they discovered him.

Sven nailed him with gimlet eyes.

'Sissela said that you'd run up there with another proposal. That you've been out sailing your own sea.'

Erik looked up, felt his cheeks flush. What had Anna said? That he was following her?

'It's all well and good that you take the initiative,' Olof said, 'but you have to pass things by us first. We have to show a united front.'

'You can't just give the client an alternative,' Sven said. 'That way you're communicating uncertainty.'

Anna hadn't said anything. Of course not. What could she say? Nothing. Not without telling.

'It wasn't anything concrete,' Erik said. 'I was just sounding it out. Trying to get a handle on what they wanted.'

'What did you find out?'

Erik shrugged.

'I don't think they're willing to pay anyone outside the company for their advertising.'

'So we're wasting our time?'

Erik didn't answer.

'Well,' Sven sighed, 'there's nothing to be done. We'll just have to find a new client. But next time, talk to us first.'

His expression was paternal, nurturing. Erik couldn't help smiling. What a boor! The uneducated, mediocre, overweight small-town failure was being strict with *him*. That was very funny.

Sven and Olof exchanged uncertain glances.

'We're serious,' Olof said.

Erik nodded.

'I am too,' he said, and picked up his computer and left.

23

'Hello, love, what are you doing here? What a nice surprise.'

'Have you got a minute?'

'Of course.'

Anna went into her mother's flat and closed the door behind her. She took off her shoes.

'I've just put on the kettle. Come in, sit down. Don't you want to take your coat off?'

Anna sank down on to one of the kitchen chairs, and immediately and automatically turned into a morose teenager.

'And to what do I owe the honour?' Kathrine asked.

'Nothing in particular, just thought I'd say hello,' Anna said, playing with the salt cellar on the table.

'I see,' her mother said, and opened one of the kitchen cupboards. 'I've got Earl Grey and Söder tea.'

'Earl Grey.'

Kathrine looked at her daughter on the sly as she scooped the tea into the strainer. Anna was staring out of the window. It was windy and wet, typical Helsingborg weather. The kettle boiled and switched off.

'It's always nice to get visitors,' Kathrine said, as she poured the tea. 'Doesn't happen every day. Milk?'

'Mm.'

'Do you want anything to eat with it?'

Anna shook her head.

'I'm fine, thanks.'

Kathrine put the cups on the table and sat down.

'Have you done something stupid again?'

'What? No, never.'

'You haven't told him? Magnus, I mean.'

'No.'

'Good. What's up then?'

Anna pulled the cup towards her, took a careful sip but still managed to scald her lips.

'Well . . . ' she started.

This time she left nothing out. She told her that he'd lied about his mother, about the broken glass, about the camera on his mobile phone, that he'd just appeared from behind the bus, phoned her drunk and come to the office without calling first.

'Gosh,' Kathrine said, when she was finished. 'That's quite a lot to take in over a cup of tea.'

She looked at her daughter, who was sitting all hunched up and staring blankly at the table.

'Are you sure that you deleted the photographs on his phone?'

Anna nodded absentmindedly. She was off in her own world.

'Good, you have to be careful with things like that.'

Kathrine reached across the table and took her daughter's hand.

'It feels creepy,' Anna said.

'Oh, I'm sure he's just a little in love. And I can understand that.'

Anna pulled a face at her mother's compliment.

'I lay awake all night.'

'But now you've told him and you don't have to work

together any more. Everything is as it should be again. It's a good thing you put your foot down.'

Anna looked up, leaned forwards over the table.

'And the guy he said he was visiting, Johan Andersson. He doesn't exist.'

'Are you sure?'

'No, but . . .'

'In which case he's out there, hiding behind the bushes. And so what? Have you never gone past the home of someone you're secretly in love with and hoped that you might bump into them by accident?'

'No.'

Kathrine looked at her daughter, with amused arched eyebrows.

'That was at high school, Mum. That's not quite the same thing. Erik is an adult.'

'Has he been nasty or threatening? Violent?'

Anna shook her head.

'No, apart from the glass.'

Kathrine nodded as if she were digesting all the information she'd been given.

'Don't worry, just take it easy. He'll tire of it soon enough.'

'But I have to tell Magnus,' Anna said in despair.

'If he goes far enough, you'll have to, yes.'

'But don't you understand? If I tell him, he'll leave me.'

'No, he won't. He'll play the self-pitying martyr for a while. Until it gets to the point where it's so ridiculous that you tell him to stop. And then he'll be quiet. And when he's cowed and suppressed, you'll gradually lose all respect for him. I can't imagine anything else. If you want to keep him, the wisest thing to do is to keep it to yourself and don't spill your heart.'

24

Anna opened the door and took in the smell. Clean, roast pine nuts, flickering light from the candle flame.

'Hello?'

'In the kitchen.'

She took off her shoes, hung up her coat and went in. Magnus was grinding basil and the pine nuts in a mortar. He took a short break to hand her a glass of wine.

Anna scrutinised him.

'Where's Hedda?'

He clinked his glass against Anna's.

'Cheers. At Louise's. She's having dinner there.'

Anna held the wine glass up to the light and the beautifully laid table.

'And this is?'

'Dinner on Monday.'

'Dinner on Monday?'

Magnus nodded.

'Am I missing something? The date or something else?'

Magnus put down his glass.

'Exactly fifteen years ago today,' he started, with great ceremony. 'Nope, you're not missing anything.'

'Have you got a new job?'

'No. Just thought that for once. You know, the days slip by, and you forget the most important thing.'

'The most important thing?'

'That I got the best.'

'The best?'

Anna smiled, bewildered. Magnus nodded earnestly.

'Best luck of all,' he said. 'Nothing special, just home-made pesto.'

'Just and just,' Anna said, and sat down. 'I popped into Mum's on the way home.'

'Why?'

'Don't know, just felt like it. We had a cup of tea.'

'We both just felt like it on the same day,' Magnus concluded.

'If it's a Monday, it's a Monday,' Anna smiled.

Her phone pinged. A text message from Erik. She turned away from Magnus and read it.

Lost my job today because of you. Hope you have a nice dinner.

She turned all the way round and peered out of the window. The street was dark. She saw her own reflection in the window and felt her heart hammering hard inside her ribs.

'Who was that?' Magnus asked.

Anna swallowed hard.

'Oh, just work.'

She put her hand on her stomach and forced a smile.

'Just have to . . .'

She pointed in the direction of the bathroom and left the kitchen. She locked herself in and caught her breath, without turning on the light. She opened the message and read it again. The bathroom was illuminated by the text on the screen.

Hope you have a nice dinner.

Was he standing outside?

'Are you okay?' Magnus called, from the other side of the door.

'Yes, fine. Just a bit of a sore tummy. Will be there in a minute.'

She heard her husband go back out into the kitchen. She deleted the message and held the screen up like a torch. The stool that Hedda had used when she wanted to reach the sink had for many years now stood under the high window that they opened when they wanted to get rid of the steam after a shower. Anna turned off her phone and stepped up on to the stool, looked out cautiously. The wind was dancing in the treetops. Otherwise deserted. No people.

Hope you have a nice dinner.

It was a normal enough expression. An ironic dig from a hurt young man. I'm unemployed and you're having a feast.

Unemployed? Had he really lost his job? It sounded improbable. And surely it had nothing to do with Sissela saying no to their stupid campaign proposal? Had he resigned in a huff? Whatever, it wasn't her problem.

Anna got down from the stool, turned on the light, flushed the toilet. She splashed her face with cold water and looked at herself in the mirror.

'Take it easy,' she said to herself. 'Don't lose it.'

Kathrine logged on to birthday.se, the website where you could look up people's birthdays. She had spent a whole afternoon looking up old friends and checking their birthdays, so that she could surprise them with cards or a telephone call on the right day. It was perhaps a bit extreme, but it was one of the many things she had done in order to avoid sitting at home alone in front of the TV. All you needed was the person's name and possibly an address when they had a usual name, like Erik Månsson. So much the better that her daughter had told her that she had gone to his flat on Drottninggatan.

Kathrine typed in the information and got a hit that informed her Erik Månsson had been born on 29 July 1984. In other words, he was twenty-eight years old. Not an unusual age for a bachelor, but definitely unsuitably young to be chatting up a woman who was fifteen years older with a family.

She wrote down his address and his six-digit personal ID

number. Then she went out into the kitchen and rummaged around on a shelf full of recipes she'd torn out, batteries, paperclips, pens, card games, boxes of toothpicks, almost empty nasal sprays, scraps of paper with long-since forgotten names and telephone numbers, plus half a million other bits and pieces that had no special place in the home but that weren't to be thrown away immediately.

Kathrine was sure that she'd pulled out a newspaper article about how to find information about people. She'd kept it for the day when she was going to write a crime novel, which was more or less a grassroots movement these days, certainly among middle-aged women. The phenomenon had caused considerable indignation among middle-aged writing men, who, as soon as the opportunity arose, declared that such works could not be considered Literature. The male genius was a sensitive organism that required constant care.

Finally she found the article. HOW TO CHECK UP ON YOUR NEIGHBOURS was the appealingly small headline. It said clearly that the first thing she should do was contact the Swedish Tax Agency. Which, to be honest, she could have worked out for herself. Who knew anything, if not Big Brother?

Kathrine looked at the clock. It was past six. Her snooping would have to wait until tomorrow. It was high time to get some food in her stomach.

Anna twisted away. Magnus looked up from between her legs.

'No?' he asked.

'I'm too stressed.'

He crept up and lay down beside her.

'I'll give you one.'

'It's fine.'

'No, really.'

'Another time.'

They both looked up at the ceiling. Anna had glanced over at the gap between the drawn curtains, screwed up her eyes and was almost certain that she saw Erik outside. Obviously it was just her imagination, but it was enough to stop her relaxing.

'Is it work?' Magnus ventured.

Anna sent him a quick look.

'It's all a bit much at the moment,' she said.

Magnus nodded.

'You have to learn to relax.'

'I know.'

The whole evening with candles and wine and home-made food was an easy ticket into the sack. Which Anna didn't mind, quite the opposite. The sex was predictable, a well-practised routine, but Magnus was a gentle and sensitive lover, ambitious to the extent that he always satisfied her first. After that, things generally moved along swiftly. A few seconds of extra effort. You scratch me and I'll scratch you. The fact that he was so content irritated her sometimes, the smug smile that assumed that she couldn't possibly want anything else. Maybe she had too high expectations of life. A deep desire that it should be greater, more intimate.

Why couldn't Anna allow herself to be fooled by the sort of philosophical messages and thoughts you got on fridge magnets? Life is what happens when you're thinking about something else. Tomorrow is the first day of the rest of your life. *Carpe diem*.

Not bad advice for those who were susceptible. That's to say those who were under fourteen or soft in the head. Often both.

Magnus got out of bed, pulled on his pants, apparently unbothered by the decline in his physique.

'How's the car sale going?' Anna asked.

'Good. I've got someone coming to look at it tomorrow. He asked about the price, so I guess we have to be prepared to knock off a few thousand.'

'Still more than we would have got for trading it in.'

'Hopefully.'

Anna slipped past him out of the room. He reached out his arm and gave her a quick, loving stroke as she passed. She smiled in answer.

Sitting on the toilet, she wondered if she was looking for the wrong things in Magnus. Looked for them too actively, as it were. Constructing a defence in her own favour.

An unfaithful man could blame his animal lust, that it was against nature to let an opportunity go. A woman could construct a world of underlying causes.

Sissela often said that someone who was happy at home didn't play away. What grounds did she have to make such a claim? It sounded like the Old Testament. Sissela said it with good intentions, to free the unfaithful Trude from guilt. Maybe it wasn't true at all. Maybe Trude had a fantastic sex life at home, which only increased her interest in the activity, outside the confines of her home as well.

There were surveys that claimed that men were more unfaithful than women. A mathematical impossibility if you didn't accept the myth of the fallen woman, the absolutely abnormally active temptress. The truth was probably something else. Being unfaithful was probably a matter of subjective judgement. Men had a bit on the side, women fell in love. And under the guise of love, no wrong could be done.

Half an hour later, Anna turned on her phone and saw to her relief that there were no text messages or missed calls. Magnus was outside walking round the car in the dark, rubbing off the spray from the bottom edges of the body and wiping the windows before taking out the mat on the driver's side and giving it a shake. Hedda came cycling home on tyres that badly needed pumping.

'Hello, sweetie, have you had a good time?' Anna called when her daughter came into the house.

'Yes.'

'What did you eat?'

'Burgers.'

'Umm, yummy,' Anna said, quickly.

'It was okay.'

'And how's Louise?'

'Okay.'

'And her mum and dad?'

'Okay.

'I was just about to have some ice cream. Do you want some?'

'What flavour?'

'Don't know. Vanilla, I think.'

Anna opened the freezer.

'Yes, it's vanilla.'

'Okay.'

'Ask Daddy if he wants any.'

Hedda went to the front door, opened and shouted.

'He doesn't want any,' she informed her mother when she came back to the kitchen.

'Have you got homework?'

'Nah, not really. We did it together.'

'You and Louise?'

'Yeah.'

The situation eased Anna's anxiety. Something as simple as scooping the ice cream into dessert bowls reminded her of the greatness of everyday life and pushed back thoughts about her mistake, which in turn threatened to destroy her daughter's world.

'Can I borrow your phone?' Hedda asked. 'I want to play games.'

'Not if you're having ice cream.'

'But I can play with my left hand.'

Anna handed her the mobile. Her ten-year-old daughter tapped her way skilfully through the files and apps.

'Why's it on silent?'

'Is it?'

'Yes.'

Hedda switched it to normal. A stupid tune accompanied by action sounds from screeching tyres and exploding barrels filled the kitchen. Anna looked at her daughter with the same look of loving indulgence that her mother had given her only a couple of hours ago. The sound of the game suddenly stopped and was replaced by a ping.

'Text message,' Hedda said, and handed it over.

Anna recognised the number, and anxiety returned immediately. Didn't he understand? What was wrong now?

Call me when you can. Important.

Anna deleted it and reluctantly handed the phone back.

'Who was that?' Hedda asked.

'Work.'

'Are you not going to answer?'

'Not now, I'll do it in the morning.'

Hedda went back to her game. Anna looked out of the window, watched Magnus do a final inspection of the car and he seemed to be pleased with the result.

'Can't you just do one thing at a time?' Anna said, and reached for her phone.

Hedda turned away.

'Can I have my phone, please?'

'In a minute, I just want to finish this game.'

The sound of a water drop announced a death and the game was over. Hedda gave her the phone.

'Thank you,' Anna said, and turned it off completely. 'Don't understand why you have to use mine when you've got your own.'

'What does it matter?'

Magnus came in.

'What are you quarrelling about?'

'We're not quarrelling.'

'Mum won't let me use her mobile.'

'You've got your own.'

'That's what I said,' Anna exclaimed. 'Are you sure you don't want any ice cream? There's not much left.'

'I'm fine, thanks.'

Magnus turned to Hedda.

'Just leave Mum's phone alone. Maybe she's got a secret lover who's sending her juicy text messages.'

'Very funny,' Anna said.

'Juicy?' Hedda repeated.

'Quite funny,' Magnus smiled.

25

Magnus gave Anna a lift to the bus stop, leaned across the seat and kissed her on the lips.

'Have a good day, darling.'

'You too. See you this evening.'

Anna got out and waited until the car had disappeared from sight before taking her mobile phone out of her handbag and turning it on. It seemed to take forever to connect to the provider. Anna stared at the display screen, every second a painful wait in expectation of what might happen. Nothing, she could confirm after about thirty seconds. Had she wound herself up unnecessarily? Lain awake half the night, twisting between the sheets, because of some fear she'd made up? Was it she who had an overactive imagination, not he who was harassing her?

The bus came and she got on, nodded to a couple of familiar faces and walked down the aisle to the back. She had just sat down when her phone started to vibrate. The screen showed an undisclosed number.

'Anna.'

'Hi, it's me,' said Erik. 'Am I calling at a bad time?'

'I've just got on the bus.'

'Can you talk?'

'I'd rather not. What's it concerning?'

'"What's it concerning?"' Erik mimicked, as if she had expressed herself far too formally. 'I just want an answer to one question, or maybe a couple.'

'Please.'

'I'm sorry, but I think you can spare the time to answer a couple of questions, I think you owe me that much.'

'I'm sitting on the bus.'

'You said. So you can just answer yes or no, okay?'

Anna took a deep breath.

'Okay,' she said.

'One: do you know how insulting it was when you, out of nowhere, accused me of stalking you?'

'What kind of a question is that?'

'It's a simple yes or no question. Do you understand how . . . ?'

'I heard. And yes, I do understand.'

Anna glanced quickly around the bus to make sure that no one she knew could hear, then leaned forwards and lowered her voice when she spoke on the phone.

'It wasn't my intention to hurt you, I hope you understand that.'

'Well, I have to say, you managed to all the same.'

'And I really do apologise for that. I was only trying to make myself clear.'

'The end justifies the means, in other words?'

'I don't understand.'

'You can trash my honour and reputation as long as it serves your purpose?'

'I really didn't want to trash your honour and reputation. Look, I'm sitting on a bus. Can you email me instead?'

'No, now that I've finally got hold of you, I do in fact want some answers.'

'What do you mean, finally?'

'Your mobile has been switched off all morning.'

'It's only eight o'clock.'

'And?'

Anna looked around again. The man on the other side of the aisle was twitching a bit, but that wasn't a problem.

'But that's exactly what I mean,' Anna said. 'You can't just call me at any time of day or night, don't you understand that?'

'It's your phone, isn't it?' Erik retorted. 'Just say it's someone else.'

'No, I can't.'

'Why not? Can't you lie? Do you get embarrassed? Does Mr Wimpy ask who it is?'

'That's out of order,' Anna snapped. 'Well out of order.'

'So it's okay for you to be out of order and accuse me of this and that, but it's not okay for me defend my honour in any way? A simple yes or no question. Answer it.'

'Right, I'm hanging up now.'

'Okay, so that's the way we're playing? Anna, let me say just one thing: you have no idea how much I've got on you. Believe me, you don't want to get on the wrong side of me.'

Anna disconnected the conversation and turned the screen off, but kept the phone in her hand. She looked around. The passengers close by who might have heard something were looking in the other direction. Their faces were almost consciously turned away. Or was she just imagining that?

How loud had she been talking? What had she said? She tried to recall her own answers. Had she made a scene? Fortunately the faces she'd recognised when she got on the bus were sitting further forwards and could hardly have heard any of the conversation, but there were eyes and ears everywhere on a rush-hour bus in Helsingborg.

Anna considered getting off and waiting for the next bus. But then she risked meeting someone she knew who would ask why she was getting off there and not at her normal stop. That was the town she lived in: nosy, prying and well informed. It was probably wiser to stay where she was. When the bus stopped at Knutpunkten in the centre of Helsingborg, the last of the silent witnesses got off and Anna's pulse slowed down a fraction.

What did he mean when he said he had so much on her? Had he somehow managed to salvage the photos on his mobile phone? Had she disclosed some deep secret to him? Promised him her love? She hadn't said anything derogatory about Magnus, she knew that. She would never do that, not under any circumstances. So what did Erik have on her? Did he know of any crimes she'd committed? Or was it just something he said?

She could worry herself to death. What was important was to avoid any further conflict. No escalation.

She went into the publishing house, said a chirpy good morning to Renée in reception. No one who came in or went out of the building could fail to be smitten by her open, friendly smile. If there was anyone who was in the right place in this world, it was Renée.

Anna took the lift up to the editorial offices and went over to her desk. She turned on the computer and opened her email. The column of semi-bold headings rolled down the screen. The final and top email caught her attention.

DO NOT DELETE – READ!!!

Three exclamation marks. Theatrical was only his first name. Anna opened it.

> I'm sorry. I don't know what got into me. I was totally out of order. I'm sorry.
>
> When I came to your office, I had been longing to

see you for days. And the shock that you weren't as happy to see me, not happy at all, in fact, was bad enough. But then when you accused me of following you, you rocked the ground under my feet.

Our meetings have meant so much to me, but obviously not as much to you. Nothing at all, in fact, it would seem – even though there is plenty that would indicate the opposite. However, it is obviously something I need to learn to live with. It's not the first time a man has had his heart broken by a woman, and it won't be the last.

Let's not part on bad terms. Let's remember and nurture the moments we did have together. I beg you, call me so we can talk things through.

Anna deleted the email and stared vacantly out of the window. She had assumed that Erik could write: after all, it was his job. Not even in the worst of the magazine's sometimes corny love stories did the ground rock under someone's feet, and only very occasionally did you nurture the moments you'd had together.

Was he mad? He had to be. Anna wondered if she'd been so caught up with his appearance that she hadn't noticed. She couldn't think of any other explanation. Her original desire was now a mystery. There was nothing more repulsive than stupidity.

Should she call him one last time, let him finish crying? Maybe it was for the best. Give him a chance to walk away without losing face. Because that was obviously where the problem lay, wounded male pride.

'Good morning, early birds.'

Sissela announced her arrival in editorial in a loud voice. Any conversation with Erik Månsson would have to wait.

26

An automated voice told Kathrine that the service she required was handled by forty-three providers and she was number seventy-four in the queue. The estimated waiting time was thirteen minutes.

Kathrine switched to loudspeaker and turned on the computer. She had time to read the evening papers on the internet and play a game of patience before a real live person answered the phone and asked how he could help her.

'Well,' Kathrine said, and blushed even though she was alone. 'You see, I'd like to know a bit more about a certain person.'

'Personal ID number?' said the employee at the national registry.

'Whose? Mine?'

Kathrine already felt guilty. Prying into another person's life was so abominable that she had to fight the instinct to apologise, put down the phone and find a wardrobe as quickly as possible where she could crouch down in the dark and chant to herself and the universe for forgiveness.

'The person in question,' said the man.

'Right, yes, I've got his name and date of birth.'

'Okay.'

'Do you want me to give it to you?'

'That would help.'

Kathrine gave him what information she had.

'Erik Månsson, Drottninggatan in Helsingborg,' the man repeated, 'yes, then there's only this one.'

He read out the complete personal ID number and Katherine wrote down the last four digits.

'What would you like to know?' he asked.

'I don't know,' Kathrine said. 'What information is available? Everything, I suppose.'

'Everything,' the man repeated. 'Let's see what we've got here then. He was born in Stockholm. Lived at various addresses there until six months ago when he moved to his current address in Helsingborg.'

'His last address in Stockholm?

He gave her the address and Kathrine wrote it down.

'Thank you so much.'

'Is that all you want?' the man asked.

'Is there more?'

'I see here that his mother is dead, died on 4 July 2010.'

Kathrine caught her breath. Of all the things Anna had told her, his tasteless lie about his mother's death was what had made her react most. So it wasn't a lie? Had he been telling the truth and then regretted it? Maybe he'd just laughed off the terrible tragedy because he realised it was far too personal and not something to be shared with just anyone. In which case, it changed everything.

'She can't have been that old,' Kathrine commented.

'She was born in 1968,' the man said.

'1968?' Kathrine exclaimed. 'So she was only sixteen when she had Erik?'

The national registry man assumed that it was a rhetorical question and didn't answer.

'Does it say what she died of?'

'No, it doesn't. Anything else?'

'Is there more?'

'Not much. His father moved to Finland in 1985, the year after his son was born.'

'Thank you so much, I'm so grateful,' Kathrine said.

'Not at all,' said the man.

'Just a moment. What was his mother called?'

'Anneli Månsson.'

'And where was she living when she died?'

'At the same address as her son.'

No editorial job was so demanding that Sissela didn't find time to slander those who weren't there. Anna had stopped listening, but was still forced to nod in agreement at regular intervals. The alternative was actively to take a stance and cause conflict, which wasn't worth the effort. When the telephone started to ring, it was a relief. Anna lifted the receiver, pressed the red flashing light and answered.

The half-second pause told her that it was Erik on the other end.

'Can you talk?' he asked.

'You're ringing at a bit of a bad time. Can I call you later?'

'Promise?'

'Yes, let's say that.'

Anna hung up and nodded at Sissela, who continued to gossip. Trude joined them.

'Oof,' Sissela eventually said, 'here I am chatting away, and we still have to go through the wall.'

They went over to layout, where the proofs of the magazine's editorial material had been pinned up in sequence to give an overview of the content. Every week, Sissela, Trude and Anna wandered over and, like generals in front of the troops, made a final inspection of the features and articles before putting the magazine to bed. There were a few small changes in the titles, boxes, introduction and picture captions that were important to give the reader the right mix and rhythm.

Three spreads in a row had quote boxes that started with the word 'I' and the editorial heads were discussing how best to change it in order to avoid the repetition when Anna's phone rang at the other end of the open-plan office. The head of features, who sat nearest, started to get up and pointed at it questioningly. Anna nodded.

The head of features answered. Anna could see from her body language that the person on the other end didn't say anything. Anna's colleague said, 'Hello?' a few times before giving in and hanging up. She was on her way back to her desk when the phone rang again. This time there was someone at the other end, Anna realised. The head of features reached for a pen and a Post-it. She nodded as she wrote. Anna followed every movement. Her colleague finished the call, pulled the Post-it from the pad and stuck it to Anna's screen.

'Excuse me,' she said, and went over to her desk.

She turned to the colleague who had answered the call for her.

'A reader,' she said. 'Something about a recipe. I wrote down the number.'

Anna glanced quickly at the number. It wasn't his. It was only the relief that made her realise how tense she was. She lifted the receiver and called Renée in reception.

'Hi, it's Anna. Can you hold all my phone calls, please? We're going through the wall.'

She put the phone down and went back to Sissela and Trude.

As a rule, Kathrine believed the best about people. She didn't like the fact that the majority of the population, at least mentally, seemed to live in the parallel world created by the tabloid press where all strangers were potential assailants unless proved otherwise.

Her daughter's worries were obviously coloured by her bad conscience. She had been unfaithful to her husband and enjoyed it. Now she just wanted to forget her impropriety as quickly as possible, whereas the motherless boy had fallen in love with her.

It had the potential to end badly, she realised that. But Kathrine had never met anyone you couldn't talk to. Fear was in practice the only thing you could really fear and she hadn't thought of going down that road. She had friends who were so obsessed with all the terrible things going on in the world that they barely dared to leave their flats.

And there was no doubt, Kathrine pitied Erik Månsson. An absent father and a teenage mother who died far too young.

Erik had told Anna that his mother took her own life, only to say the next moment that he'd made it up. And if it was true after all, perhaps the young mother had had mental health issues. In which case, that would explain why Erik had stayed with his mother, even when he was well into his twenties.

Kathrine realised she was feeling a bit self-righteous. As

if she had all the answers. What did she think would happen? Should she go to visit Erik Månsson and talk to him, get him back on the right track? In which case, what was she going to say?

'I can understand that you're in love with my daughter, she is a fantastic woman. But the fact is that she already has a husband and they have a daughter whom they both love very much. So I'm asking you to accept that, and to try to find happiness elsewhere.'

Kathrine shuddered. How ridiculous. The moral police, protector of the good, champion of law and order.

The Phantom and her.

And all the snooping around she'd done. No, she couldn't say anything. Not to anyone.

27

The review of the wall was always followed by an editorial meeting. The magazine staff gathered on and around the large sofa to discuss content and the next number. The meeting was led formally, but in a relaxed style, by Sissela. Whoever felt the need to express their views and give suggestions was welcome to do so, which in practice meant that the same people said the same things week in and week out. But that was fine as the main purpose of the meeting was to give the staff an opportunity to grumble if they wanted to and the illusion that they had some influence. Anyone of a more cynical nature might notice that the editorial staff were more dissatisfied in good times and less so when sales numbers started to fall and cutbacks loomed.

Everyone went back to their places after the meeting. People checked the time and their mobiles. How long was it until lunch? Had anyone tried to contact them in the past half-hour, since they last checked?

Anna went to her desk. The red voicemail diode was not flashing. She checked her mobile without taking it out of her bag. Nothing there either. She opened her email. A handful of new emails, all job-related, nothing from Erik.

Had he finally realised that he couldn't behave in that way?

She understood that he was upset. It was insulting to be dumped and told to stay away. The rules were always set by the person who wanted least from the relationship. She might just as well call him and give him a chance to walk away with his honour intact.

She went to the toilet, locked herself in a cubicle and checked the reception. No worries. She dialled his number from memory. After four rings, she was transferred to his voicemail.

'Hi, Erik, it's me. I got your email. Thank you. You said that you didn't want us to part on bad terms. I don't want that either, I really don't. And I'm so sorry that I hurt you, it was never intended. I hope that we can sort all this out. I'll try to catch you later. It's probably best if I call. I'm busy and there's someone watching all the time. Hope you'll be patient.'

She hung up and tried to remember exactly what she'd said. Was there anything that might be misunderstood? Hardly. Had she said anything that could be misinterpreted? No. She had been as clear as she could be and, at the same time, her voice was humble and positive. She had held out her hand. It was up to Erik now to take it.

'Hi, Erik, it's me . . . I'm so sorry that I hurt you, it was never intended . . . It's probably best if I call . . . Hope you'll be patient.'

To add insult to injury, she was trying to sound upbeat and self-important. First false concern, almost upset, then over-jolly.

Don't call me, I'll call you. That's what she said.

Well, that's exactly what she could do. He wasn't going to make any more effort. Did she think he was sitting by the phone waiting? Even self-righteousness had limits.

Anna sat towards the back of the bus and got out her telephone. No missed calls. Erik hadn't phoned back. To be fair,

Anna had said that she would call, but the question was whether it might be wiser not to. Let sleeping dogs lie. And if he was now finally over her.

Over her?

Anna felt ashamed, it sounded so self-centred. She had hurt his pride when she accused him of stalking her. In the same way that a man had hurt her mother when he saw through her attempt to chat him up and brushed her off without so much as a pardon. The difference was that the man in the library had rebuffed her immediately. Anna had slept with Erik Månsson. And not just once, but three times. Four, in fact, if you counted the time in the car up on the cliff. Which obviously made the whole thing far more serious.

How could Anna get Erik to understand that she didn't want any contact without him feeling insulted and forced to defend his reputation? It would be best to call after all. If nothing else to find out how the land lay.

Anna let the thought mature. By the time the bus stopped outside Sofiero Palace, she had made up her mind to take the bull by the horns. The extra fifteen-minute walk would give her plenty of time.

She got off the bus, fished out her phone and dialled the

number. The line connected, one ring, two. Erik answered on the third.

'Hello.'

His voice sounded strained, as if she were interrupting, a constant hum in the background.

'Hi, it's me.'

'I can't really talk right now, I'm driving.'

He sounded irritated and Anna felt stupid. How easily the balance of power between two people could change, it was almost depressing.

'Of course, I . . .'

Even though it was a relief too. He wasn't mad, at least not at her. And that was the main thing.

'Call me in an hour.'

He disappeared.

'Hello? Erik?'

Anna looked at the screen. The call had been disconnected. Had he hung up on her? Strange. She clicked on to the call log to delete the number, and just then a loud car horn made her jump.

She spun round and saw her own car. There were two people behind the windscreen and her eyes immediately swung to the passenger seat, where she expected to see

Hedda, but her husband was sitting there instead, waving at her. She looked back to the driver's seat.

Erik Månsson was sitting behind the wheel.

Her husband rolled down the window.

'Hello, darling. What are you doing here?'

'What? Well, I got off the bus early, thought I'd walk a bit, the nice weather, and . . .'

'This is Erik,' Magnus said, and leaned back.

He leaned forwards over the gearstick and held out his hand.

'Hi.'

'He's a potential buyer for the car,' Magnus explained. 'So we're out on a test drive.'

Anna nodded silently, she couldn't get a word out. She wondered whether Magnus had seen that she was talking on the phone and hung up at the same time that Erik did. He must have done. He was just too slow to make the connection. Wrong, not slow. There was no reason in the world for him to make the connection. He wouldn't even dream that his wife could do something like that.

'Hop in,' Magnus said.

Anna felt that her chest was clammy and cold.

'No, I don't know,' she said, sounding uncertain. 'I think I'll go by the shops and get some food.'

'Jump in, we're just going to drop Hedda off at the stables first.'

Magnus pointed his thumb over his shoulder. It was only now that Anna saw that her daughter was sitting in the back. She looked bright and happy. Anna wanted to get her out of the car, but didn't know how she could do it.

Magnus turned to their daughter.

'Move up, sweetheart, so there's room for Mummy.'

Anna had no choice. She opened the car door and sat down in the back seat, a stranger in her own car. She was glued to the spot, couldn't do anything. She held her hand out to Hedda.

'Hello, darling.'

Hedda held back as if she were suddenly too big for intimacy, certainly when there was a stranger there. Erik swung out into the road.

'The ultimate family car,' Magnus said. 'Three adults sitting comfortably in the back. Enough room for everything. The boot just swallows everything up. It's not for nothing that it's so popular. Straight ahead here.'

He pointed out the direction. Erik's driving was calm and gentle; he slowed down for the speed bumps.

'Do you have a family?' Magnus asked.

'Not yet.'

Erik looked at Anna in the rear-view mirror, she turned her face away.

'Are you expecting a child?' Magnus exclaimed. 'Sorry, rude of me to ask.'

Erik shook his head.

'Not at all,' he said, smoothly. 'No, I'm waiting for her to make up her mind. One day she does, the next day she doesn't.'

Anna turned to Hedda, pretended not to be part of the conversation.

'How was school today?' she asked. 'Did anything fun happen?'

'No,' Hedda said in a dismissive tone and demonstratively turned to look the other way.

Had she turned into a teenager overnight?

'Perhaps she's too young?' Magnus suggested. 'To start a family, I mean. Maybe she wants to wait.'

'No, she's not too young,' Erik said, and again tried to catch Anna's attention in the rear-view mirror. 'She's my age, a bit older, in fact.'

'Well, then maybe it's time for her to make up her mind,' Magnus said, paternally. 'We're not getting any younger, any of us. What do you think, darling?'

He sounded obscenely content when he included himself in the 'we'. As if he liked Erik's company and wanted to draw it out.

'Oh, I don't know,' Anna said, uninvolved.

Erik was looking at her annoyingly often in the rear-view mirror now.

'Excuse me,' he said, eventually, and turned round. 'I recognise you.'

'Me?'

Anna felt the fear. She was scared in her own car in the company of her husband and daughter.

'We must have met,' Erik said.

'I'm sorry?'

'Hang on, I know. Mölle, the hotel. Weren't you there a few weeks ago?'

'Yes.'

'We met very briefly. You were there with two other women, and you were talking to my colleagues. Two advertising men.'

'Oh yes, I remember.'

'I was pretty beat that night,' Erik said, 'so I went to bed early. But I understand you had a good time.'

'Yes, we had a good time,' Anna said, with an uncertain smile.

'Isn't that funny?' Magnus said. 'The world is so small. Especially in Helsingborg.'

'Good hotel,' Erik said.

He chatted away without a worry. As if it were already his car, and he set the rules.

'Were you there for a conference?' Magnus asked.

'I don't know that I'd call it that. We played some golf, celebrated closing the books.'

'You play golf?' Magnus lit up. 'Then this car is perfect. Plenty of room for two bags in the back. To the left here and then straight on.'

They reached the stables.

'To the right here, down the gravel track.'

'We'll come and pick you up later,' Anna said when they'd parked alongside the paddock.

'Mm,' she said, grumpily and then with more enthusiasm: 'Bye.'

The friendly goodbye was for Erik. So that was why she was being so mean to Anna. She had a crush and wanted to appear grown-up.

'See you. Have fun riding.'

Anna felt the hate surge through her. He had no right to play to her daughter, not even in a friendly and amenable way. How did he support himself? Anna's flushed cheeks quickly darkened.

'So,' Magnus started. 'Have you had enough, or would you like to drive some more?'

'That's fine,' Erik said. 'I think that's plenty.'

'Maybe we should switch places then.'

Magnus undid the safety belt and opened the door. Erik sat where he was with his arms stretched to the wheel and looked at Anna in the rear-view mirror. Magnus came all the way round and was slightly confused. He knocked on the window and opened the door.

'Sorry,' Erik said, and undid the safety belt and got out. 'Just wanted to savour the feeling.'

'It's important,' Magnus said.

Erik sat down in the back seat beside Anna. She got out and went to the passenger seat. It was all one movement.

'What do you think then?' Magnus asked when they parked outside the house, where Erik had left his own considerably smaller car.

Erik pretended to think.

'I'll go home and sleep on it. Is the price negotiable?'

'Well,' Magnus drew it out, what he thought was a smooth dealer technique. 'A couple of thousand, maybe. But the mileage is low, relatively speaking, and the condition as good as new, so . . . '

'I understand.'

'I've got several others who are interested,' Magnus said. 'So if you are, you'll have to make up your mind relatively swiftly.'

'Okay,' Erik said. 'Let's say that if I'm interested I'll give you a ring before eight this evening. Does that sound fair?'

'Absolutely. Let's say that then.'

Erik held out his hand. Magnus took it first, then Anna. She had no choice.

'Nice to meet you again,' Erik said. 'See you both around.'

He got into his own car and drove off.

'Nice guy,' Magnus said. 'Strange that you didn't recognise him.'

'I didn't really see him properly.'

'A looker like that?'

'When I got in the car, I mean.'

'Well, there you go. Now, what do we need from the shops?'

28

Magnus wandered back and forth and kept looking at his phone.

'I guess he's not interested,' Anna said, from where she was sunk deep in the sofa.

'No,' Magnus agreed, reluctantly. 'Strange, I really thought he would take it.'

'Obviously not.'

She turned towards the television, didn't feel sure enough to meet her husband's eye.

'Ah well, whatever,' he said.

He sank down beside Anna.

'It's quite fun selling cars,' he continued. 'Think it would suit me. Walking around the showroom, a bit of chitchat, high fives with my colleagues when I close a deal. Ka-ching, high five.'

'Sounds just like you.'

'Have the special of the day in a restaurant with strip-lighting on the ceiling, and salt cellars the size of sugar shakers.'

Anna gave him a questioning look. He nodded obstinately.

'Real workers put salt on their food.'

Anna couldn't even be bothered to comment on that. She turned back to the TV, picked the remote control up from the table and started channel hopping. She went through the whole lot before stopping at the first channel, a national, commercial channel with a mixture of stuck-up pretensions and abysmal productions that did more damage to the country than all the 1970s town planners who just wanted to pull everything down.

Anna's body was hopping. Fear and anger were fighting for domination, tossing her back and forth. She felt seasick and nauseous, as if she were on a ferry with red fitted carpets and drunk, ugly passengers. The fear sloshed around and crashed over her.

'No,' she said, and stood up in one movement.

Magnus looked at her in surprise.

'Can't bear to sit watching this rubbish. I'm going out.'

'Out?'

'Get some fresh air, whatever.'

She walked past him out into the hall.

'Do you want me to come with you?''

'I'm quite happy to go on my own.'

She put on her coat and discreetly took her mobile phone out of her bag.

'I'm sorry,' she said. 'I just feel grumpy and fed up.'

I'm not interested in the car.

The message had been sent at five to eight. The cheeky bastard, wasn't afraid of anything. Did he seriously believe that Anna would leave her family and start a new life with him? Surely he couldn't think that? No, he was entertaining himself at her expense, trying to frighten her. Punish her for wounding his male pride.

Anna walked down to the water and phoned her mother. As usual, Kathrine didn't let herself get agitated.

'But don't you get it?' Anna said. 'He's just getting at me.'

'You don't know that.'

'Do you really think he was looking for a new car?'

'I don't understand why that's so unbelievable. How would he find the advert otherwise?'

'Because Magnus put his name underneath. Don't you understand? He sits at home googling us. And now he's met Hedda as well.'

'Calm down, dear.'

'Mum, don't tell me to calm down.'

'Okay, I'm sorry. All I'm saying is, don't always think the worst. He hasn't been aggressive, has he?'

'No.'

'And he hasn't threatened you?'

'No.'

Kathrine didn't say anything. Anna recognised the technique from her childhood. Her mother had always let her draw her own conclusions, never rubbed her nose in it.

'Go to see him,' she said, eventually. 'Talk to him.'

'I don't trust him. He's weird.'

'He won't be any less weird if you keep pushing him away.'

'He's just so . . .'

She searched for the right word.

'He's got no boundaries,' she said in the end.

'Yes, that's a very popular expression in amateur psychology these days,' Kathrine said.

'I called you,' Magnus said, and gave her an accusing look. 'It was engaged.'

Anna still had the cold wrapped around her. She took off her coat and hung it up.

'I was talking to Mum,' she said.

'About what?'

Anna looked at her husband.

'Why?'

He gave an exaggerated shrug.

'That's enough. I went out because I couldn't bear to just sit here evening after evening watching rubbish.'

She shook her head and pushed past him. It wasn't until they were in bed that he mustered the courage to ask a direct question.

'Are you getting tired of me?'

Anna had just managed to read a page in the book that had been lying on her bedside table for over a week.

'Am I what?'

She stared at him, he looked grey and miserable.

'No, no, never,' she said. 'How can you ask such a silly question?'

'I don't know, the thought just struck me and then everything went black. The ground disappeared from underneath me.'

'Oh, my love.'

She put her book down and rolled over on to her side, held him close and stroked his hair, with her chin nestled on his shoulder.

The ground disappeared? Again?

Men should read more books, expand their vocabulary.

29

Anna held the bell in, pure provocation in a country where unity and compliance are deemed to be national virtues.

'Take it easy, I'm coming.'

Erik Månsson opened the door and Anna stepped past him into the flat. She stopped in the hall and turned around. Her eyes were black. She was charged, had been stewing in her anger all day.

'What are you playing at?'

There was not a trace of the conciliatory tone her mother had advised.

'I haven't a clue what you're talking about,' Erik said, amused.

'What do you think you're doing, contacting my husband, pretending to be interested in buying our car? You have got nothing to do with us. I don't want you in my world. How bloody hard is that to understand?'

'Tea?'

Anna stared, not sure that she'd heard correctly.

'I was just about to make a cup,' Erik said, and went out into the kitchen.

Anna followed him, at a distance.

'Erik, are you listening to me?'

He filled the kettle and switched it on.

'Hard not to, given that you're shouting,' he said, tersely.

Anna slammed her hand against the wall.

'Erik, you listen to me and you listen well, do you hear?'

She held her finger up in the air in warning.

'If you come anywhere near my family again I will kill you, do you understand?'

'You're threatening me,' he concluded, nodding. 'Exciting.'

Anna was shaking.

'What do you want? What have you got on me? I'm not interested, I've told you. Have I wounded your male pride? Tell me what I've done.'

Erik cast her a glance before he opened the cupboard above the fridge and took out a box of teabags.

'Are you sure you don't want any?'

'Erik, I don't want anything to do with you. In any way.'

'And yet you're still here,' he said.

Anna regulated her breath.

'Erik, I came here to sort everything out. I'm here for closure. I don't want you to call, email me or contact me or anyone in my family in any way, understand?'

The kettle started to boil. Anna had a horrible feeling that Erik might at any moment get it into his head to throw the boiling water in her face. She took half a step back towards the hall and changed her tactic and tone of voice, from confrontational to conciliatory.

'Erik, I come with an open mind. I don't want to argue. Tell me what I can do to make you happy. Tell me what I've done to hurt you so much. Please, tell me, and I promise I'll do everything I can to rectify it. If you only leave me in peace.'

He moved over to the kitchen window, looked down on to the street.

'I can't stand this any more,' Anna said. 'It was a fantastic night at Mölle, it really was. And our meetings here too. But I'm married, happily married. We've got a daughter. You and I are something else, you should be able to see that. Please, Erik, I'm begging you. Leave me alone.'

The kettle clicked off. Erik went to the sink and poured some water in a cup. He dipped the teabag up and down, smiling as if he were enjoying the situation.

'Erik, what are you doing?' she said, trying hard to stay calm.

'Right now, I'm making tea.'

'Stop it, please.'

'Please?'

'My life is complicated enough as it is. I really am so sorry that I've hurt you in some way, truly I am.'

'"Truly"?' Erik parroted and smiled at her.

'Please, I can't bear this any more.'

'Come,' he said, and went out into the sitting room-cum-bedroom.

Anna followed him reluctantly but stopped in the doorway.

'Erik, please, talk to me. Tell me what I can do.'

He put the tea down on the windowsill next to the only

plant in the flat, which was half-dead, then went over to the bookshelves.

'Come over here.'

'No, Erik. I'm not coming over there. I'm not interested.'

'Stop saying my name, like some sort of salesman. I want to show you something.'

'I'm not coming into that room again.'

'Why ever not? Don't you trust yourself to withstand temptation? Is that why you're here? You're hoping that I'll fuck you again?'

'If you so much as touch me, I'll report you,' she snapped.

Erik reached out and picked up a T-shirt that had been slung on to a bookshelf.

'This is a web camera.'

He took the cup from the windowsill and went over to the desk. He opened his laptop, clicked a couple times and turned the screen towards Anna. She heard herself, saw herself. Swaying breasts and loud lovemaking. Erik sipped his tea and closed the laptop.

'You were there, so that was nothing new to you,' he said.

Anna stood with her arms hanging by her sides. Her face was beetroot.

'You, you . . .'

'I know, the sound isn't great. But the picture is surprisingly good.'

'I'm going to report you, I am. This is too much. No more. You're going down, you are going fucking down.'

She darted across to the desk, but Erik was in the way.

'Get out of the way,' Anna said. 'I'm taking that computer, I'm confiscating that computer.'

She was shaking with rage.

'You have no right to film me on the sly like that,' she carried on, stabbing her finger into Erik's chest.

'To the contrary,' he said. 'I've got every right to record both sound and picture if I'm an active participant. However, I don't have the right to distribute it.'

'I want you to delete that video immediately. That's harassment, sexual harassment.'

Erik lifted the cup to his lips and took a sip.

'Delete it now,' Anna said again. 'Did you hear what I said? I'm going to report you for rape.'

'Might be difficult,' he said. 'You can hear a lot of yeses on the clip, but not a single no.'

'You ... you're sick, that's what you are. I came here wanting to sort things out, so we wouldn't part on bad terms. Consider yourself reported.'

Erik put down the cup.

'The end is the best,' he said. 'When you focus on my, what shall I say, natural talent? I don't know why, but I almost get the feeling that you're comparing me with someone who doesn't quite fulfil your needs.'

Anna shook her head. She was breathless, but unable to breathe. It was as if she had forgotten how to fill her lungs with oxygen. Her head rocked aimlessly like some dashboard doll.

30

The man who was half-lying on the swivel chair bore the title Chief Inspector, but had introduced himself as Karlsson. He didn't use his first name. He spoke in a drawling Helsingborg dialect that gave the impression that he was a man of the world and not easily impressed, certainly not by anything that might be found outside the county boundary.

'So what you're saying is that there's nothing I can do?' Anna concluded. 'I've got no rights?'

'Weeell,' Karlsson drew it out, 'if the bloke you're talking about decided to distribute the material, that would be a different story. But from what I understand he recorded the video for his own pleasure.'

'And you think that's all right?'

'In purely legal terms, it's permissible as long as he himself is a participant. If, however, you had both been unaware of it and filmed in secret by a third party, it would be another matter.'

Anna shook her head.

'But that's crazy.'

Karlsson shrugged.

'New legislation in the area is being discussed. But it's bloody chaos because tabloids are screaming censorship. And as you know, the discussion is really only about one thing . . .'

Anna didn't know what he was talking about. When she realised that he expected a prompt, she tilted her head questioningly instead.

'That they can write and claim whatever they like without having to think about the consequences,' Karlsson stated.

'Well, I'm actually a journalist, and I'm not entirely sure that I agree.'

Karlsson sat up.

'What I meant is that . . . a lot of journalists . . .'

'I work for *Family Journal*. We don't really cover traditional news.'

Karlsson nodded.

'*Family Journal,* that's a fine old magazine. My mother . . .'

Anna waved her hand. She wanted to return to the subject.

'So there really is nothing I can do?'

'As long as he doesn't distribute or threaten to distribute the video, no.'

'Why would he record it otherwise?'

Detective Inspector Karlsson scratched his neck.

'Well, I guess he sits there roughing up the suspect like all the other masturbators.'

Anna didn't feel comfortable with the image the jolly policeman gave her.

'But what if he posts it on the internet?' she said. 'He could pretend that someone has hacked into his computer or say that it was stolen.'

Karlsson leaned forwards, folded his hands on the table.

'You're not the first person to get caught up in something like this. My personal advice is to let the whole thing die down. If you start making a noise, the video is guaranteed to end up on some website. And then you'll never be able to get rid of it, no matter how many courts you appeal to.'

'What about the rest then?' Anna asked. 'The fact that he calls me and emails me and appears all over the place?'

'You can always report him for stalking. But then it would be official and public.'

'What should I do?'

'Hard to say, really. Is the bloke a nutter or just unhappy?'

'I don't know. Both, it would seem.'

'Could you talk to him? Do you have any men you could use?'

'What do you mean?'

'A brother or someone who might help the lad to understand that you're serious.'

'You mean frighten him? No.'

'Sorry, stupid idea. I can't just sit here and recommend vigilantism, can I? What I mean is that blokes like that, if he is one, are often cowards. They're all macho in front of women, but not quite so beefed up with other men.'

Karlsson looked at the desperate woman on the other side of his desk.

'You know what,' he said. 'I know what we can do. I'll have a word with him tomorrow morning, see if that can make the idiot see sense. Shall we do that?'

31

'But what if he puts the video on the internet?' Anna howled. 'What will I do then?'

She stared straight ahead. For once her mother had neither sage advice nor comforting words to offer.

'He can't,' Kathrine said. 'He simply can't. It's a crime. So?'

'I don't think Magnus could deal with it,' Anna said, as if she were talking to herself. 'I really don't think he could. And it would affect Hedda. Every child at school would know about it.'

She looked up at her mother.

'We'll have to move,' she said. 'We can't stay here.'

'Of course you can.'

'And it doesn't matter where,' Anna carried on, as if in a trance, 'it still won't be far enough. Someone there will always be able to find it.'

'Calm down. He hasn't posted anything yet, and if he was to do it, there must be ways to remove it. And who on earth watches things like that? It would say more about them than about you.'

They sat in silence.

'Perhaps it's just as well if you talk about it,' Kathrine said, finally. 'To Magnus, that is. So that he hears it from you.'

'He would demand to see the video.'

'The boy's bosses,' Kathrine started. 'Didn't you meet them at Mölle? Couldn't you talk to them?'

'He doesn't work for them any more. He either resigned or got the sack. And in his world, it's because of me. The video exists, Mum, and it will always exist. It doesn't matter what I do, it exists somewhere and will eventually be shown and people will see it.'

Kathrine moved her chair closer, put her arms round her daughter.

'Sweetheart, oh, my darling.'

'Magnus would never be able to deal with it,' Anna snuffled. 'I don't sound like that with him, you see.'

Kathrine let her cry.

'I'm horrible,' Anna said, drying her cheeks. 'A worthless mother and a terrible wife.'

'You're a fantastic mother and wonderful wife.'

'No, I'm not.'

'Of course you are. Stop being silly.'

Anna laughed, embarrassed.

'Do you remember when I was little, do you remember Alexander?'

'Ugh, that one.'

The love of Anna's life from junior high had made a career as a celebrity lawyer in adult life. And that, in Kathrine's eyes, was one of civilisation's lowest life forms.

'Do you remember when I bit him?' Anna giggled. 'We were doing a slow dance and I was so happy that I didn't know what to do.'

'So you took a bite of him. Yes, I remember.'

It had been a huge drama. The teacher had switched on the lights and turned off the music. The other girls fought to comfort Alexander and to blame Anna, and it wasn't clear which was actually higher on their wish list.

When Kathrine came to pick up her daughter, the heinous crime was reported to her. The teacher's witness account had an underlying accusation: there was something wrong with the girl.

'Do you remember what you said when we got home?' Anna said and looked up at her mother.

It was more than thirty years since the great event.

'No.'

'You said that one day I would make a man very happy.'

'And I was right. You do make him happy. Every day.'

Anna's chin started to tremble, her mother opened her arms.

'Oh, my darling.'

Anna didn't know what to do. There was no answer. The world carried on and would continue to do so, no matter what.

Hedda was irritable when she came home from school. She muttered like a prepubescent, kicked off her shoes in the hall and walked into her room on hard heels.

Normally, Anna would have showered her daughter with love, peppered her with loaded questions. But now she stayed in the kitchen, looking out at the street. She saw a certain beauty in the situation. Her daughter was an independent individual who was, for the moment, in a bad mood. Maybe she'd had an argument with a friend, or been given a ticking off at school, justified or not, or maybe she had a bad conscience about something or was in a hurry or whatever. It was what it was and would quickly pass. Anna was just glad to be able to witness it. In all of Hedda's ten-year life, Anna had never been away from her for more than two nights in a row. They had lived under the same roof, eaten at the same table and generally laughed at the same things. Anna didn't know how much longer that would last.

Perhaps she was blowing it up out of all proportion. As her mother had pointed out, she wasn't the first woman in history to be unfaithful. Nor was she the first one to appear naked in a film. However, the short clip she'd seen had reminded her of just how sexual their encounters had been.

Was that why Erik had reacted in the way he did? Was that why he expected more? Because he believed the strength of her response stemmed from powerful underlying emotions?

'Are you going deaf?'

Anna spun round. Hedda was standing with her hands on her hips like an old busybody.

'The phone's ringing.'

Her daughter already had her hand on the receiver. She answered the call.

'Nothing in particular,' she said.

Anna could tell by her voice that it was Magnus.

'In the kitchen,' Hedda said.

Anna guessed he'd asked where she was. Strange, given that he'd phoned the landline. Anna looked at her daughter, who was inspecting the floor as she always did when she was on the phone.

'But why? Oh, okay.'

Hedda finished the conversation and looked up at her mother.

'Dad,' she said. 'We're to stand by the window and look out.'

'Look out?'

Hedda shrugged.

'Why?'

'He didn't say.'

They looked out through the window. Five seconds passed, ten. Then they started to laugh when a red SUV glided majestically into view. Hedda ran out, Anna took her time. Magnus had just got out of the car when she came to the door.

'What do you think?' he asked, proudly. 'A hundred and fifty thousand, and it's ours.'

'Is it second-hand?'

'Of course it's second-hand, good God, a new one costs five or six hundred thousand kronor. What do you think?'

Anna nodded.

'Absolutely.'

'Jump in.'

'I'll just lock the door.'

'Oh, don't worry about that, just a quick spin.'

They cruised slowly around the streets of the neighbourhood. Magnus was unstoppable, told them all the about the car's merits, the many finesses, the superior finish.

'You really sit quite high up,' Anna commented.

'Just that in itself. The feeling it gives you, the overview.'

'Like lords,' Anna teased.

'*Ganz richtig*, real gangsta wheels. What do you think, sweetheart?'

He turned and looked at Hedda in the back seat.

'Nice,' she said.

'It sure is.'

'How much fuel does it guzzle?' Anna asked.

'About one to ten, which isn't bad. Not much more than the one we've got. What do you reckon?'

Anna turned to face her hopeful husband.

'What's the mileage?''

'Six thousand.'

'Almost the same as our old car.'

'God, there's no comparison. This is German quality, a totally different car.'

Anna looked straight ahead again, thought how strange it was that something so meaningless could be so important. And how difficult it was not to be certain of the obvious fact that her husband's boyish must-have joy would be replaced by everyday indifference within a fortnight.

'Yes, why not,' she said. 'If you want it, so do I.'

Magnus grinned. He leaned forwards and put on the radio, turned it up loud, stretched his arms out to the wheel and with immense pleasure pushed back into the seat.

Magnus stopped outside the house.

'I'll just drive back into town then and finish up the deal,' he said.

Anna nodded.

'Still a hundred thousand less than the one we looked at.'

Magnus was pleased that she'd approved.

'Exactly. I think that's wise. Don't always need to buy new. It's the first two thousand miles that cost. And this is a very different car.'

Anna patted him on the knee, opened the door and got out. She turned to Hedda.

'Are you coming, sweetie?'

'I want to go into town with Dad. Can I sit in the front?'

'Of course.'

Anna stood on the road and watched them drive off. She went into the house, closed the door behind her and caught a whiff of strawberries. A faint, barely perceptible trace. The air felt different. As if someone who had been out in the cold had just passed through the room. She stood absolutely still, with her hand on the door, listening for sounds.

'Hello?'

She slowly let go of the doorknob and took a step into the room.

'Hello?'

She looked around for something she could use as a

weapon, grabbed an umbrella, held it out in front of her and called again.

She sniffed. The smell of strawberries wasn't so strong any more. Had she got used to it or had she just imagined it?

'Erik?'

She went into the kitchen, swapped the umbrella for a kitchen knife, and swallowed to wet her throat.

'Hello?'

She pushed open the door to the bedroom. Looked under the bed, carried on to Hedda's room. She stopped by the stairs down to the cellar, hesitated.

'Hello? I'm going to get the neighbour. And if there's anyone down there I want you to show yourself.'

A neighbour. How would she explain that to her husband? If it really was Erik and the neighbour detained him and called the police? Everything would have to come out.

'Erik?'

She went down a step. And one more.

'I have to warn you, I'm armed.'

She listened. The feeling that someone was down there was overwhelming. She didn't dare continue. She backed her way up, retreated down the hall with the knife out in front of her.

'Listen. If there's anyone down there, I want you to leave the house immediately. I'm going to get help. You'll have time to get away.'

She darted towards the front door, threw the knife down on the floor and ran to her closest neighbours, an elderly couple who had stayed in their big house, even though the children had long since left home. The woman opened the door. Anna was nervous and talked very fast.

'Hello, I'm sorry. We just went out for a spin and I forgot to lock the door and now I think there's someone in the house. Probably just my imagination, but . . .'

'Göran, can you come here a minute?'

Anna explained the situation again to the husband. She was ashamed that she lacked the courage, but Göran seemed happy to be charged with such a dangerous task, despite his age. He put on his shoes and went back to the house with Anna.

'I'm probably just imagining it,' she said, embarrassed, 'but it really felt like someone was in there.'

'In the cellar?'

'I don't know.'

They went through the house.

'Thank you, thank you so much,' Anna said ten minutes

later when they'd established that the house was empty of intruders. 'I just got so scared, I don't know what's wrong with me.'

'Not to worry, it was a pleasure. If it happens again, just ring the bell.'

'Thank you. Really. I feel so embarrassed now.'

He put a hand on her shoulder.

'Well, you shouldn't. I know that feeling only too well. And it's better to be on the safe side. I would have done exactly the same thing.'

'Thank you.'

He left and Anna closed the door behind him, filled her lungs and let out a loud sigh.

32

'I'll have to go over with a bottle of wine.'

Hedda was sitting in front of her computer in her room and Anna had just told Magnus about the imaginary intruder.

'I still don't understand,' Magnus said. 'It smelt odd?'

'But it was like, like someone had just walked through the room.'

Magnus gave her a sceptical look.

'The white lady sort of thing?'

'Okay, okay, has your imagination never run away with

you? I did in fact want to lock the door. It was you who said I didn't need to. But don't say anything to Hedda. It'll only make her nervous.'

Magnus smiled at her, held his hands up in the air and wiggled his fingers.

'Whoooohoooo.'

Anna let out an unimpressed sigh.

'I'm sorry,' Magnus said. 'You did the right thing. You never know. Always best to be on the safe side.'

He opened the fridge, grabbed a beer and looked out at their newly purchased car. Anna went into the sitting room and switched on the TV. The phone rang and Magnus answered it. Anna saw him put it down again.

'Who was it?'

'No one.'

The phone rang again. Magnus answered it again.

'Yes? Hello? Hello?'

He hung up.

'Probably some salesperson who got an answer elsewhere.'

It was generally only salespeople who called on the landline. With the exception of Kathrine and a few parents from school who didn't have their mobile numbers. The phone rang for a third time. Magnus looked at the display before he barked: 'Yes?'

He stood silently for quite a while.

'Hello?' he said, finally, before putting the phone down in irritation.

'Someone messing around?' Anna suggested.

The phone rang for a fourth time and Magnus shouted up to Hedda.

'There's someone who keeps calling but doesn't say anything, maybe it's for you.'

Hedda answered.

'Oh, hi, Granny. Fine, thank you. Yes. No. Not today. Of course.'

She came into the sitting room with the phone.

'It's Granny.'

Anna took it.

'Hi, Mum. Did you just call?'

'Wasn't me.'

'Okay.'

Anna was worried that her mother might ask whether it could have been Erik and quickly changed the conversation.

'We've bought a new car.'

'Have you? Why?'

'The other one was getting a bit old.'

'But it was such a nice car.'

'A BMW,' Anna said, and noticed Magnus grow a few inches in the background.

'Is it difficult for you to speak?' her mother whispered.

'Second-hand,' Anna said.

'So you haven't told him. Good. I think it might be wisest to wait. I called the national registry a few days ago, checked up on Erik Månsson. I didn't tell you earlier because I felt so ashamed.'

Anna didn't know what to say. Her mother had phoned the authorities? Why on earth had she done that?

'His mother is dead,' Kathrine continued. 'I don't know how, but she died a couple of years ago now. And his dad disappeared out of the picture early on, moved to Finland when Erik was just a baby.'

'Okay.'

'I don't think he's had an easy life.'

'Mmm.'

'I can tell that it's not easy for you to talk. Can we maybe speak tomorrow?'

'Of course.'

'Take care then, dear. Bye.'

'You too, lots of love.'

Anna put down the phone and saw Magnus was looking at her, full of anticipation.

'She wondered how we could afford it,' Anna said, and saw her husband grow even more

As if the borrowed money bought status and increased his value as a person. The telephone rang again.

'Hello?'

'Can you tell Mr Wimpy to stop answering the phone?'

Anna felt her cheeks burning.

'You must have got the wrong number.'

'I have to meet you. We need to talk.'

'Not a problem.'

She cut off the conversation and struggled to swallow.

'Wrong number.'

She put the telephone down on the table in front of her. Stared at the TV, but saw only the phone in the foreground. Her ears shut down and a shrill sound filled her head, a sound that she couldn't block out. She barely heard the phone when it started to ring again. She grabbed it, quick as a flash.

'Anna.'

'If you answered your mobile phone I wouldn't need to call the landline.'

'Hello?'

'You're such a bad liar.'

'Hello?'

'And yet you're living a lie.'

'Hello?'

Anna looked at Magnus, who had left the kitchen and was walking towards her.

'Come here and I'll fuck you like I fucked you on the video. I'm watching you right now.'

Anna heard herself moaning in the background and hung up. She held the red button in until the phone was completely dead.

'No one there?'

Anna nodded.

'Just as well to keep it off then.'

She glanced at her husband and then turned to the TV again. She could feel him looking at her, and reached out for the remote control. She couldn't even change channels naturally.

Magnus turned and left the room.

'Hedda? Someone keeps calling our landline. Do you have any idea who it might be?'

33

Kathrine barely recognised her daughter's voice. She sounded frightened and stressed. Erik Månsson really had knocked her off kilter and it couldn't continue.

Who might know more about this motherless, misguided young man? Kathrine logged on to ratsit.se and typed in the address in Huddinge where he and his mother had been registered. A list of all the other people living in the block came up. Plus their ages. She chose a man of thirty-five and searched for his phone number.

'Lars Johansson in the middle of eating,' he answered, humorously.

Kathrine could hear children's voices and a woman scolding in the background.

'Oh, so sorry, didn't mean to interrupt,' she said. 'Can I call you back later?'

'What's it about?'

Kathrine guessed insurance broker, but she wasn't sure why.

'Well, my name is Kathrine Hansson and I'm trying to get in touch with an old friend who used to live at this address. Anneli Månsson. I'm coming up to Stockholm and thought it would be nice to meet her again, but the number that I've got doesn't seem to work any longer.'

'Oh,' said Lars Johansson in the middle of eating.

'I'm sorry?'

'Just a moment, I'll just go into the next room, so the kids don't hear.'

'Sorry, would you like me to call back later?'

'There,' the man said, when, by the sound of it, he had locked himself in the family bathroom. 'You're an old friend of Anneli Månsson, did you say?'

'Yes. We met on a holiday a few years ago, and had a lovely time together. And as I'm coming to Stockholm, I thought I'd surprise her.'

'Well, I'm very sorry to say I've got bad news for you then,' Lars Johansson, the insurance broker, said. 'Sadly, Anneli Månsson has passed away.'

'Passed away? But she wasn't that old.'

'She took her own life.'

'T-t-took her own life?' Kathrine stammered. 'Why on earth would she do that?'

She tried to sound shocked and suitably upset.

'I guess you never really know with that kind of thing,' Lars in the middle of eating replied.

'But she was so full of life,' Kathrine said, and really felt very sorry for herself.

'Yes,' Lars Johansson agreed, stoically. 'You just never know.'

Kathrine changed tack.

'Did you know her well?' she asked.

'Not at all.'

'Did you know her son?'

'No. But from what I understand, he was the one who found her.'

'Oh, the poor boy,' Kathrine said, and finished the conversation.

She rang the next person on the list of Erik Månsson's

former neighbours, a woman her own age, a few years older in fact.

'Barbro Wellin.'

'Hello, my name is Kathrine Hansson and I'm calling from Helsingborg.'

'I see.'

Kathrine explained the situation to her, without leaving anything out. She found it hard to make up a story and lie to a peer.

'Your daughter had a fling with Erik Månsson and now he won't leave her alone?' Barbro Wellin summarised.

'Yes. And that's why I'm calling. Is he . . . dangerous?'

'I don't know,' Barbro said. 'He lived with his mother, who committed suicide. But you knew that. To tell you the truth, I never really knew them. There was a wall of silence around them. And then there was all the gossip.'

'What gossip?'

'That he and his mother . . . Well, I don't know how seriously to take rumours like that, but well, there was something going on.'

'You mean that there was something going on between them?' Kathrine guessed.

'Yes, at least, that's what was hinted at between the lines,' Barbro Wellin replied.

Anna was in the bathroom brushing her teeth.

'Oh, how sweet,' Magnus shouted from the bedroom.

Anna had her mouth full of toothpaste and couldn't say anything. Their curious daughter asked instead.

'What?'

'Your mother,' Magnus said. 'She's left a racing car sweet on my pillow.'

'Why?'

'It's the kind of thing you do in posh hotels, leave sweets on the pillow. And Mummy's put a racing car on mine because we've just bought a new car.'

'I want one too.'

Anna listened to it all and blinked furiously at her own reflection. She hadn't put a racing car sweet on her husband's pillow. And Hedda obviously hadn't done it either.

Anna had finished brushing her teeth, but continued so she had time to think. There was only one answer. Someone had been in the house. Wrong, Erik had been in the house.

Erik had been in her house, walked in like it was the

most natural thing in the world and left a sweet on Magnus' pillow. But why? Why on earth would he do anything as bizarre as that?

'You can have mine,' Magnus said to Hedda, 'but you can't eat it until tomorrow, because you've just brushed your teeth.'

There were no limits to what Erik could do, he really was sick. The best thing would be to admit everything, tell Magnus about their encounter at Mölle and her subsequent visits to his flat, the video. No, not the video. Magnus must not find out about that, under any circumstances. If he ever saw the recording, it would be over. He would never recover.

Anna stopped brushing, spat and rinsed. She went into the bedroom.

'You're so sweet,' Magnus beamed.

Anna gave a quick smile, got undressed and crept into bed. She reached over for her book and opened it. A piece of paper fell out. It wasn't her usual bookmark. Anna looked at the piece of paper and read the handwritten message.

Small car, big ... Who do you want beside you in bed?

A currently contented husband, an unhappy daughter and her own emotional life in disarray – all because of some idiotic fling at a hotel in Mölle.

The first and the last didn't matter so much. His pleasure in the car would gradually be replaced by complaints about the costs. She had sold her own peace of mind for a few incredible orgasms. Which might seem like an unreasonably high price, but it was nothing compared to what Hedda was suffering. Magnus' insinuation that someone was making prank calls to her could not be magicked away.

When they dropped her off at school, she looked so unsure as she walked towards the entrance.

'Maybe it's someone who's in love with you,' Anna tried.

Hedda glared at her.

'Yuck,' Magnus said. 'That must be it.'

He turned and Anna noticed how happy he was with his hands on the steering wheel.

'It might be someone who's wanting to annoy us too,' she said.

Magnus smiled as if to say it was a nice thought, but not plausible.

'You don't need to drive me,' Anna said. 'I can take the bus.'

'Of course I'll drive you,' Magnus objected. 'You can't take that pleasure from me.'

'What do you mean by pleasure?'

'I would love to give you a lift.'

'Have I taken any other pleasure from you?'

Magnus didn't understand.

'What are you talking about?'

'When you said *that* pleasure it sounded like you thought I'd clipped your wings in other areas.'

Magnus shook his head.

'What's up with you?'

Anna didn't answer. She just stared ahead, but could feel his gaze switching between her and the road.

'Is everything okay?' he asked.

Anna put her elbow up by the window and rested her head in her hand.

'Just a bit stressed at work.'

'Do you need to work overtime?'

'I don't know.'

'Don't worry if you do. I'll look after supper.'

He dropped her off outside the publishing house. Sissela was walking round from the parking place.

'New car?' she said, and waved blithely at Magnus.

'Newish, second-hand,' Anna said.

'Nice.'

They went up in the lift together, observed each other in the mirror.

'You look tired,' Sissela said.

'Thanks,' Anna said. 'That's just what I needed to hear.'

'I'm sorry, it was well meant.'

Anna backed down.

'Barely slept last night,' she explained.

'What? Again?' Sissela said. 'Why not?'

'I don't know.'

They got to their floor. Anna went into the toilets and took out her mobile. She'd had it turned off all night. She tapped in the pin code, sat down on the toilet seat and waited while the phone connected to the server. A text message from the server told her that she had seven new voicemails. She called.

Received yesterday at seventeen fifteen.

Anna heard him put down the phone.

Received yesterday at seventeen twenty-seven.

Another click.

Received yesterday at nineteen o-five.

'Hi, it's me. How did it end up like this? I just want to see

you. Don't you realise how much you hurt me? Okay, so you were led astray once, I can understand that. But four times? I believed in you, you fooled me.'

Received yesterday at nineteen twenty-one.

'What's my crime? Explain. What did I do wrong? The difference between you and me is that I don't jump into bed with just anybody. It really means something to me. I lost my job because of you. What did you lose? Nothing. You can carry on living the high life in the suburbs as if nothing has happened.'

Received yesterday at nineteen fifty.

'I think it's ironic, I really do. You disassociating yourself from me. You! What happened to self-insight?'

Received yesterday at twenty-two o-nine.

'Oh, how clever. To turn off your phone. You think you can get rid of me by not answering, do you really believe that? So you think I'm a problem? Don't you realise how crazy that is? How back to front? You think I'm a problem? You're about a hundred years old and not particularly attractive anyway.'

Received yesterday at twenty-three forty-five.

'Sitting here reliving old memories. Listen. Jeez, you'd think you'd got a jellyfish up your cunt, you're so wet. Listen. That's all.'

Anna turned off her mobile. She didn't want to have it

on while she was at work. She went into the editorial office. Sissela was standing by her desk.

'Your phone rang,' she said. 'I tried to answer, but whoever it was just hung up.'

'Thank you.'

Sissela went over to layout and Anna immediately phoned down to reception.

'Hi, Renée, it's Anna. Can you hold all my calls. I'm going to be in a meeting and busy all day.'

'Of course.'

'Thank you.'

She hung up and then tried to call her mother.

34

'Erik Månsson?'

'Yes.'

Karlsson held out his ID card.

'Police. I'd like a few words with you. Have you got a minute?'

Erik shifted his weight.

'Of course,' he said, hesitating. 'What's it concerning?'

'I've had a visit from Anna Stenberg.'

'Right,' Erik sighed heavily.

'You know who she is?' Karlsson asked.

Erik put his hands sulkily on his hips.

'Yes.'

'She says that you're harassing her.'

'I'm sorry?'

'I'm sure you heard. Are you perhaps of a different opinion?'

'You could say that.'

'Interesting,' Karlsson said. 'Could I come in so we can discuss it?'

Erik hesitated again, but had no reason to say no. He opened the door and took a step to the side.

'Shall we sit in the kitchen?' Karlsson suggested.

Erik nodded and led the way.

'The name's Karlsson, by the way.'

Erik gave an uninterested nod.

'Everything okay?' Karlsson asked.

'How do you mean?'

'You seem bothered.'

'Well, it's not very nice being accused of things like this.'

'So, there's no grounds for it?'

'Absolutely none.'

'So if we were to request a printout of your phone log, we wouldn't find an unhealthy number of calls to her?'

'We're in a relationship. I don't know whether she told you that? It's not like we don't know each other.'

'I don't think she actually used the word "relationship",' Karlsson said.

'She didn't?' Erik sounded aggressive. 'How come we've had sex together quite a few times then? She's come to my flat. Does that count for nothing?'

'And apparently you made a film as well?' Karlsson added.

Erik didn't answer.

'Nice,' Karlsson nodded to himself. 'Considerate, manly.'

'What do you want?'

'I wanted to hear what you had to say. And to make sure that you leave Anna Stenberg alone in future. No visits, no sudden appearances, no phone calls, no text messages. No contact with her whatsoever. Agreed?'

'I'll contact who the fuck I like, and I have every right to do so.'

'Yes, but Anna Stenberg is already married and not interested in your attention.'

Erik muttered something.

'What did you say?' Karlsson asked.

'I said she should have thought of that before.'

'Is that what you think? You feel that you've got some kind of an alliance?'

Erik stood up straight.

'I want you to leave. I've tried to be patient, but this is too much.'

Karlsson nodded and got up. He went into the sitting room and stood by the window, clasped his hands comfortably behind his back.

'Nice view,' he said.

'I want you to leave,' Erik repeated.

Karlsson turned round and studied him, nodded in amusement.

'If you contact Anna Stenberg again, in any way whatsoever, she'll report you for stalking. And you will be charged and sentenced, I can assure you. If the video you made is distributed in any way, I personally will make sure that you are charged with blackmail.'

'Blackmail?'

Karlsson went over to him.

'Your purpose is to defame another person. And that is against the law. I agree that legislation can seem a bit unwieldy at times, but I promise you, when interpreted correctly, it's very effective.'

He gave Erik a hard pat on the cheek.

'Don't know what you're after,' Karlsson said. 'She's old enough to be your mother.'

Erik's eyes went black, his lips tightened.

'You've been warned,' Karlsson continued. 'Now, be a sensible young man and lay off. Swallow the bitter pill and accept that she's not interested.'

He whistled as he left the flat and went down the stairs. At the bottom he held the door open for an attractive older woman who was talking on her mobile phone. He saluted in jest and she smiled her thanks.

'Protect, help, reprimand,' Karlsson chanted.

35

It was Kathrine's firm conviction that all people were basically the same. Even the wildest ideas were driven by a desire to belong. Everyone was steered by more or less the same compass.

Kathrine understood why Erik Månsson was fascinated by her daughter, his desperation at losing his job, his loneliness as a newcomer and outsider in a closed place like Helsingborg. His hurt feelings when Anna suddenly didn't want to know him and refused to see him after several intense encounters.

Kathrine was going to talk to him. Get him to understand. Surely it must be possible.

When she got to the address, all her good intentions were stymied. She didn't know the entry code. She rummaged around in her bag for her mobile and rang her daughter. The call went straight to voicemail, which meant her mobile was turned off. Kathrine tried her direct number at work instead.

'Please hold the line while your call is transferred.'

The automated voice was replaced by the familiar voice of the receptionist.

'*Family Journal*. You were trying to get hold of Anna Stenberg?'

'Yes, hello. It's Kathrine, Anna's mother.'

'Hi, Kathrine,' Renée said. 'How are you?'

'Very well, thanks. And you?'

'Fine, thanks. Listen, Anna's in a meeting for the rest of the day. Shall I ask her to call you?'

A man came out of the door and Kathrine grabbed hold of it. The man saluted her.

'Protect, help, reprimand,' he chanted.

Kathrine smiled in answer.

'No, it's not important,' she said, into the receiver. 'Just let her know I called.'

'Will do,' Renée assured her. 'Bye for now.'

'Yes, goodbye.'

Kathrine stopped by the stairs, looked up at the name board and then took the lift to the top floor. She rang the bell and heard quick steps approaching. The door was pulled open in an almost aggressive manner. Erik Månsson looked surprised, but the surprise swiftly disappeared as his guard immediately went up.

He looked younger than Kathrine had imagined. Somehow not fully adult, despite his age. He was good-looking, no doubt about it, if a little stressed and bothered.

'Hello. My name's Kathrine Hansson. I'm Anna Stenberg's mother.'

She held out her hand. He hesitated but then took it, as it would be far too rude not to.

'I wanted to talk to you.'

Erik shifted his weight, stood up straight.

'About what?'

'My daughter. Can I come in?'

She gave a kind smile.

'Anna doesn't know that I'm here,' she added.

Erik held open the door.

'Thank you.'

She went in and he closed the door. She turned around and tussled with the uneasy feeling that she was making a mistake. She took off her coat and hung it up, put her handbag on the floor below it.

'Is it okay if I keep my shoes on? They're a bit difficult to take off.'

Erik grunted his agreement and went into the kitchen. Kathrine followed tentatively behind. She pointed at a chair, he gave a curt nod. She sat down. Erik crossed his arms and leaned back against the worktop.

'So,' Katherine started gingerly, when it became clear that he wasn't going to help her with any small talk or charming questions. 'Anna's told me about what happened and how you met. To your mutual pleasure, I believe.'

She tried to read his response but was uncertain whether her words were having any impact.

'But she also said that it's all started to go a bit off the rails now,' Kathrine carried on, opened out her hands. 'I've only heard her version. So I wanted to hear yours.'

Erik scrutinised her.

'So she sends her mum here, eh?' he exclaimed. 'She doesn't dare tell her husband, but she cries on her mum's shoulder. Mummy who's always there to comfort her and put things into perspective. Mummy who promises to sort things out and talk some sense into the naughty boy.'

'Anna doesn't know that I'm here.'

'I didn't believe you the first time,' he said. 'And repeating the lie doesn't make it any more convincing.'

'It happens to be the truth.'

'Okay,' he said, and hopped up on to the worktop. 'So you're here of your own accord. That means that Anna's told you my name and where I live. Did she give you the entry code as well?'

'A man came out just as I wanted to get in.'

'How handy.'

He'd gone from being aggressive to being facetious. Kathrine didn't know if it was a step in the right direction.

'Can't you just say what the matter is?' she asked. 'Surely you can talk it through.'

'It's pretty hard to talk when she doesn't answer my calls.'

'Would you like me to talk to her?'

Erik laughed until it made him cough. Kathrine didn't let it bother her.

'As my representative, you mean? Yes. That would be

really good. Because you wouldn't be at all biased in that situation.'

Kathrine straightened her back and changed her sitting position.

'I am of course here for Anna's sake. She said that you'd recorded a film.'

'She did, did she?'

'Without her knowing about it. Do you think that's fair?'

He shrugged.

'I haven't done anything illegal.'

'I don't know whether it's legal or not. I asked whether you thought it was fair?'

Erik looked over her shoulder.

'I've got every right to document my daily life.'

'Your daily life?' Kathrine repeated.

He nodded.

'So it's something you do regularly?' she asked. 'Make that kind of film?'

'I didn't say that.'

Kathrine held up her hand.

'Wait,' she said. 'Let's start again. Is that okay?'

She gave him a questioning look, he flung out his arm with ironic generosity.

'This is what I know about you,' Kathrine started. 'You met at the hotel in Mölle. You had sex. You met a couple of times later here in this flat, same activity. And from what I understand, you both enjoyed it.'

Erik made no comment.

'And since then,' Kathrine continued, 'you've tried to contact Anna in different ways, even though she's expressly asked you not to.'

She looked at him: not a twitch. Kathrine bobbed her head down between her shoulders and opened out her hands, a physical question mark.

'Am I wrong?' she asked.

Erik jumped down from the worktop, took a glass out of the cupboard, turned on the tap and felt the water with his finger. When he thought it was cold enough, he filled the glass. He drank half of it straight down before he answered.

'Did she forget to tell you that I lost my job because of her? Something she felt forced to do so she wouldn't need to tell her colleagues that she'd been unfaithful.'

'She said she had nothing to do with it.'

'She said that?'

He poured out the rest of the water and put the glass on the dish rack. He shook his head.

'What are you doing here?'

'Why argue?' Kathrine asked. 'It seems so unnecessary. Please stop. And if you don't want to do it for Anna's sake, then think of her daughter.'

Kathrine pushed her behind back in the chair and leaned forwards, rested her arms on her thighs and clasped her hands between her knees.

'I believe that most people are basically the same,' she said. 'There's very little that differentiates us. When things get out of hand, it's usually because of hurt feelings or a mis-understanding.'

'If I was at all interested in that kind of thing I'd be watching Dr Phil,' Erik said, curtly. 'You want to help your daughter. Is that why you're here?'

'Of course.'

'Do you want to help me?'

'I don't know you.'

'So you want to help your daughter, but not me?'

Kathrine tried to change tack.

'I want to understand,' she said.

'Understand what?' Erik asked.

'Why you can't leave her be? You met a few times, fair enough.'

Erik grinned, as if she'd said something funny.

'You come here and preach about morals. Your daughter used me for her sexual gratification. Then she was overcome by guilt and is trying to blot out the whole thing now. Do you think that's fair?'

'You slept together. Good God, you're both adults.'

'Ah,' Erik said. 'You mean the pleasures of the flesh. Disassociated from the loneliness of the soul. She wasn't responsible for her actions? It just happened.'

'You got something out of it as well, didn't you?'

'So I should be there for her pleasure? I should be there whenever she feels the urge, but otherwise I should keep away and not disturb? Anna fooled me into believing. She owes me.'

'Owes you what? She's not interested. How hard is that to understand? Move on. Surely you won't have any problems meeting other women?'

Kathrine let the question hang in the air, almost like an accusation.

'Do you know why I recorded the video?' Erik said, calmly. 'To document what it was like. To prove to myself that it wasn't just my imagination. If you saw it, you'd believe me. What Anna and I have together is real. She's lying when she says she doesn't want to see me, lying to her-self.'

'Can I see it?' she asked. 'Can you show me the record-ing so I can make up my own mind?'

Erik looked at her with disgust.

'I would never show anything that private to anyone else.'

'Is that a promise?'

Erik didn't understand.

'That you won't show the video to anyone else? Do you realise how terrifying it is for Anna? That you're threaten-ing her entire life?'

'Her suburban lie, you mean?'

'Call it what you like, think of the girl. She's only ten years old.'

'Marvellous,' Erik said, amused. 'Bloody marvellous.'

'What?'

'The constant chat about children. Unashamed.'

Kathrine looked at him, puzzled.

'As soon at things get difficult, the middle class cries "but the children, the children, the children". Artificial concern in order to hide whatever it is that's threatening their false self-image. Children are accessories in their world, nothing more.'

He was so agitated, he was spitting.

'Do you think it's right to use the children as an excuse just because you're too lazy to get divorced and too tired to fight? It's a construct, a convenient lie. You know just as well as I do that Anna would never have stayed with that boring fart if it hadn't been for Hedda.'

Kathrine felt sick hearing him say the girl's name.

'She'd have left him ages ago,' Erik continued. 'You know that too. If she was so in love with her husband she would hardly have been looking for pleasure elsewhere.'

'Anna loves her husband,' Kathrine stated. 'They're happy together and have a good relationship. What you had was a flirt, a bit of spice. Why can't you be happy with that?'

'Can I ask you something?' Erik interjected. 'If Anna loves her husband so much, why did she go to bed with me? Please tell me that. And be honest.'

'I don't know. I guess she was attracted to you.'

'She was attracted to me?'

'Obviously.'

'And that makes it okay to be unfaithful to your husband?'

'No, it doesn't. But good grief, have you never made mistakes? You were both at a work do, for Christ's sake.'

Erik laughed and shook his head. He went over to the window and looked down at the street.

'A work do? And that excuses everything, you think?'

'No, I don't. But I think we all do strange things every now and then. And her judgement wasn't the best just then.'

'Just then?' he said, turning round. 'We've done it four times. Four.'

He held up the same number of fingers as proof, like a child.

'Whatever,' Kathrine said. 'I don't suppose it will happen again. If Anna had known how this would end, she would never have done it in the first place. You must understand that. You need help, professional help.'

Kathrine crossed the kitchen and stood next to him.

'I've found out a few things about you,' she said. 'I admit, I phoned the national registry. They told me that your mother died a couple of years ago. I even spoke to a couple of her, well, your previous neighbours. They hinted that you and your mother were perhaps closer than normal. If you don't leave my daughter alone, I will make your life very difficult. Do you understand what I'm saying? I'll publicly humiliate you.'

Erik's lower lip twitched once, though it was hard to tell whether it was nerves or repressed anger. Possibly the latter. Kathrine was not going to back down.

'It's up to you,' she said.

36

Sometimes Anna became blind to individual words. Often, it was an everyday word or one that was repeated so often that it became unrecognisable, hard to articulate and impossible to understand. This was something else.

The individual letters were swimming. Black spots on a white background, familiar enough in their own right, but meaningless together. Anna forced her eyes to move from left to right, row after row, from the top to the bottom. And still she didn't understand the words, even less the sentences.

Her brain wasn't working. Wrong, it was overloaded and

couldn't take in what her eyes were registering. All the familiar sounds and voices of the office had gone too. Someone had pressed the mute button and the only thing Anna was aware of was her own tight lips. They felt as swollen as those of a surgery-happy porn queen.

She turned the page, kept on pretending to read, but all she saw was the silenced mobile.

Anna licked her lips. They were numb, as if she had eaten poison.

Turning the telephone off had not given her peace. It was almost growling. As if it were vibrating on its own. And the vibrations spread and made the desk shake, made the lights on the ceiling and the bookshelves shake so much that the files and books and paper spilled out on to the floor while people screamed and took cover under their desks, but to no avail.

'Hello, earth to Anna Stenberg.'

She looked up and saw Sissela shaking her head.

'What?'

'Lunch?'

'Absolutely. Yes.'

Anna dropped the printout she was staring at blindly and got up.

'She didn't get any sleep again last night,' she heard Sissela explaining to Trude.

Erik looked down at the floor, his eyes darting back and forth.

'I don't what it is,' he said. 'This past year, since Mum died. Everything's falling apart. I thought moving here would change things. Then I met Anna, I thought that finally . . . '

His eyes pleaded with Kathrine.

'Have you never met someone and just felt that it was right, almost like fate?'

Kathrine scrutinised his face, didn't know what to think.

'I didn't mean any harm,' he said. 'I'm just lonely.'

Kathrine hesitated. Erik lowered his head, resigned, with a sheepish smile.

'I feel so stupid,' he said. 'It's as if I've become someone I don't want to be, that I've been forced into it. And not being able to explain myself just makes things worse. A bit like when someone says that you're weird. There's no way to answer it. What can you say? That you're not? How normal does that make you sound?'

Kathrine nodded, encouraging him to continue.

'It's a vicious circle,' he said. 'Anna decides it's over and I have no choice but to accept it. If I try to do anything, I'm accused of being difficult and a pest, and worse. And suddenly there you are with your hands out, swearing and promising that you're normal.'

He shook his head in despair at the impossible situation.

'You're the first person who's spoken to me,' he continued.

'The video . . . '

'I've deleted it,' Erik said, and lowered his eyes. 'To be honest, against my will. It was the only thing I had. But at same time, I understand . . . '

He looked up.

'My reasons for recording it weren't dishonourable, I want you to know that. I realise that it seems slightly perverse to even think of it, but I just wanted something to remind me of our time together. Anna and me.'

'So the video is gone? Doesn't exist any more?'

'I wouldn't want to risk it falling into the wrong hands.'

'What do you mean?'

Erik shrugged.

'You never know. It was wrong of me to do it in the first

place and it's not something I normally do. I hope that you'll believe that.'

Kathrine didn't say anything. Her silence forced him to continue. He laughed with embarrassment and waved his hands, shifted position.

'I don't know what to do now,' he said. 'I don't have a job, I don't know anyone. I'll probably move back to Stockholm. There's nothing here, really.'

'Maybe it's just as well,' Kathrine said.

He reacted strongly. As if he'd been hoping for her to object, to persuade him otherwise, and felt let down.

'It really meant something to me,' he retorted. 'For Anna it was just a bit of fun, a welcome break from boring every-day life. Something to boast about to her friends.'

'You don't know my daughter. She would never say a word.'

'Wouldn't she?' Erik objected. 'You seem to be very well informed.'

'The only reason she told me is that you frightened her.'

'I frightened her? She's the one scaring me. How can a grown-up woman jump into bed with someone without it meaning anything? Explain that to me. And then when it no longer suits them, they just leave with a supercilious "Thanks, bye".'

He regretted this outburst and tried to recapture his humiliated mood by adopting submissive body language. Kathrine watched him. She breathed through her nose and nodded to herself.

'Just like my daughter said,' she concluded.

'What did she say?'

'That you seem to be perfectly normal, but you're not.'

'Did she say that?'

Erik's look was amused and patronising. Kathrine had a sad expression on her face.

'I normally credit myself with being naive and believing the best of people,' she said. 'And contrary to what most people think, it comes at a price. It requires hard work and conscious effort. You have to dismiss the thought that people don't wish you well. If you don't, you become suspicious of everyone and end up bitter and cynical.'

Erik ran his tongue along his lower lip, pulled a bored face. Kathrine looked at him long and hard.

'So why do I get the feeling that you don't wish me well?' she said. 'Neither me, nor my daughter.'

The telephone interrupted her. It was in her bag out in the hall. She got up to answer it.

'I'm going to take this call. I think you and I have said all there is to say.'

Anna's lips felt less swollen after some food and she had returned to reality. She heard what was being said and could even make small comments to prove her existence. Which was important. Sissela was an anxious general who needed constant reassurance. Anyone who held back or wasn't present could reckon on getting a veiled dressing down that was hard to counter. In a way, her insecurity was justified: Anna and Trude made a far more natural unit. They enjoyed each other's company, laughed at the same things and not necessarily at the expense of others. Sissela's humour depended on having a victim as it was the exclusion of others that gave her a sense of belonging.

'So, what do you reckon? Shall we have coffee upstairs?'

They left the canteen in good humour and walked towards the lift.

'Anna.'

Renée stood up behind reception.

'Your mum called.'

'Oh, thank you.'

'Will you be in a meeting all afternoon as well?'

Anna could feel her boss's curious eyes on her neck.

'No, not this afternoon,' she replied.

They went into the lift.

'In a meeting?' Sissela quipped. 'I didn't notice.'

'I had to say that so I could get my work done. Everything gets so fragmented when the phone rings all the time.'

'Oh to be so in demand,' Sissela said ironically, and sent a glance to Trude. 'I wish I was as interesting.'

Anna left them in the kitchen, went to her desk and called her mother. She looked around while she listened to the ring tone, on and on. The office was almost empty and none of her colleagues was within earshot. The call was transferred to voicemail, so she hung up.

She dialled the direct number to Karlsson, the policeman she had spoken to.

'Yes, I went over and had a chat with him,' he said, pleased with himself. 'And I think I got him to realise how serious the matter was. If you hear from him again, just give me a call.'

'Thank you,' Anna said, and felt her body relax. 'If you knew how much that meant to me. Thank you so much.'

She finished the call and was on the verge of crying for joy. Suddenly she became aware of the pain. She felt an ache in her back and shoulders, and her head was pounding with released tension, as if she'd been in an exam for hours.

'Did you hear what I said?' Kathrine exclaimed. 'Let me past.'

Erik had stood up and was blocking her way.

'What's wrong with you? I need to get this. It's Anna. I'm going to tell her. That she was right all along. It wasn't her imagination.'

Kathrine tried to push Erik to the side. He put his arm across her chest and pulled her back.

'What are you doing? Let me go!'

She screamed and Erik put his hand over her mouth.

'Be quiet,' he said, 'don't scream.'

Kathrine tried to get free and Erik responded by pressing harder. He pinched her nose between his thumb and index finger. She flailed with her arms. He had no choice, he was forced to hold tighter. Kathrine tried to claw herself loose, but Erik had no problem holding on to her. She twisted in desperation, screamed for air and kicked out in a futile attempt to free herself. He hushed in her ear.

'Please, don't scream.'

The telephone stopped ringing, but the last signal seemed to fill the flat.

'Shhh,' Erik commanded. 'Take it easy.'

Kathrine's back was arched like a bow and she kicked powerlessly into thin air. Erik closed his eyes and kept a firm grip. Kathrine shuddered and her body slumped into an ungainly mass. Erik kept hold of her for a while before gently releasing her on to the floor.

'Promise to be quiet,' he said. 'Promise.'

37

Anna put the phone down and went out into the kitchen. She got herself a cup of coffee, then went to join the others.

'We're sitting here wondering if anything has happened,' Sissela said.

'We?' Trude objected. 'Speak for yourself.'

'Happened? What do you mean?'

'You're not sleeping at night, asking for all your calls to be held. Then he drives you to work. Has he done something stupid?'

'Who?'

'Magnus. Has he been unfaithful?'

'What are you talking about?'

Sissela held up her hands in innocence.

'Okay, okay, sorry. We just wanted to make sure you're all right.'

'Again,' Trude said. 'Speak for yourself.'

Sissela turned to her.

'Don't you want to make sure that Anna's all right?'

Trude gave a resigned sigh.

'Sissela, give it a break.'

Anna got up.

'Excuse me,' she said, and went back into the office.

'What?' Sissela exclaimed. 'I was only joking.'

Anna went over to her desk, picked up the mobile phone, which was turned off, played with it for a while, then turned it on again. She waited anxiously while it found the server. Thirty seconds later she saw that no one had tried to get hold of her, at least, no one had made the effort to leave a message or send a text.

The feeling of happiness made her cheeks glow. She called her mother again. Four rings until the voicemail kicked in.

'Hi, Mum, it's me. You rang. Sorry I was so short with you yesterday. He called. But the police have been to speak to him now. Hope he'll stop. Hope, hope, hope. I'll try again later. Lots of love.'

Erik sat on the floor, sweating. He looked at Kathrine, stretched out his arm and pressed his fingers against her neck. Looking for a pulse. He slapped her lightly on the cheeks. No reaction. Her face was sagging, which made her look different.

Erik got up abruptly, looked around before pointing at her.

'I told you to be quiet,' he said, and nudged her with his foot. 'Kathrine?'

He backed into the kitchen table, forced himself to breathe slowly.

'I wasn't holding that hard,' he said. 'You only have yourself to blame, you wouldn't listen.'

Her eyes were wide open, empty and accusing at the same time. Erik turned away, didn't want to look at her.

'You forced me.'

Kathrine's phone started to ring again. He edged past her lifeless body as if it were a poisonous snake, opened her handbag and looked at the illuminated screen on the mobile phone: Anna.

Erik wanted to answer, to hear her voice. He had to fight the impulse.

The phone stopped ringing. He looked at Kathrine. There were no signs of asphyxiation. He hadn't held her mouth that hard, just stopped her from screaming. And now she was lying there. Not moving, with a sagging face and staring eyes. He bent down and poked her gently on the shoulder.

It wasn't his fault, he hadn't done anything. Just restrained her, and not particularly hard. It wasn't his fault. She'd been completely hysterical, like a different person.

Maybe she suffered from a congenital heart defect. It wasn't impossible, in fact it might be quite possible. An aneurysm or something that suddenly, without warning . . .

'Think,' he admonished himself. 'Think, think, think.'

He couldn't let an unfortunate mistake ruin his future. It wasn't fair. Life had never been fair, not to him, enough was enough. This was yet more proof that he always drew the short straw. Why was he being punished? It was wrong. Wrong from a divine perspective. He was young, she was old. Old and meddling and smug. The world was no worse off without her, that was for sure. Not in any way.

It was Anna's fault. She had poisoned her mother with

her malicious stories. She was a pathetic coward who had rewritten events so she could walk free.

Erik had tried. He'd listened. And how had she thanked him? By accusing him of awful things. Just like her daughter, Kathrine claimed to know how the world worked and refused to see that her truth wasn't necessarily the same as someone else's. A self-righteous and obnoxious know-all, and when something didn't suit her, she simply closed her eyes and smiled like a dissenting pastor when Darwin was mentioned.

He needed time. Anna would continue to ring. He looked at the clock. Quarter to one. Anna was at work.

There was a ping on Kathrine's telephone.

A text from the operator to say she had a voicemail. He picked Kathrine's phone out of the handbag and listened to it. Anna's familiar voice. He'd now heard it in so many variations.

'Hi, Mum, it's me. You rang. Sorry I was so short with you yesterday. He called. But the police have been to speak to him now. Hope he'll stop. Hope, hope, hope. I'll try again later. Lots of love.'

He called.

The way she said it. As if he were a madman who was

stalking her. As if she didn't want his attention and would rather he stayed away. As if he were the only one who was interested. Erik felt his face flush with anger. She was lying. Shamelessly and wilfully.

Another thought forced its way into his conscience. Anna hadn't mentioned Kathrine coming to see Erik, or asked how it went. In other words, Kathrine had been telling the truth when she said that she was there of her own accord.

Good, good, good, very good. Practical, if nothing else.

He went back to the messages. Opened the thread with Anna, read through what had been written. Short, witty messages: reminders, congratulations, questions about birthday presents, comments, exclamations. Nothing about him, nothing.

He went through Kathrine's other messages, the majority of them to and from old friends. About everything possible, but generally family and practical arrangements for cultural outings. Galleries, art centres, trips to the theatre and cinema. The longest thread, apart from the one with Anna, was with a someone called Ditte. Erik read all the messages and decided that she was a Danish culture vulture and Kathrine often went to the opera and the Kongelige

Teater in Copenhagen with her. He almost felt he knew the woman when the phone started to ring and vibrate again. The screen showed ANNA and Erik pressed FINISH CALL in sheer panic.

Not good. Or maybe it was good. Maybe it was perfect.

Anna was obviously used to getting hold of her mother without any difficulty whenever she wanted and would therefore carry on trying until Kathrine answered.

Erik needed time. Time and an alibi. He went into messages and wrote:

In Denmark with Ditte. Will call tomorrow.

He hesitated momentarily before pressing SEND. The text message winged its way. He was glad. For about half a second. Then it hit him that he had no idea who Ditte was or what she did. Maybe she was abroad or lying in a coma. He'd taken a chance and that was stupid. And what's more, you could trace telephones. He would have to get rid of it.

He put the phone down on the kitchen table and walked around the flat. He had to keep calm. Not give in to panic. He looked at Kathrine's lifeless body. She wasn't a big woman. Couldn't weigh much more than sixty kilos. He got her handbag and put it on the table, then went through the contents. A purse containing six hundred and forty kronor in cash, about twenty receipts and half a dozen loyalty cards from various retail chains. He put the cash and keys in his pocket and closed the handbag.

Sixty kilos was nothing. He'd filleted halibuts that weighed three times as much when he worked behind the fish counter. He looked at her, caught a whiff of urine and faeces. He rolled up his sleeves as far as he could, bent down and lifted her up. Her head flopped to one side and he dropped the body in a panic. Kathrine fell to the floor with a bump and he stared at her without breathing.

When he realised that she hadn't moved of her own voli-tion, he bent down and picked her up again. Her behind sagged and he had to fold her arms in a rocking position in order not to drop the body.

Her weight wasn't a problem. She was probably closer to fifty than sixty kilos. He put her down in the bath and washed his arms in the sink. Not because they were dirty, more for the sake of it. They felt unclean.

He inspected the floor. It was wet, but that was all, just urine. Any shit was in her pants. He dried the floor with kitchen roll.

He would have to get the body out of the flat as soon as possible, but without doing anything rash and desperate, or he risked being discovered. But how could he get a body out? He couldn't, certainly not in one piece.

Erik went back to the bathroom and studied her body. She was a fish, he'd just have to look at it like that.

Another ping on the mobile phone. He went over to the kitchen table and had a look. New message.

Copenhagen? Again. Have fun and say hello.

Erik replied:

Thank you. Will do.

Lots of women were terrified of becoming their mothers. Whether it was their voice, or movements, sagging skin, unwillingness to change or whatever. Few things seemed to scare middle-aged women more than any similarity with the source of their origins.

The opposite was true of Anna. She couldn't imagine a better fate. There were times when she wished she could be exactly like her mother. She even envied Kathrine her age.

Anna wanted to be at the stage in life where she no longer worried about silly things, where she felt strong enough to say what she thought and humble enough not to judge. Her mother never forgot that everyone had their story and all you had to do was scratch the surface with a nail.

Anna's mother was able to enjoy life, and she still wanted to improve herself.

Copenhagen, for example. Nine out ten people were forever banging on about how close to the continent they were, but how often did they actually cross the water? It wasn't exactly every day.

Anna lifted the receiver and called reception.

'You are letting calls through again, aren't you?'

'Yes, absolutely,' Renée assured her.

'It's just the phone's so quiet.'

'That's because no one has called.'

'Okay, that's good. Thanks.'

Anna picked up the printout with the incomprehensible soup of letters and made another attempt. This time the letters formed words that made sentences that combined made a largely understandable, if not particularly interesting, text.

*

Erik found a piece of paper and pen and sat down at the kitchen table. He tapped the bottom of the pen against his teeth. What did he need?

Meat cleaver

Alternatively, one of those square Asian knives that could be used for everything. Ikea probably had an adequate variation. His own bread knife certainly wouldn't do and the filleting knife was really only meant for skin and muscle. Good to open things up, but not much else.

Heavy-duty refuse sacks

How many? He went out and looked at Kathrine. Her legs were bent. He pushed them up even more. Folded the arms more. When rigor mortis set in it would be a lot harder. The torso was a problem. He could always divide it just below the ribs. And remove the head.

Two bin liners for the arms and legs. One for the pelvis and head, one for the upper torso. Four in all. And double, obviously, to avoid the risk of leakage. So eight. Plus a couple more for clothes and waste.

He sat down at the kitchen table again. What else? He couldn't carry out twenty-kilo rubbish bags, that would look suspicious.

Removal boxes

Naturally. Easy to carry, wouldn't attract attention. They were sold in packs of ten at Ikea.

Entrails. What about the contents of her insides? Another brainwave.

Blender

He could flush the mix down the toilet.

It would be important to close the rubbish sacks properly before he took them out, because of the smell. If he decided to dump them in the sea, he would have to open them again to put in some stones or something else suitably heavy before he pressed out as much air as possible and closed them again. In other words, he needed something that would allow him to open and close the bags safely.

Cable ties, clippers

What else? Of course.

Gloves, apron

Normal washing-up gloves would be fine. And it would be good if the apron was plastic so he could just wipe any mess off.

He folded the list and put it in his back pocket, felt his front pocket to see if the car keys were there, and left the flat.

38

Erik turned Kathrine's phone to silent, wiped it against his top and threw it into a rubbish bin outside Ikea. He left it on so that if it was traced it would show that she had left Erik's flat and gone to Väla. He got a trolley and raced through the prescribed consumption path that was the furniture giant's trademark.

He picked out the items he had on his list. He didn't manage to find a suitable apron, so he picked up an extra roll of refuse sacks instead. He could make his own apron. He put all the things in the car and drove home to the flat. He was lucky enough to get a parking place right outside the entrance. That certainly made things easier.

A quarter of an hour later he'd carried everything in and was dressed in a black rubbish bag, with holes for his arms and head. He had a T-shirt on underneath and yellow rubber gloves on his hands. A pair of scissors, the filleting knife and meat cleaver were lying on the toilet seat. He'd arranged the empty refuse sacks on the floor.

At one point he was close to giving up. A person wasn't a halibut. He had to cut, hack, prise and sweat to get the limbs off and when he split open her belly like a surgeon, the entrails spilled out. It smelt fucking awful and he had to run back and forth between the bathroom and the kitchen in order to cut and blend her innards into something that could be flushed down the toilet. And then there was a problem with the torso, which was too big to fit in a removal box, even without the head. He was forced to break and remove the pelvis.

It was five o'clock by the time he could finally take off the gloves and rinse the blood from his arms. He went to get a removal box and cursed Ikea several times before he managed to fold it together. He then made up a further three, before checking that it was dark outside. That suited him perfectly.

A whole afternoon without any reminders. Her relief edged into anxiety. Anna had thought the danger had passed a couple of times before. Erik Månsson was like two people. One who was friendly and charming, the other who was unreasonable and ruthless.

She hadn't been ambiguous. To the contrary, she had been too harsh and offended him. That was obviously it, otherwise he would never have reacted so aggressively.

She stood at the bus stop and looked around. She was keeping an eye out for his car, terrified that he would pop up at any moment.

Was he mentally ill? Genuinely? Psychopaths were said to be experts at reading people and winning their trust. Only to suddenly turn. Erik Månsson had a screw loose, there was no doubt about it. Whether he was actually dangerous as well remained to be seen. But it was unnerving enough to have him sneaking around in the bushes.

The video, oh my God, the video.

Immediately Anna was all hot and sweaty. How could she even doubt it? Erik Månsson was sick, completely mad. Or was it down to his age, something that his generation did? God knows, they seemed to document everything else in their lives and publish the most uninteresting thoughts for everyone's perusal.

She saw the bus approach in the distance, got out her

pass. The bus stopped, she got on and looked closely at every passenger as she made her way down the aisle. She sat right at the back, so she had an overview, didn't want to risk any nasty surprises.

Erik cleaned Kathrine's nails and scrubbed them with a brush. He had no scratch marks but she had tried. He rinsed every body part with the shower, then dried them carefully with a towel before putting them in double refuse sacks. He put the sacks into the removal boxes, rinsed out the bath and the sink and then took a quick shower himself.

How did you get rid of a body? Obviously, the best thing would be to dump the body parts with something heavy somewhere out to sea. But you needed a boat to do that and even if Erik had access to one, he couldn't load it up with removal boxes or heavy black rubbish bags without attracting attention. The coastline was watched. There were always people looking out at sea and keeping an eye on what was going on on the shoreline.

An alternative was to drive up to Kullaberg and throw the sacks over the cliffs under cover of darkness, but he guessed that it wouldn't take more than a couple of weeks before some diver would be splashed across a double spread in the local paper, telling the story of his macabre find.

Rubbish tip? No, they had cameras and checked everything that was driven in or out.

Was it even necessary to hide the body? The main thing was that he got rid of it without being caught.

He went out on to the landing and called the lift, carried the boxes out and went down.

'Oh, are you moving?'

A helpful neighbour held open the door.

'Just helping a friend with a few things.'

Erik carried the boxes out and stacked them in the car.

It was so easy when you didn't try to hide anything. It was stupid to make things more complicated. If everyone was screaming, you'd only hear the person who whispered. Erik could leave the boxes outside the Salvation Army in town and no one would notice. But perhaps that was being a bit foolhardy. It wouldn't be a bad thing if the body wasn't discovered for a few days.

He headed north, without knowing why. Somehow it felt most natural. Perhaps because she lived there. He saw that the façade of a building was being renovated on Margaretaplatsen. Big skips on the street. He got as far as Pålsjö before he turned around and drove back. He parked in front of a skip, opened the boot and took out the removal boxes. Then he lifted out the black refuse sacks and dumped them over the edge.

An elderly couple walked by. They looked at him and Erik gave them a friendly smile. They reciprocated, no doubt knowing themselves how hard it was to get rid of bulky waste. Erik put the removal boxes back in the car and drove away. He found a recycling station further south, tore the boxes to pieces and stuffed them into the green igloo marked 'Cardboard'.

When he got home, someone else had taken the perfect parking place. His bad luck never ran out.

39

'Where did you say your mother was?'

'Copenhagen. She was going to see Ditte.'

Anna's reply was mechanical. Her thoughts were elsewhere, in a happier space. As the bus had passed Erik's flat, she'd seen him filling the car with removal boxes. Whatever had the policeman said to him? It didn't matter. If it meant that Erik was leaving town, she was eternally grateful.

'Theeeeaaaatre?' Magnus exclaimed.

Anna shrugged.

'No idea.'

'Don't see what pleasure she gets out of it. Sitting there,

crammed in with four hundred dentists pretending to be intellectual.'

'Dentists?'

'The only profession that goes to the theatre.'

'I didn't know that.'

'There's a lot you don't know,' Magnus quipped, happily.

Then he became serious again.

'I don't get it. It's a dead art form. What's wrong with the cinema?'

'The one doesn't exclude the other, does it?'

Hedda laughed with delight in her room. She was skyping a friend with the door shut. Anna and Magnus looked at each other and smiled.

'At that age, even the theatre was fun,' Magnus said. 'It's behind you! No, it's not.'

'She's not that little any more.'

'Almost feels like it.'

They settled down in front of the television. Sat beside each other on the sofa and with relative indifference watched news reports on various ways to die. Magnus took Anna's hand. She glanced up at him and smiled before looking back at the telly and swallowing.

Hedda bounced out of her room, a happy reminder of how life had once been before it petrified into its current form.

'Mum, can I borrow your phone?'

'You've got your own.'

'But yours has got better games.'

Magnus looked at his wife with reproach.

'I think I might have left it at work,' she tried.

Hedda was already in her handbag.

'No, here it is.'

'Sweetheart, I don't like you going through my handbag.'

'You've got a missed call.'

Anna knew that it showed. She blushed and started to blink. She couldn't hide it, had never been able to. Even strangers could read her like an open book.

'It's a long number,' Hedda said.

Anna got up quickly from the sofa and went over to her daughter.

'Sweetie, can I . . . ?'

Hedda gave her the phone.

'It's a Danish number,' she said with relief, and wondered if it was unnatural to give Magnus that information.

'It's probably your mum calling from Ditte's,' he said, his eyes not leaving the screen.

'Maybe I should call back?'

And why on earth should she ask her husband's advice on something so trivial, which in fact had nothing to do with him?

'Weren't they going to go to the theatre?' Magnus asked.

'I don't know.'

'It's what they normally do,' Magnus said. 'Did she leave a message?'

'No.'

'Well then.'

To be so submissive, to consult her husband. It was so unlike Anna.

'Can I have the mobile?' Hedda asked, impatiently.

'Yes, yes, of course.'

Anna handed it to her.

'But only for a while.'

'Right.'

'After all, it's actually the magazine's phone.'

Hedda went back into her room and Anna had no choice other than to return to her husband on the sofa. She stared into thin air. The mobile was an undetonated bomb that threatened to blow her family to pieces at any moment.

'Why's it suddenly so important?' Magnus wondered.

'What?' Anne said, evasively.

'Your mobile.'

'Well, she changes all the settings and mucks about with it. I don't like it. And if it were to break . . .'

Magnus let out a weary sigh.

40

Erik slept well, despite having a sore back after all those hours stooped over the bath. When he woke up it was broad daylight outside. He stretched, blinked his way into the present, looked at the clock and realised that it was nearly lunchtime.

He tried to think logically, go through the remaining details. He would have to scrub the bathroom with chlorine, get rid of Kathrine's clothes and handbag, as well as the bloody towel that he'd used to dry the body parts with. None of it was such a big deal; in fact, compared to yesterday, they were relatively easy tasks.

He was assailed by a wave of emptiness, an overwhelming emotional understanding that there was no meaning to anything. He could barely move, he just lay there on the mattress and stared at the wall.

It wasn't the things he was forced to do under the rather unfortunate circumstances, they didn't matter. Kathrine had been a challenge he'd had to face, and he'd won. No, what made him almost stop breathing was the realisation that it didn't matter. The outcome of all his efforts would be as good as nothing. Kathrine's disappearance would, if anything, bring Magnus and Anna closer together. At least temporarily.

On the other hand, Erik was suddenly full of hope: it wasn't Kathrine who kept them together. The only thing that bound Anna to her boring husband was their daughter. Kathrine's disappearance might remind Anna of her own mortality, make her mature, in the sense that she would understand that life is short. Because it was. The days raced by at high speed and life wouldn't go on for ever. Anna couldn't keep lying to herself.

Erik got up from the mattress, felt much happier. He went over to the window and looked out to see what was going on down on the street. Not much. The moment rush hour was over, the traffic flow was so meagre that no more than four cars gathered at one time for the red light by Stadsteatern.

He might as well get started with what he still had to do. He went out into the bathroom, rinsed the clothes and towel clean of blood, wrung them out and put them into several plastic bags. He scrubbed the walls and sink, the toilet and floor. First with Ajax and a scrubbing brush, then again with chlorine. The bath sparkled white, except for a few chips in the enamel from the meat cleaver when he'd got the angle wrong.

Erik had a long, hot shower.

Who might know that Kathrine had come to see him? he asked himself. Not Anna, judging by the text message. Kathrine had looked him up on her own initiative, out of her concern for her daughter. When Erik asked her how she had got hold of the entry code, she said that a man had let her in, a man on his way out. Erik tried to visualise his neighbours. It took a few seconds before he realised that it probably wasn't one of his neighbours, but the policeman, that fat, stupid local guy who Anna had pumped full of lies, the pompous loser who'd had the cheek to try to frighten Erik in his own home.

That made things more complicated. But no more so than that he would have to be open and honest about Kathrine having come to see him. She had been there and then left, that's what he'd say. Which would be confirmed by the location of her mobile phone.

Erik got out of the shower, dried himself and dressed. He was on his way out when he caught sight of the bowls and the blender. He'd washed the parts carefully, but decided to bin them all the same. Maybe he was chicken.

He glanced quickly around his newly scrubbed flat, picked up the bags and went out.

41

Well rested, happy and ready for work. Almost a bit horny, now that she thought about it. Maybe Anna would surprise her husband this evening. He deserved it.

She had worked efficiently all morning, cleared all the things pending from her desk, written half a dozen photo captions for a feature that was set and ready, gone through all the mail in her in tray and booked two photo shoots.

Her phone rang and she lifted the receiver without a moment's hesitation.

'Anna.'

'Hello, it's Ditte.'

'Hi, Ditte. How are you? Has Mum left?'

'What do you mean?'

It took a while to sort things out. Kathrine hadn't been to visit Ditte. Nor had there been any agreement that she would.

'Where has she been then?' Anna wondered.

'Has she met a man?' Ditte asked, delighted.

'I don't think so. She would never have kept that secret.'

'Well, could you maybe ask her to phone me when she has the time?'

'Yes, of course. I will. Bye.'

Anna put down the receiver and stared straight ahead. Had her mother wanted to surprise Ditte with a spontaneous visit? Could something have happened to her on the way? She dialled her mother's number again. After the fourth ring, it switched to voicemail.

'Ditte called,' Anna said. 'Where are you? Has something happened? Please give me a ring.'

Trude saw the worry in her face.

'When did you last hear from her?'

'Yesterday,' Anna told her. 'She sent me a text to say she was going to visit a friend in Denmark. But she's not there and her friend says that they hadn't arranged anything.'

'Oops,' Sissela joined in and raised her eyebrows in the usual manner.

The most likely explanation was that Kathrine had met a man, which was what Ditte had suggested, but Anna didn't appreciate them questioning her disquiet. Especially not Sissela, who just wanted attention.

Anna rang the hospital in Helsingborg. No Kathrine Hansson had been admitted. The main hospital in Copenhagen gave the same answer. They were even kind enough to check the central register. No, no Swedish woman of that name had been admitted.

She got up and put on her coat.

'Maybe it's best if I pop over to her flat. Check that nothing's happened.'

'Take my car,' Trude said, and threw her the key.

Anna caught it.

'Thank you.'

Anna rang the bell and listened for any movement. She stood there with the key at the ready, but didn't want to just barge in. No steps to be heard on the other side, so she opened the door.

'Mum?'

She closed it behind her. The morning papers were lying on the floor.

Anna walked through the flat. The kitchen, bathroom, knocked tentatively on the closed bedroom door.

If her mother was lying in there with a man, it was only fair that she should give her a chance to say something first. Those self-chosen snatched moments, Anna thought to herself. As a teenager, lying there touching each other with the constant fear of being discovered by well-meaning but curious parents. Now her mother was in the same embarrassing situation. Anna could hear her own excuses already: *I was worried. You know that I don't begrudge you the company, I was just worried that something had happened because you weren't answering your phone . . .*

Maybe he was married. Which was why Kathrine didn't want to burden her daughter with her secret.

Anna opened the door to the bedroom and poked her head round. The bed was empty and tidily made. If her mother had met someone she was at his place. Anna got out her phone and tried again. And again the call went to voicemail after four rings. She couldn't face leaving another message.

She found a pen in the cupboard over the sink and used

one of the Asian takeaway menus that was attached to the fridge with a magnet.

Hi Mum, she wrote on the back, *where are you? Getting a bit worried. Please call me as soon as you see this. Kisses from Anna.*

She drove back to the office with a nagging doubt. She spoke to her mother almost every day. Why would she suddenly be so secretive?

42

They bloody well needed security on the northside with all those posh people. Kent only had to turn his back and they were out there filling the skip with their fucking furniture and stuff. He had a mind to haul out the sofa and desk and wooden chairs and bin liners and leave it all on the pavement. Because they'd certainly kick up a fuss then.

Why couldn't they hire a trailer and take their rubbish to the tip themselves? That's what they did on the southside. Big difference from the north. Weird bunch of people. Probably why they were so rich, never paid for anything themselves. Fucking tax dodgers, the lot of them.

He got out his mobile and phoned.

'Hiya, Kent here. Just wondered if you could maybe come and pick up the skip you delivered yesterday ... Yep, it's full already ... No, you can just dump it all in the incinerator ... And I'd like a new one, please. With security cameras and electric fencing. Not before tomorrow? Okey-dokes, at least I know. Thanks.'

A passer-by craned his neck to see if there was anything of interest in the skip. Kent glared at him and the young man scurried on.

Fuck, if they weren't putting their shit in, they were looking to see what they could take out.

Like rats they were, Kent mused, no better.

'Have you still not heard anything?'

Anna shook her head. Magnus pulled his chin in.

'Strange. And she said she was going to see Ditte?'

'Yes.'

'Could she be with anyone else?'

'No, I've phoned everyone.'

'Do you think something's happened?'

'I've called the hospitals. And the newspaper was on the floor, so she wasn't home last night.'

'Hmmm,' Magnus insinuated.

Anna half-smiled.

'I just don't understand why she'd keep it a secret.'

It was almost a pleasure to focus on the mystery. It was the first time in weeks she was on the same wavelength as her husband and could tell him what was on her mind.

'Has she been internet dating?' Magnus asked.

'Not that I know of . . .'

'But?'

'It wouldn't surprise me.'

'So long not as she's not met some nutter.'

Anna gave her husband an anxious look.

'Don't say that,' she said. 'Why would she meet anyone like that?'

Magnus shrugged.

'There's a lot of strange people out there, that's all.'

'Stop. Can't you see you're making me nervous?'

Anna turned away. Magnus reached out.

'I'm sorry.'

'What time is it?' Anna said, and looked at her watch. Quarter past five. 'I think I'm going to go to the police. Just to be sure. She's been gone more than twenty-four hours now.'

'Isn't that a bit extreme?'

'Maybe, but I don't care. You stay here until Hedda gets home.'

Karlsson lounged on his swivel chair and played with a ball-point pen. Had he made a mistake, big-hearted and generous as he was? It was certainly starting to look like it. The woman who had said she was being stalked by the young film enthusiast was back at the station with another problem. This time it was her mother who had disappeared.

Karlsson was beginning to get the picture: a lonely woman who needed attention. He would have her here constantly if he didn't say something sharpish.

'My mother . . .' Anna started.

'Your mother,' Karlsson repeated, and felt vaguely guilty when he thought of the young man he'd almost scared to death yesterday morning.

' . . . she's disappeared.'

'Disappeared,' Karlsson said, and comforted himself with the fact that a bloke who made his own porn on the sly was perhaps not someone you would call normal.

'She said that she was going to visit a friend in Denmark, but she never went.'

'Oh, so she didn't go, no.'

'No, and the newspaper was lying on the floor, so she obviously hadn't been home last night. And I've phoned round all the hospitals here and in Denmark.'

'There you go. And Bergman?'

Anna looked at him blankly.

'Your film director,' the detective inspector explained, and thought to himself that perhaps they were both mad.

Birds of a feather and peas in a pod and all that.

'I'm so grateful I haven't heard anything from him. But this is about my mother.'

'So you said.'

'She's not answering the phone.'

'Really?' Karlsson nodded.

'Mum always answers when I ring,' Anna insisted. 'And if she can't answer right away, she calls me back.'

'That kind of mother.'

Anna sent him a puzzled look.

'Do you think I'm making this up to get attention?'

Karlsson stopped playing with the pen, sat upright and grabbed hold of the edge of the desk. Without lifting his posterior, he pulled himself towards the desk.

He woke the computer to life and put on his glasses.

'Name, address and ID number,' he said.

Anna gave him the information and he typed them into the computer with his index fingers. Every tap on the keyboard followed by an inspection of the screen. It took a while, but he got there in the end.

'Is she senile?'

'Why would she be?'

'Lots of old people who disappear are senile.'

'My mother is clear as a bell. Have you not been listening? Something has happened. Could you perhaps try to locate her mobile phone?'

'Do you know how helpful it actually is trying to position a phone in a city?'

'No, how would I know that? And Helsingborg is hardly a city.'

'Whatever – it's no help at all. We get an angle from one of the masts, plus or minus thirty degrees, at a distance of up to two kilometres. So we're talking about quite a wedge of cake. Seventy-five per cent of all senile people are found within a radius of—'

'My mother is not senile.'

Karlsson wasn't listening.

'Everything outside that radius is called the Rest of the

World. We use an American system, MSO, management search system. We nearly always send the dogs in first. If that doesn't work, then we might do a group mailing to all the newspaper delivery folks, and security firms and other people who are out and about. In that way, we get help from the local community, you see. Positioning is just a waste of resources, really.'

43

'Is Granny missing?' Hedda asked.

She was standing by the sink, eating an orange.

'No, no, of course she's not,' Anna said, sending Magnus an irritated glance because he hadn't been able to keep his mouth shut, as they'd agreed. 'We just haven't heard from her. Obviously she's somewhere.'

'Why don't you check her phone?' Hedda suggested.

'She's not answering. I've phoned her several times.'

'On the computer, I mean. She's got one of those apps. If you lose your phone or it's stolen, you can just check on the computer where it is.'

'What are you talking about?'

Hedda groaned because her mother was so slow. She rinsed her hands, then went to get her computer. She typed in a website address, while Anna and Magnus looked on, impressed.

'What's her number?'

Anna rattled it off and Hedda's fingers danced over the keyboard.

'The password is you and me, Mum.'

'Does no one use Magnus?' Magnus bleated.

'Mine is "poo",' Anna informed them.

'Not good,' Hedda said. 'Loads of people have that.'

She pointed at the screen. A blue flashing bubble appeared on the map. Anna looked at Magnus.

'What on earth is she doing there?'

The mobile phone was somewhere outside Ikea at Väla shopping centre. It hadn't moved at all. The blue bubble was still in exactly the same position. Anna was holding the computer.

'It must be in one of the cars,' she said. 'Hedda, you stay here. If the bubble moves, let us know.'

Her daughter nodded obligingly.

Anna and Magnus got out of the car. They looked around uncertainly before starting to walk between the cars and peer in through the windows.

A father came out of Ikea. He was pushing an overfull trolley while his five-year-old son was eating a hotdog. The father stopped, let go of the shopping trolley and pulled a serviette out of his jacket pocket. He wet it with his tongue.

'Don't you feel sticky?' he said, in irritation. 'Come here, let me . . .'

He wiped around the boy's mouth.

'Please try to get it in your mouth, not just on your cheeks.'

He threw the serviette into a rubbish bin and carried on towards his car, loaded his purchases into the back and strapped his son into the back seat.

'Don't drop anything now.'

Anna turned back to her daughter with a questioning look as the car drove away. Anna shook her head. The blue bubble was still there.

'It has to be in one of the cars,' Magnus said. 'Where else could it be?'

The confidence with which he said it made Anna think laterally. If it wasn't in one of the cars, where could it be?

She went down on her hands and knees and peered under the cars. But all she saw was rubbish from a nearby hamburger chain. She got up again, looked slowly round as if she were a periscope.

She went over to the rubbish bin, lifted the lid and rummaged around in the discarded paper plates, paper cups and scrunched-up serviettes. The phone was lying at the bottom of it all.

'I've found it,' she cried, and held it up triumphantly.

They drove home via Ödåkra and Allerum. As the sky darkened, the headlights swept over forest and fields, avenues, houses and farms. In the passenger seat, a faint blue light shone from Kathrine's mobile phone. Anna scrolled through the list of missed calls. Most of them were from her, three from Ditte and one from another friend. The last dialled call was to Anna and she was also the recipient of the last text message.

'What was it doing in the bin?' Hedda asked.

Hedda's question made Anna's skin crawl.

'You steal a mobile because you want it,' her daughter continued. 'Why put it in the bin then?'

'Can you be quiet, sweetheart? I want to listen to Granny's voicemail.'

She heard her own voice, then Ditte's, then her own again, several times. No one else had left a message. Anna went back to the list of recently dialled numbers. The last two were to Anna's mobile and her direct line at work. The day before that, her mother had spoken to two Stockholm numbers that Anna didn't recognise, for three and nine minutes respectively.

'You'll have to contact the police,' Magnus said.

'Darling.'

She sent him a stern look.

Too late.

'What?' Hedda piped up from the back seat.

'Nothing, sweetheart.'

'Has something happened to Granny?'

'I don't think so, I'm sure there's an explanation.'

'Why are you going to talk to the police then?'

'Just to be on the safe side. Oh, is that the time? Straight to bed when we get home. Did you have anything to eat before we went out?'

'Yes.'

Hedda looked out of the window. Anna stretched back her hand and patted her on the knee.

'Clever of you to find Granny's phone.'

'It was you who found it.'

'Thanks to you. I had no idea there were apps like that. Hedda, are you crying?'

Anna looked up the Stockholm numbers on the computer. They were both at the same address in Huddinge. She went out into the garden to phone. The noise of the waves down in the sound was almost like traffic. Lars Johansson didn't answer and Barbro answered Major Erik Wellin's phone with the same name. She sounded quite old.

'Yes, hello, my name is Anna Stenberg. I'm sorry to be calling you so late, but it's important and I hope you can help.'

'I'm not going to buy anything.'

'And I'm not trying to sell you anything. I'm Kathrine Hansson's daughter.'

'Sorry, who?'

'Kathrine Hansson.'

'I'm afraid I don't know anyone by that name.'

Anna broke out into a sudden sweat. Was her mother having an affair with the major? And his wife had no idea? No, that would be some farce at the theatre.

'My mother has disappeared and I'm sitting here with her phone. Apparently she called this number on Monday and talked to someone for nine minutes, shortly after six in the evening.'

'I'm sorry?'

'Nine minutes is quite a long time. Might she have talked to ... anyone else?'

'No, I'm the only one on this number. My husband died a while ago. But wait a moment, now that you say that, someone did call to ask about Anneli, yes, that's right.'

'Anneli?'

'A neighbour. She's dead now. I didn't quite understand the connection, something to do with her son, I think.'

'Her son?'

Magnus opened the terrace door and looked out. Anna held up her hand to show she didn't want to be disturbed.

'Sorry, I'm not quite with you.'

'A big, grown man still living at home with his mother. Though, who knows, maybe he looked after her. Someone who commits suicide can hardly be of sound mind. The police asked lots of questions, they certainly did.'

'What was the son called?'

'Erik. Erik Månsson.'

Anna couldn't get out a word. Magnus took it to mean he could say something.

'Hedda wants you to come.'

'Was there anything else?'

'No, thank you,' Anna said and hung up.

She stayed standing where she was with the phone in her hand. Her mother had been making enquiries about Erik Månsson. And now she'd disappeared. And Erik Månsson had stopped terrorising her. It couldn't be a coincidence.

'Has anything happened?' Magnus asked, anxiously.

Anna looked at her husband.

'Darling, we have to talk.'

44

They had sat up the greater part of the night and not slept in the few hours that remained. Surprisingly little had been said, and yet there was nothing more to say. The atmosphere was oddly polite. No shouting or dramas, they were remarkably relaxed with each other.

Tiredness lulled them into a mental trance and as they drove to work they discovered a shared world that had always been there, which they'd never been aware of before: Bäckström's extension, the windswept tree by the stables, the newly painted line down the middle of the road that made it all look so clean.

'Thanks for the lift,' Anna said, when he dropped her off outside the police station.

When she leaned forwards to kiss him, he turned his face away.

'Are you sure you don't want me to come in?' he asked.

'Yes. But thanks.'

She didn't want him there. She had just told him the bare minimum. That they'd met at Mölle, ended up in bed together and now he was obsessed. Nothing about the video, no details and no comparisons. He had asked. After hours of silence side by side in the darkness of the bedroom, where every breath was registered, he had finally asked the question that was inevitable for men.

How was it then?

Said gruffly, almost in passing. Anna had sighed with a heavy conscience and said that it was just something stupid that had happened.

'Call as soon as you hear anything,' he said.

Anna went into the police station.

'Detective Inspector Karlsson,' she said to the woman in reception, who immediately lifted the phone and dialled a short number.

'Who can I say is here?'

'Anna Stenberg. I know where he sits.'

She marched towards the lift and the woman behind the desk leapt up.

'You can't just ...'

Detective Inspector Karlsson became quite agitated when Anna stepped into his office.

'I'm afraid I haven't got time.'

She put the mobile phone down on his desk.

'My mother's mobile phone,' she said. 'It was in a rubbish bin outside Ikea.'

'Well, there you go,' Karlsson answered, and made a mental note that he must have a serious word with the civilian employees at reception, tell them they couldn't just let any old eccentric in. 'And how did you find it?'

'My mother has an app that makes it possible to see where the phone is. My daughter checked on the computer.'

'How smart.'

'I checked the last numbers she'd called.'

Karlsson folded his hands on his belly and leaned back in the chair. It might be just as well to think of it as entertainment.

'One of the numbers was to a woman in Stockholm who

was a neighbour of Erik Månsson's mother. My mother talked to her.'

'Erik Månsson?' Karlsson said.

'Who made the video. You obviously managed to talk some sense into him.'

Karlsson nodded.

'Yes, yes,' he nodded. 'And so? Your mother talked to his mother?'

Karlsson was already finding it hard to follow. Strange how crazy people really believed their own stories. They lived in parallel worlds. For them it was real.

'No, my mother spoke to Erik's mother's neighbour. Erik's mother is dead, she committed suicide.'

'Aha, I see,' Karlsson said.

Anna glared at him in such a way that he straightened up.

'You think I'm nuts,' she said. 'You think I'm sitting here making it all up.'

Karlsson opened his hands, palms to the ceiling.

'I'm no psychologist.'

Anna leaned forwards and lowered her voice.

'Now you listen to me carefully and don't interrupt with any of your idiotic comments, which neither I nor anyone else is in the slightest bit interested in.'

Karlsson didn't dare say a thing. He sat in silence for some time after Anna had finished talking. It wasn't until she gave him a stern look that he pulled himself together, stretched and cleared the lump in his throat.

'This woman that both you and your mother spoke to,' he said, looking through his notes. 'She was a neighbour of Erik Månsson's mother?'

'Yes.'

'And how did you mother get in contact with her?'

'I have no idea. The only thing I know is that my mother is missing and that my mother loathes Väla shopping centre more than anything else in the world. She would never go there.'

Karlsson's breathing was weary and audible.

'Your mother,' he said, 'do you have any pictures of her?'

Anna got her mobile out of her bag, found a photograph and held the phone out over the desk. Karlsson put his glasses on, held the mobile up in front of him and studied the picture. Anna could almost swear that he was taken aback.

'What is it?' she said.

'Nothing,' Karlsson replied, handing back the phone. 'But tell me, in what way would this lad ... ?'

'Erik Månsson.'

'Quite. What makes you think he's got something to do with your mother's disappearance?'

Anna shook her head, exasperated.

'I don't know. My mother has disappeared and he's stopped calling and harassing me. It might be because you went to talk to him, but I've got a horrible feeling that there's a connection. Does that sound strange? Maybe it's just my imagination working overtime, I'm sorry.'

She looked at Karlsson with uncertainty and he shrugged.

'Do you think that Erik Månsson is dangerous?'

'I don't know,' she shook her head. 'I really don't know.'

'Was he violent towards you?'

'Violent? No, not physically.'

She looked down at the photograph of her mother. Karlsson stood up.

'Look, I'll take one of my colleagues and go round to see the troublemaker. But we mustn't think the worst. After all, your mother hasn't been missing more than . . . '

'Forty-eight hours,' Anna said. 'Nearly forty-eight hours.'

45

Karlsson tugged at the mint that he'd found nestling in his coat pocket. He'd bought a big bag on the Denmark ferry a couple of weeks ago, and this poor, lonely sweet must have fallen out and stayed there. Every day was full of small surprises.

'What do I think?' he said, and popped the mint in his mouth. 'I don't have a bloody clue, I only know that Anna's mum went in the entrance to Erik's stair as I went out. Thought she was quite a lady, full of energy and life.'

'Sixty-seven?'

'It's in the eyes. You don't necessarily have to hop into bed with everyone you meet.'

Karlsson was pleased with the way he'd formulated that, proof that he was on top of the impossible gender politics of the day. The lift stopped on the top floor and he and Gerda got out. Karlsson pressed the bell. Erik Månsson opened the door. When he saw Karlsson his shoulders sagged despondently.

'What is it now?'

Karlsson gave him a broad smile.

'Have you got a minute?'

'I haven't been anywhere near that crazy lady. Haven't phoned, sent a text message, nothing.'

'Take it easy, we know.'

'Her mother was here as well,' Erik said. 'Came just after you. Same thing. It's not me that's harassing her, it's her that slandering me. Totally absurd.'

'Can we come in?'

Erik held the door open reluctantly.

'This is my colleague, Gerdin.'

Gerda held out his hand.

'Are you moving?' he said, pointing at the removal boxes that were stacked against the wall.

'Seriously thinking about it,' Erik replied. 'It's not easy to be accepted in this town. You just get accused of one thing after the other.'

Karlsson looked at him.

'So Anna Stenberg's mother was here?' he said.

'Yes,' Erik nodded. 'She came just after you. Why?'

'No one's heard from her for a couple of days. What did she want?'

'Same crap. Ranted on about me leaving her daughter in peace.'

Erik took a deep, jagged breath.

'How can you even listen to her? Can't you see that I'm the victim here? Anna Stenberg is obsessed. I mean, honestly, why would I be interested in her? Yes, we had a night together at Mölle, a couple of afternoons here in the flat. Yes, it was stupid of me to film our afternoons together, but it wasn't that serious. And I've deleted the video.'

'Sorry, could I use your toilet?' Gerda asked.

Erik pointed him in the right direction, thankful for even the brief change of focus.

'How long was Anna's mother here?' Karlsson asked, forcing him back to the awkward situation.

'I don't know. Quarter of an hour, half an hour maybe?

Why? I tried to talk to her, she refused to listen. Just took her daughter's side.'

'Did things get heated?'

'Heated? No, I wouldn't say that. But it's not very nice when people come round and question you, first the police and then someone you've never met.'

'So you argued?' Karlsson prompted.

'I wouldn't say that. I think she was worried that I'd upload the video on to the internet or something like that. Which I would never do, by the way. The truth is that Anna wanted to spice up her dull suburban life with an affair and then tried to make herself even more interesting by pointing me out as a mad stalker. All I want is for you all to leave me alone.'

Karlsson nodded glibly, watching Erik with interest.

'She's making it up?' he suggested.

'She's twisting it, at least. I'm not the crazy one here.'

Gerda came out of the bathroom.

'Phew, that's a relief,' he said, and started to wander around the flat. 'Smelt of chlorine in there. Have you been bleaching clothes?'

'What? Oh yes, yes.'

Karlsson demanded his attention again.

'Did Kathrine say what she was going to do after she'd been here?'

'Why would she do that?'

'And you don't know how long she was here?'

'I've already said.'

'But if you were going to guess a bit closer, would you say fifteen or thirty minutes?'

'No idea. It might have been more.'

'An hour in fact?'

'I don't know, I tried to be helpful.'

'But it wasn't longer than an hour?'

'I shouldn't think so. Why?'

'Nice flat,' Gerda shouted, unnecessarily loudly, from over by the window, where he was standing admiring the view.

Erik turned towards him, took a breath as if to say something, but couldn't find the words.

'Might be interesting to compare it with the log on Kathrine's phone,' Karlsson continued.

'The log?'

'To check any calls she made or where the text messages were sent.'

'Why? Has she disappeared or something?'

Erik blinked and swallowed. Karlsson saw it quite clearly.

'I said that when we arrived,' he said, and smiled.

'I don't understand.'

'Why do you think we're here? We're trying to establish her movements before she disappeared. Strange isn't it, don't you think? That an older woman should just disappear.'

'Maybe she's gone somewhere.'

Karlsson nodded in agreement.

'Good thinking. Easy to imagine, given that Denmark's right across the water. She might be there.'

Erik shifted the weight on his feet.

'Someone called while she was here. She cut the call. Like it was someone she didn't want to talk to.'

Karlsson grinned at Erik. That was information he hadn't asked for. Erik felt uncertainty creep in.

'I mean, if she's disappeared. Maybe she felt threatened.'

Karlsson patted Erik hard on the cheek, as he had done the first time they met. Gerda snuck up behind them and held out his hand. Erik refused to take it.

'No?' Gerda said. 'Oh well, goodbye then.'

'That's fine,' Karlsson said. 'See you again.'

46

Bugger, fuck, shit ... and what's more, it was his own fault. *In Denmark*, he'd written in the text he'd sent from Kathrine's phone in the hope of buying himself some time and breathing space. *In*. They would immediately see that it had been sent from his address. Straight after an incoming call from her daughter had been cut off. They would know exactly what had happened. A child could work it out.

'Think,' he said out loud to himself and stamped his feet. 'What's done is done. Think.'

He wandered aimlessly around the flat. It didn't matter what they knew, he tried to convince himself, what was more interesting was what proof they had. They had no body, that was his salvation. As long as they didn't have Kathrine's body, they couldn't prove that she was dead.

So stupid, so rash and badly planned. So cocksure. He was an arrogant fucking twat.

They would come back, they'd come back with dogs and a forensics team, a whole bloody army. Was there anything left in the flat that was hers? Her scent, definitely. The dogs would pick that up. Could they smell if people were dead? He didn't dare search for information on the internet. Everything could be used against him. From now on he would have to be careful.

He who had been so pleased with himself when he'd realised what Kathrine had said, that a man had let her in the front door, and that it was probably the policeman. Erik had weighed every move and yet still had let himself down with one fucking preposition.

In. Why not *On the way to*?

But even if they'd understood, they would need more. A text message sent from a phone was hardly enough, not by a long shot.

You claim that my client forged a text message and sent it from the deceased's phone? Yet this message referred to information that he couldn't possibly know. How could my client know who Ditte was? Or that she lived in Denmark? You believe that my client thought fast enough to send this red herring? Laughter. My client is no fool, I would be the first to accept that, but that he should be so cunning.

The body. Everything depended on whether they found it or not. No matter what, they would come back with dogs as soon as they'd matched Kathrine's location with the message he had sent from her phone.

Erik had gone through her bag. Were his fingerprints still on it? No, he'd taken great care to wipe everything. And the bag hadn't been found yet, had it?

If the technicians found any splashes in the bathroom he could say that she'd used the toilet. How had her blood got there? How could he know? Maybe she cut herself on purpose to make it look suspicious. He didn't have a clue.

No, he was going to do as little as possible. That was important. Not to prepare his answers, but to improvise as needed. One thing at a time. And no thought of the consequences. Life was so contradictory, who could remember what they'd done the day before?

First and foremost, he needed time to himself. He had to clear his brain of anything that was still stuck there. The cloying and stabbing that never granted him peace. That left a bad taste in his mouth, an itch on his scalp and heat in his cheeks.

Erik gave the flat a final check, then went down to the car.

Once again he drove north, there was nothing in the other direction. Just Råå as a creative alternative for those who saw themselves as different and free-thinkers, shallow and vapid.

Erik passed the skip by Margaretaplatsen. He could see boards sticking up over the sides. Full to the brim, good. It would soon be collected and taken to the tip. And as soon as the contents of the skip were mixed with other rubbish no one would be able to separate it from the rest of the waste. The elderly couple who had seen him dump the four black refuse sacks could witness as much as they liked. And what was to say that the content of the bags would be discovered? Even if there was a hole in one of them, no one would react, given the stench at the tip, and in time they would be burned with all the other rubbish.

Erik put on the radio and turned up the volume. He sang at the top of his voice and out of tune, drumming the beat on the steering wheel. When he got up to Kullaberg, his ears were ringing. He got out and went over to the edge of the cliffs, filled his lungs with briny air and listened to the sound of the sea.

This was how it was meant to be, this was how it would be. If that sexed-up slut he'd fucked out of sympathy refused to let go.

He went back to the car, got out his ropes. He wanted to climb one last time.

47

Magnus phoned. And even though he mostly talked about Kathrine's disappearance, Anna could hear it in his voice, the injured martyr, the only faithful person in a world of cheats.

'Have you heard anything?' he asked.

'Nothing.'

'What did the police say?'

'I've just spoken to them. They've requested the phone log so they can see where she's been.'

'Good,' Magnus said.

'I don't know what to think,' Anna whispered, with a tremble in her voice.

'Maybe the phone wasn't working,' Magnus suggested. 'So she went to Väla to buy a new one and dumped the old one ...'

'... in a rubbish bin?' Anna snorted. 'She said that she was going to Ditte's. Why would she lie about that?'

Magnus breathed slowly.

'You said that she'd phoned the national registry.'

'Yes.'

'They have information about where people live, what their parents are called, if they're married. Maybe she's gone to search out the guy's father.'

Anna heard the pause. She couldn't work out whether her husband wanted to avoid the issue or draw attention to it.

'Or maybe someone nicked or found the phone,' he continued. 'And then saw that it had that search app on it and got rid of it as quickly as possible.'

'Magnus.'

'I'm trying to be constructive. We mustn't always think the worst, even though that might be harder from now on.'

'Darling, I'm so sorry. If there was anything I could do to ... Total madness, I don't know what got into me. It won't happen again. I promise.'

'Be careful what you promise.'

Anna said nothing.

'Well,' Magnus concluded, 'the main thing is that we find your mother. We can deal with the rest later.'

'I'll phone as soon as I hear anything.'

'Outgoing call to Anna's mobile, two seconds, Drottninggatan 11.47.'

'Two seconds?' Karlsson exclaimed, half-lying on his chair as normal, with his hands folded on his belly.

'The answerphone kicked in and she hung up,' Gerda explained, and carried on. 'Outgoing call to Anna's direct line at work, thirty-three seconds. Drottninggatan 11.48.'

'Thirty-three seconds? But Anna didn't talk to her mother, did she?'

'She was transferred to the main switchboard.'

'Okay,' Karlsson nodded to himself.

'Missed call from *Family Journal* 12.33, also received at Drottninggatan. Text message sent at 13.04: "In Denmark with Ditte, will call tomorrow". Sent from Drottninggatan. Text message received from Anna 13.07: "Copenhagen? Again? Have fun, say hello". Text message sent 13.10: "Thank you, will do".'

'All from Drottninggatan.'

'Yep. After that, the Danish friend tried to get hold of Kathrine through the afternoon and evening. As did the daughter, repeatedly. And the phone was lying in a rubbish bin outside Ikea the whole time. A wonder that the battery lasted as long as it did.'

'But Kathrine sent all the text messages from Erik Månsson's flat?' Karlsson asked.

Gerda nodded.

'After the thirty-three-second call, she didn't talk to anyone, only sent and received text messages.'

They sat in silence for a long time.

'Could Erik Månsson have sent the texts from Kathrine's phone?' Gerda asked, eventually.

'But he wouldn't know who Ditte was, would he?' Karlsson said, as he spun halfway round on his chair and looked out over the main road into Helsingborg from the north, and the local newspaper's building on the other side of the road that resembled a gull.

'Maybe he went through everything on Kathrine's mobile, found a long conversation and guessed that they were friends and that they usually met in Denmark,' Gerda said.

'Sounds a bit far-fetched,' Karlsson objected. 'Don't you think?'

'It fits timewise. Kathrine goes to Erik's flat, they have an argument about the dirty film, things get out of control.'

'And afterwards he sits down, cool as a cucumber, and answers a text message received on her mobile phone?' Karlsson was sceptical. 'Before going up to Väla and dumping the phone? No, no. And where's the body? What's he done with it?'

'It stank of chlorine,' Gerda said.

'Yes, yes, yes, I'm sure there's a natural explanation. Didn't he say he'd been bleaching clothes? Gerda, please, don't always think the worst of people. Just because he's a pervert and a pornographer doesn't mean to say he's a butcher.'

Little by little, Karlsson had slipped further down in his chair. His behind was now more or less hanging off the seat. He yawned indifferently and sat up.

'If the guy had done the dirty he would hardly have told us that Anna's mother had been there.'

Gerda shrugged.

'No,' Karlsson said, in a grown-up manner. 'The lady has slipped off with a man for a couple of days. She lost her mobile and so can't contact her daughter. Someone found the phone, picked it up, then regretted it and dumped in the nearest rubbish bin. Does he have a record?'

'I don't know. You were going to check.'

'Was I?' Karlsson retorted. 'It was you who was going to do that, we agreed.'

'I contacted the operator, you were going to look through the databases.'

Karlsson waved his hand in front of him before turning on the computer.

'Well, well, let's not get too hung up about that. Now, let's see what we've got.'

He typed in the information, called up a personal ID number which he then fed into a search of the police records. Erik Månsson was mentioned in a report about his mother's suicide. Karlsson skimmed quickly through the report and then suddenly froze.

'Come over here,' he said, without taking his eyes from the screen.

Gerda got up and walked round the desk.

'What?'

'Look,' he said, and pointed at a photograph. 'Erik's mother. Who hanged herself from the banister at home.'

'She looks just like . . .'

'Like Anna, precisely.'

Karlsson reached for the phone and rang the officer who had written the report.

'The son's name has popped up in connection with something else,' he said, once he'd explained who he was and why he had called.

He listened for a while.

'Yes, yes, absolutely,' he said, put the phone down and turned to Gerda. 'He's going to call back.'

They both stared at the phone until it finally started to ring.

'Karlsson.'

Five minutes later he finished the call. Gerda waited in anticipation. The single-syllable words that came from Karlsson's lips during the conversation bore witness to the fact that Stockholm Police had a story to tell.

'Oi, oi, oi,' Karlsson said, rubbing his nose.

Gerda was sitting on the edge of his chair.

'What?'

Karlsson pointed at the phone.

'Nice guy. Probably wasn't a Stockholmer.'

'What did he say?'

'That our friend the pornographer was a mother-fucker as well, if the rumours are true. He was also convinced that Erik murdered his mother. But it was impossible to prove.'

'Jesus.'

'Yep, that certainly changes things.'

'So, what are we going to do?'

Karlsson clasped his hands over his stomach and twiddled his thumbs while he thought.

'I think we'll get a little help from our four-legged friends.'

48

'I understand. No, I'll come. As soon as I can.'

When Anna put the phone down, she could feel Sissela and Trude's eyes on her.

'They're going to take the dogs in,' she said. 'I have to get something that smells of Mum.'

Anna collapsed on the floor, her hands shaking. The editorial team were quick on their feet. Sissela commandeered the rescue and ordered someone to fetch some water.

'Oh, love, don't think the worst. We don't know anything yet.'

Trude and Sissela helped her up on to the chair. The

water arrived and was handed to Sissela, who gave it to Anna. In the office, even compassion was hierarchical.

'I have to go,' Anna said, lowering the glass from her lips. 'I have to go to my mum's and get a top or a jacket or something.'

'I'll drive you,' Trude offered.

Anna reached over to put the glass down on her desk. Her arm wasn't long enough. A resourceful person from layout took the glass from her hand.

'I'm sorry,' Anna said, and laughed with embarrassment when she realised how much drama her collapse had caused.

Sissela put an arm round her.

'Please, don't be sorry. Don't worry. It doesn't necessarily mean anything. Just you wait, the police will find her.'

Anna got up, looked at the dozen or so concerned colleagues who had gathered round her.

'Thank you.'

Trude took her by the arm and Anna let herself be steered out to the car.

'The advertising guy at Mölle,' Anna said, as Trude pulled out into the traffic. 'We slept together.'

'I know,' Trude said.

Anna stared at her.

'I went to knock on his door,' Trude said. 'You weren't exactly being quiet. Made me quite envious. Just a good thing that Sissela wasn't on the same floor. You seemed to be enjoying yourself.'

'It's him,' Anna said, now looking straight ahead.

Trude didn't understand what she meant.

'Him what?'

'He's killed Mum.'

'What are you talking about?'

'We had sex together several times. In his flat. He made a video. I told Mum. I think she went there to talk to him. Mum thinks you can talk everyone round, she doesn't believe that anyone is evil.'

Anna turned towards Trude again.

'I know that it's him,' she said.

'Have you spoken to him?'

Anna wasn't listening.

'He stalked me. This will just go on and on. He won't stop. I've only told part of it to Magnus, not everything. If you saw the video ... I'm never like that with Magnus, nowhere near.'

Trude changed gear and then reached her arm out to Anna. She took hold of her hand.

'It might not be as bad as you think. Do you hear me?'

Erik drove back along the coast, he was in no rush. He made a point of following the gentle flow of traffic, slowing down for the speed bumps and flower boxes, keeping within the speed limit. Even though he didn't need to. Nor did he need to sit behind the wheel like some chauffeur, for that matter. Wrong from start to finish.

He took the road through the mock-timber idyll of Viken, drove through Domsten's sad streets slow as a Sunday driver on a rich man's safari, accelerated a touch in the forest up towards Kulla Gunnarstorp Castle before turning off by the old windmill on to the northern approach to Hittarp.

Erik Månsson wasn't just anybody. He couldn't be expected to play by the same rules as everyone else. What his mother had said was true. He was a pharaoh, a ruler destined for greater things. Not just to flog fish in a supermarket, not waste time with a bunch of old advertising has-beens who called themselves creatives. There was a meaning and a purpose. What he and his mother had had was neither sordid nor wrong. It was part of the plan, she had schooled him.

He made his way down to the water, parked by the sandbank and went for a walk. Along the water's edge through the sparse pine trees to the castle that reminded him of Manderley in Hitchcock's film *Rebecca*. That's where he should have lived, instead of being boxed in in a studio flat in the centre.

Erik went up the slope, wading through a thick blanket of beech leaves that hadn't yet started to decay. He entered the woods that were so full of promise, walked beneath the vault of tree tops that were hundreds of years old.

Kathrine made no difference. Whether she existed or not was of no significance. She was irrelevant to what happened next. Hedda was the one who was important. Without her, the husband would soon be ditched. And Erik wasn't guessing that, he knew. Fact.

Ten-year-old Hedda was the only reason that Anna stuck with her uninteresting husband. Without the girl, Anna would leave him.

Erik made his way back to the car, shivered off the raw air that had got in under his coat, and set off towards Laröd school.

Anna and Trude took a top and a coat from Kathrine's flat and then drove to the police station.

The woman in reception had been informed of Anna's imminent arrival and let them go up before she phoned to say they were there. Anna and Trude stepped out of the lift on the third floor and headed towards Karlsson's office. The door was open and voices could be heard inside. When Anna appeared in the doorway, they all fell silent. There was no doubt that they were discussing Kathrine's disappearance. Anna made her way into the room and handed the clothes to Karlsson.

'Thank you,' he said, and took them.

'Do you know any more?' Anna asked.

'Nothing substantial. We'll do a search with the dogs based on the last known positions of her mobile phone.'

'Väla?'

'I'll contact you as soon as I know anything new.'

Anna turned towards the other policemen in the room, her face crumpled. She had a thousand questions, but didn't know how to formulate a single one.

'I'll drive you home now,' Trude said, taking her by the arm.

Anna twisted herself free.

'Is it him?' she cried. 'Tell me if it's him. I thought it was over. When the bus went past the other day and I saw him loading removal boxes into his car. I was so glad, thought it was over. That you had frightened him off.'

She was shaking. Her face was trembling and her mouth twisted.

Trude put an arm round her.

'Come on, we're leaving,' she said. 'I'll take you home and stay with you until Magnus gets back.'

Anna nodded gratefully and let herself be led out.

Börje attached the skip to the hook and took out the remote control. He lifted it carefully so the contents wouldn't fall out. Kent stood beside him and watched.

'So,' he said, 'straight to the new incinerator in Filborna then?'

'Naah, it's not ready yet.'

'So on to the tip then?'

'Yep.'

The skip was manoeuvred carefully over towards the back of the flatbed truck. The angle revealed what was inside.

'When will we get a new one?' Kent asked.

'As soon as I've emptied this one. I'll be back within the hour.'

'Good.'

Börje looked at the waste.

'You sure it's all good for incineration? Those plastic bags, what's in them?'

'Haven't a fucking clue. Asbestos and plutonium,

probably. If it was only us who threw things in, then I wouldn't have to ring you all the time. Why? Does it really make any difference?'

Börje shrugged.

'Not really, but obviously it's not so good if it's impregnated wood or some other evil.'

'What do you want me to do? I haven't got time to go through all the crap that people dump in there. I'd put up a fence but there's no room.'

'No, no,' Börje placated him. 'Just saying.'

The skip lifted from the ground and lurched heavily. One of the refuse bags rolled down. Kent stepped forwards.

'Forget it,' Börje said. 'It's not a problem.'

'Might as well check.'

Kent took a knife out of the pocket on the side of his trousers, leaned over the side and made a slash. Something white, he couldn't make out what. He made another cut at a ninety-degree angle to the first. Still couldn't see. He put his fingers in and tugged at the plastic. Then he pulled out an arm, which he dropped as if it had burned him. He backed away instinctively, looked at his hands and swallowed hard.

'I think I have to wash my hands,' he said, and threw up on the asphalt.

49

Erik had parked out of sight of the school. To be on the safe side, he'd swung by the shop and bought an evening paper so that he looked preoccupied in the event that anyone reacted. He also kept his seatbelt on like a responsible man who was just about to turn the ignition key again and continue on his way.

He looked at the clock and then checked the photograph he'd taken of Hedda's timetable, which was attached to the family fridge with a magnet. Only a few minutes to go.

Then, as if by the touch of a wand, the place erupted with life and movement. Children on bikes and skateboards, bags and noise, hands in the air and shoving and laughter and the odd lonely child who walked with their head down.

He scanned them over the top of his newspaper, like some second-rate detective. He spotted her with a friend. Neither of them was a show-stopper, but they had each other. He waited until they were a suitable distance from the others, to avoid the risk of friends gathering round, and then drove up alongside the girls. He wound down the window on the passenger side and leaned over the seat.

'Hedda,' he said, appropriately strained. 'Do you recognise me? I came to test-drive your father's car and we took you to the stables.'

She lit up, almost proud of the attention in front of her friend.

'Your mother called. She's a bit caught up. I'm not sure how much she's said to you about your gran.'

'They don't know where she is,' Hedda replied.

'Exactly. Well, something has obviously come up and your mother called and asked me to collect you.'

He opened the door. Hedda hesitated.

'I'll take you to her,' Erik said.

'But I . . .'

'It's about your gran.'

Hedda looked at her friend.

'See you later then, okay?'

She got into the car.

'Put the seatbelt on, please. I don't want us to have any accidents.'

Hedda pulled on the seatbelt, happy and proud of the attention, but also the fact that she could sit in the front without having to ask.

'Has she come home?'

'Who?'

'Granny. Is she back in her flat?'

'I don't know. Have you got your mobile with you?'

'My mobile?'

'I haven't got your mother's number saved in mine.'

'I know it off by heart,' Hedda told him with pride. 'Zero, seven, three . . .'

'I don't have any battery left,' Erik interrupted, and held out his hand to Hedda. 'Can I borrow yours?'

She gave him her mobile.

'Thank you,' he said, and put it in his inner pocket.

Hedda looked at him.

'Aren't you going to phone?'

'Not while I'm driving. It's dangerous. And you don't want us to crash, do you?'

'No.'

Erik smiled and turned left on to the main road.

'Are we not going to Granny's?'

'We're going to Kullaberg. Have you been to Kullaberg?'

'Loads of times,' Hedda said, world-weary. 'Is Granny there?'

50

The police sniffer dog, Nalle, a sociable Labrador, picked up the scent of body fluids and a body in both the kitchen and bathroom.

'Are you absolutely certain?' Karlsson asked. 'The dog can smell it despite all the chlorine and other things?'

'The dog doesn't lie,' the handler said. 'Nalle is the best dog I've ever worked with.'

Karlsson sighed.

'Well, well, we'd better call forensics then.'

'And another dog,' the handler said. 'For the court.'

'Two independent dogs,' Karlsson said, and turned to

Gerda, who was standing out in the hall counting unmade removal boxes.

'Six,' he said. 'I think they're sold in packs of ten.'

'So four are missing?' Karlsson calculated. 'Do you think he carried her out in parts?'

Gerda shrugged. Karlsson went over to the window, folded his hands behind his back and looked out over the sound.

'Trouble and strife,' he said. 'I don't know what's wrong with people. Oi, oi, oi.'

His phone rang. He fished it out of his inner pocket and answered.

'Karlsson.'

He listened and mumbled short, single-syllable words to confirm that he was taking in all the information he was being given.

'We're on our way,' he said, and finished the conversation.

He turned back to Gerda.

'They've found her.'

'You'd thought of knocking on his door?' Anna asked. 'At Mölle, had you really?'

She was sitting at her own kitchen table. Trude had ushered her to a chair and was making some tea.

'Yes,' she said, as she put two mugs down on the table.

'But you're married.'

Anna stopped herself and sighed.

'But then, so am I.'

'You can't just sit in your chamber waiting,' Trude said. 'That way nothing ever happens. You weren't to know he was mad. You don't usually notice that sort of thing until it's too late.'

'It was the first time. And the last. Never again.'

'I wouldn't be so categorical. Imagine if he'd been normal. Judging by what I heard from the room, you were certainly enjoying yourselves. At that point, I mean.'

'Your husband,' Anna ventured. 'What does he say?'

'What he doesn't know won't harm him.'

'But that's terrible.'

'A terrible burden, you mean?' Trude said, and thought about it. 'Yes, sometimes. The rest of the time it's absolutely perfect. If it wasn't for my little adventures, I'd have left him years ago. I need to feel alive, can't bear all this sitting-on-the-sofa-watching-telly bliss. It's not enough.'

'But you want that as well?' Anna asked.

'Yes, of course. I love him more than anything else in the world. But it's not about that.'

'The attention?' Anna said.

'The sex,' Trude replied, and took a sip of tea. 'Sex is my hobby, all my dreams are erotic. As soon anyone says, "If you only had one month to live", I visualise myself surrounded by gigolos there to satisfy my every desire. Or I'm just afraid of getting old. I don't know, I'm not a psychologist.'

She looked at Anna.

'Attention,' she said, and snorted. 'I get enough of that from my husband. Why, do you think I'm bad?'

Anna shook her head.

'I've never thought that. I think you're fantastic. Perhaps a bit too beautiful. You frighten off men and have to make do with the dregs.'

'That's fine,' Trude said. 'That often makes them more skilled and grateful.'

'Do you know what my mother says?' Anna continued. 'She says that you should watch out for moralists as they're usually immoral.'

She laughed briefly and then looked around, distraught. She wanted to think about something else, not venture into deep waters, but fear is like a tide, it closes in relentlessly with every wave. She looked at the kitchen clock.

'I have to ring Hedda to see if she wants to eat here.'

*

'Has something happened to Granny?' Hedda asked.

Erik took his eyes off the road.

'I shouldn't think so,' he said. 'Why would something have happened to her?'

'Her mobile phone was in a rubbish bin at Väla and no one knows where she is.'

'Strange,' Erik agreed.

Hedda nodded.

'Can I have my phone back?'

'But I'm going to ring your mum.'

'You can borrow it again later.'

'You can't phone now,' Erik said.

'Why not?'

'Because we're talking. Don't you know it's rude to talk on the phone when you're with someone else? That would mean you don't like my company.'

He sent her a friendly, accusing look.

'Don't you like my company?'

'Yes.'

'Well, I don't think you do. Because if you did like my company, you wouldn't need to phone anyone. Who do you want to talk to so much?'

'Mum.'

'But we're going to meet your mum. I'm going to call her and she'll come to meet us.'

He nodded to himself and only after a while did he notice that Hedda's eyes were shiny.

'Do you want an ice cream?'

'It's cold.'

'You can still eat ice cream.'

'I want to see my mum.'

'I can turn in here and buy an ice cream. Would you like that?'

Hedda's phone started to ring. Erik took it out of his inner pocket and looked at the screen.

'I better take this,' he said. 'It's for me.'

He pressed to answer.

'Hello,' he said, smooth and relaxed.

There was silence at the other end.

Anna looked the screen. Had she dialled the wrong number? No.

'Hello?' she repeated, and felt her pulse racing.

'Hello, Anna.'

'Who am I talking to?'

She was clutching at straws.

'You know.'

'Where is Hedda? I want to talk to Hedda!'

'We're on an outing. I'm going to show her the cliffs we went to. You remember?'

Anna couldn't make a sound. Her voice box was simply not functioning.

'Hello?' Erik said.

'Listen to me,' Anna screamed. 'No matter what's happened, despite everything. Not Hedda, do you hear me? Not Hedda, for God's sake, not my daughter.'

She had got up from the chair and was leaning over the table in an awkward position. Trude looked at her aghast, her eyes open wide.

'You don't need to worry, we're having a nice time.'

'Erik, let me talk to my daughter. Give her the phone!'

'Say hello to Mummy.'

Anna heard her daughter's voice faintly in the background.

'I want to talk to her.'

'I know, come here,' Erik said. 'No blue lights. If I see any flashing lights I'll grab her hand and jump.'

He hung up.

'Hello? Erik!' Anna shouted.

She looked at the phone, pressed REDIAL.

'Yes?' he answered, unperturbed.

'Erik, listen to me.'

'No, you listen to me. Number one: don't call me, I'll call you. Keep the line open. If it's engaged, I'll take that to mean blue flashing lights. Now, do we understand each other?'

He hung up again.

'He's on his way to Kullaberg, he's going to throw her off the cliffs.'

Anna was already out in the hall and Trude rushed after her.

The tyres screeched as they drove off.

Anna's eyes fell on Trude's phone in the tray by the gearstick.

Karlsson and Gerda were more or less clear about the chain of events now. Everything fitted. The removal boxes that had been bought at Ikea, where Kathrine's phone had later been found. The strong smell in the flat of the chlorine that Erik had used in a futile attempt to clean up. The chips in the enamel on the bath.

People had started to gather on the pavement and ask questions and the traffic was snarling up due to the double-parked police cars.

'How do you tell people about something like this?' Karlsson wondered, hunching up in the increasing wind.

'You tell it like it is,' Gerda said. 'Anything else would just be worse.'

'Yes,' Karlsson gave in. 'I guess you're right.'

They were walking towards the car. Dusk was already starting to fall.

'Is the flat guarded?'

'Yes.'

'What have forensics found?'

'They've secured blood, hair and splinters of bone from the wastepipe. And something from the kitchen, not sure what it is. Hopefully just spillage from cooking.'

'We might as well go to her house.'

He rang directory enquiries and was given her home address. They went out to Laröd and rang on the bell. When no one opened, Karlsson got out his mobile phone. He took a deep breath to muster himself before dialling. Anna answered on the first ring.

'Yes?'

Karlsson regretted not having prepared what he was going to say.

'Um, hello,' he started, tentatively. 'It's Karlsson. From the police . . .'

'I can't talk.'

She hung up.

Strange. And given the circumstances, very strange indeed. What could be more important? Karlsson looked at his phone. Should he try again?

'She hung up,' he said to Gerda.

'What? Were you disconnected?'

'No, she hung up. She said she couldn't talk and hung up.'

'Strange.'

'Should I try again?'

'Yes.'

Just then, the screen on Karlsson's phone lit up with a number that was unknown to him. He pressed ANSWER.

'It's me,' Anna said, in a strained voice. 'I can't block my line.'

'Calm down. I can hardly make out what you're saying.'

'He's taken Hedda.'

'Who?'

'My daughter. Erik has got my daughter. He's on his way to Kullaberg. He said no blue lights. If he hears any sirens he'll throw her off the cliffs. Or if my phone's engaged.'

'Where are you?'

'On my way there. My colleague's driving. We're nearly at Höganäs. If he tries to call and my phone's engaged he'll assume I'm talking to the police.'

'Do you know where on Kullaberg?'

'He showed me some cliffs up by the lighthouse. We went there when we first met. It's right out on the edge, with only the sea below. No sirens. If he sees the police he'll throw her over the edge. Or if he hears a helicopter. He'll do it, I know he'll do it.'

'Wait, stay on the line.'

Karlsson ran to the car.

'Kullaberg,' he said. 'Now, like a bat out of hell.'

He put the phone to his ear again, pulled on the seatbelt with his free hand. He was forced to tense his body when Gerda put his foot to the floor and turned on the sirens.

'No noise,' Anna screamed.

'We'll turn it off in good time. We're in Laröd, in a civilian car. Take it easy. We'll soon be there. Talk to him. I have to go, we need to get people.'

'No police cars. Promise me, no blue lights.'

51

'Isn't it beautiful?'

Erik had stopped by the viewing point. Below them, Mölle lay sleeping under a damp, bluish-grey winter blanket, waiting for the short, intense flowering of summer. The wind was blowing in from the sea and dark was falling fast.

'I want to go home,' Hedda said in a thin, pleading voice. 'To my mum.'

'Your mum's coming here,' Erik said. 'She's on her way, she'll be here any minute now. I'm going to show you something I showed her a few weeks ago.'

He shifted into gear and wound his way up past the golf course towards the lighthouse.

'It's fantastic,' he said.

'I want to have my phone.'

'You'll get your phone. As soon as I've shown you the view.'

They came to the parking place up by the lighthouse. Erik opened the door and had to hold on to it so the wind wouldn't blow it wide open. Hedda stayed demonstratively where she was.

'I don't want to see the view,' she said.

Erik closed the door and smiled, in an attempt to recapture the trust between them.

'It's not dangerous,' he said.

Hedda was trembling with tears that were welling up inside. Erik gently stroked her cheek.

'Have you seen *Titanic*?'

Hedda looked at him.

'The film, I mean,' Erik explained.

Hedda nodded.

'You know the bit when they're standing right out on the prow, do you remember that?'

'Mm.'

'Well, it's like that. It won't take long. A minute or so, then you'll get your mobile phone back. Your mum loved it. You can stand there and scream into the wind. Everything you've got. It feels great afterwards, all the bad things are gone. Your mum wanted me to show you, she asked me to take you here. When she comes you can tell her that you've seen it already. It's not dangerous, I'll hold on to you.'

'Promise.'

Erik smiled at her, stroked her cheek once more.

'I promise,' he said, and opened the car door again.

'I repeat, no blue lights, no sirens.'

Karlsson was thrown against the window as Gerda took the roundabout by Viken at such speed that the car nearly lifted up on to two wheels.

'Silent after Krapperup,' Karlsson continued, when the car had stabilised again. 'He's threatening to throw the girl off the cliffs if he sees the police.'

'Silent after Krapperup,' the emergency switchboard repeated.

'And nothing in the air. I'll ring again.'

Karlsson finished the call and phoned Anna on the number he'd been given.

'Where are you?'

'Nearly there, we've passed the golf course,' she said. 'We'll be there any minute.'

'Don't challenge him. Talk to him, get him to relax.'

'I can see the car,' Anna screamed.

The wind kept blowing and increased in strength when it whipped up the cliff face. It tugged and pulled at their hair and clothes.

'Close your eyes,' Erik said, with a steady hold on Hedda's shoulders. 'Don't look. I'll hold you.'

He guided her in front of him.

'I'm scared.'

'You don't need to be. I'm here, I'll look after you. We'll do it together.'

He took her right to the edge.

'And now hold your arms out like in the film.'

'I don't want to.'

'Straight out, don't be silly.'

She obeyed reluctantly.

'Now you open your eyes,' Erik said.

Hedda had been looking the whole time. She was standing on the very edge of the cliff. It was already dark, but she could see the waves exploding on the rocks below and throwing cascades of white foam high into the air.

'I don't want to,' she said, and reversed back into Erik, who didn't budge.

'Can you feel the freedom?' he asked, and held her shoulders hard. 'It's only when you're here you really understand everything. How meaningless it all is. Our short lives. What we do and don't do. How we think, everything we learn, engage in, our feelings. God, our feelings. So petty and unimportant.'

Erik turned her round.

'We barely exist. The waves down there, they'll continue. Long after we're gone.'

'I don't want to be here.'

'Hedda. Look at me. See me.'

She stared at him, frightened.

'I'm talking, I've got something to say.'

'I don't want to.'

'You're an insignificant little girl. You listen to what I've got to say, do you understand?'

She nodded in terror. Erik smiled like a patient teacher who had given his student a talking to and was now generously going to take them back into the fold.

'Do you want your mobile phone back?'

'Yes.'

'Then I want you to scream.'

Hedda didn't understand.

'Turn round, look out to sea and scream. With all your might, as loud as you can. Scream as if your life depended on it.'

'I can't scream.'

'You can't scream?'

'No.'

'Your mum screamed. She screamed all the time. Here and other places.'

'I don't dare. Please, I don't want to. I want to go.'

'You can go. As soon as you've screamed, you can go. I'll give you back your mobile and we can go. How old are you?'

'What?'

'You've got an age. How old are you?'

Hedda didn't understand.

'Ten,' she said, hesitantly.

'Ten years old,' Erik repeated, and nodded. 'You're a child. An insignificant girl of ten. Do you know why I took you here?'

'I want to go home.'

'Do you understand why? Do you understand what it will cost, what I'm prepared to do? What a sacrifice I'm being forced to make?'

He hit her over the cheek. Hedda couldn't get a word out. The shock of his slap made her shake. Erik got down on his knees in front of her, stroked her skin.

'I didn't mean to. You ...'

He hugged her hard, pressed his cheek against her stomach, looked up with pleading eyes.

'Your mother fooled me, got me to believe. She used me. Do you know how it feels to be used? When someone pretends to be your friend, without being one? Imagine if you came home from school and your mum didn't ask how your day was. Instead she sighed as if she thought you were just a nuisance. Would you like that? I don't think you'd like that. That's what it's like for me. Just like that. Your mother sighs when she sees me. Not at first. At first she came to me. Came to my room at the hotel. To my flat in town. Everything was fine and she couldn't get enough. Then one day it all changed. And I hadn't done anything. She'd just got tired of me, regretted it.'

He laughed, suddenly aware that he was talking to a child.

'You don't know what I'm talking about, do you?'

'I don't want to be here, I want to go home.'

Erik took her hand, held it hard.

'Then your grandmother came. She wanted something as well. Everyone's the same, they all want something and I'm expected to give. To always be there, to never say no.'

Hedda was crying silently, gulping in the air.

'Always ready,' Erik continued, with empty eyes. 'Mum said I should be happy for what I've got. That there was nothing strange about it.'

He shook his head for himself, looked up at Hedda.

'I want you to jump with me.'

'No.'

'I want you to punish your mother for what she's done. Like I paid for my mother's sins, you're going to pay for hers.'

Hedda tried to pull back her hand. He was too strong. They both heard a noise and turned. The headlights from a car swept into the parking place and stopped with the beam pointing straight at them. The doors were thrown open.

'Hedda!'

Anna ran towards them. Hedda tried to wrench herself free, but Erik held on to her without any problem. He swung her round towards the cliff edge and turned to face Anna.

'One step closer and I'll let go.'

Anna stopped, held up her hands in a submissive gesture. The light from the car shone from behind her so she looked almost saintly.

'Please, Erik, listen to me.'

He shook his head, gave a nervous, accusing laugh.

'You sent your mum.'

'I didn't.'

'You sent your mum, she threatened me. Said that she knew and would tell. I tried to talk to her, really tried. She refused to listen.'

'Erik. No matter what's happened. Not Hedda. Do you understand what I'm saying? You can't, not a child.'

Erik swallowed nervously and shifted his feet. He dragged Hedda away from the edge and held her in front of him instead.

'Let her go,' Anna said, gently, and took a step towards them. 'Let her go.'

Erik didn't know how to get out of the situation.

'You fooled me,' he said in an accusing tone. 'You made me believe.'

'I'm so sorry for everything I've done. But for God's sake, not my daughter.'

She took another step towards them, and Erik backed away instinctively, his foot was over the edge and he almost stumbled before regaining his balance. Anna stood with out-stretched arms and an open mouth, frozen in terror. Erik pulled himself together first.

'Stop, or I'll jump. Back off.'

Anna took a step back, bumped into Trude. They both moved back. Anna still had her hands out in front of her in an attempt to calm the situation.

'Erik, I beg you. Let her go. She has nothing to do with us.'

He nodded frantically.

'Exactly,' he said. 'It's you and me. Why won't you see that? We're made for each other. You can't deny that it's us, you and me.'

Anna nodded.

'Let her go. I'll do whatever you want.'

'Your mum,' Erik said. 'She didn't understand, refused to see the obvious. She thought that we, you and me ... A work do, she said, made it ugly. I tried to get her to under-stand, she laughed. She forced me, she didn't give me any choice. But everything's good now.'

He nodded to himself several times.

'My mum, yours,' he said. 'It's the same for both of us, the same. We can start again, you and me.'

He was talking to himself, he wasn't looking at Anna any more, shaking his head uncontrollably.

'Erik, listen to me. Erik.'

He looked up. Anna swallowed.

'Let Hedda go. Then we can talk.'

Erik gave her a strange look, as if he'd just woken up and didn't understand what she was talking about.

'Let her go.'

Erik looked down at his arms and discovered Hedda in front of him. Almost surprised, he let go of the girl. Hedda pulled herself clear and ran towards Anna, throwing herself into her arms. Keeping their eyes fixed on Erik, Hedda and Anna backed away. Slowly to begin with, tentatively, but when there was enough distance, they turned and ran. Only when they reached the car did they see that Erik was still standing there holding his arms out towards them, in a theatrical parting.

'Mummy,' he cried, and fell to his knees.

He braced his hands on the ground and crawled towards the cliff. It looked like he was praying before he stood up and threw himself over the edge.

52

Erik fell silently to a certain death. The wind and the sea paid no heed and continued unchanging, with the same force. A tumult arrived with the police. First Karlsson and Gerda made a dramatic entrance with guns drawn. They shouted out questions and Trude answered as best she could. Anna sat on the ground, holding Hedda close. They were tightly wrapped in a human ball, isolated from their surroundings and impossible to reach.

Within the next quarter of an hour, several cars turned up with blaring sirens and flashing blue lights, despite orders to the contrary. The place was crawling with apparently disorganised police officers who ordered each other loudly to do various things. Torches danced in the dark. Some officers lay down on their stomachs and looked over the edge, searching for the body, but it was impossible see it amid all the white foam.

The sudden drama had woken the local youths with wheels and they formed a procession up to the cliffs. A young policeman who was so fresh that his uniform still smelt of naphthalene made sure that no one passed the blue and white plastic cordon that had been tied across the road between two trees. The curious onlookers had no choice but to document what was going on with their mobile phones from the parking place, as if they were at a gig.

Trude told them what she had seen. That Erik had been standing right out on the edge of the cliff with the girl, but then suddenly let her go and threw himself off. Karlsson and Gerda wandered to and fro, circling around Anna and Hedda, who were still sitting on the ground leaning against Trude's car. The policemen assured them that there was no rush, they would talk to Anna when she was ready.

Karlsson hunkered down.

'We've seized his computer,' he whispered. 'Just so you know.'

'My husband,' Anna said. 'I want to call my husband.'

Karlsson patted her on the shoulder and stood up.

'His computer?' Hedda said, and looked at her mother.

'It's nothing, sweetheart,' Anna answered, and pulled her close again.

A helicopter arrived just as they were being driven away, hovering over the cliffs with a searchlight and a rescue swimmer at the ready to fish out Erik's body. Trude had to leave her car there for investigation purposes and was given a lift home by a more-than-willing officer. The local youths snapped pictures like experienced paparazzi as the police car left the parking place.

Karlsson and Gerda drove Anna and Hedda to the hospital in Helsingborg, where Magnus was waiting. The police didn't need to speak to Hedda and Anna about this right now, the most important thing was that they all got some rest. They would, however, appreciate a few words with Magnus.

He followed them into an empty reception room.

'We've found Anna's mother,' Karlsson told him. 'But sadly, not alive.'

'Right,' Magnus said.

The policemen looked at each other.

'Do you understand what we're saying?' Karlsson asked.

Magnus nodded.

'We don't know the exact chain of events, but we know that Kathrine went to see Erik Månsson and that something went wrong.'

'I understand,' Magnus said, but his voice indicated the opposite.

'She's dead,' Karlsson stated.

Magnus nodded with dogged determination, repeated what they'd said and looked at Karlsson and Gerda. He started to blink and his face crumpled. Karlsson put his arms round him.

'Come here,' he said, and stroked Magnus comfortingly on the back.

They stood like that for about a minute before Magnus pushed Karlsson away. He smiled sheepishly, sniffed and cleared his throat.

'We haven't told Anna yet,' Gerda said. 'Perhaps we should wait?'

'What? Yes. No. I don't know. Is she here in the hospital?' Magnus stuttered. 'Kathrine, I mean. Is she here? Should I identify her?'

'Not just now.'

Magnus nodded.

'Do you want us to talk to Anna?' Karlsson asked. 'We've asked for a professional crisis management team. They'll be here shortly.'

Magnus pointed over his shoulder.

'My family, I thought that I, we ... I think I want, that we, I want to be with them.'

They went back. Anna and Hedda were sitting huddled together on the edge of a bed. Magnus went over and sat down on the other side of his daughter.

Anna looked at Karlsson and Gerda, who stood in the doorway.

'You've found her,' she said.

53

The crisis management team were no doubt skilled and well suited for their work, but Anna was not responsive. She didn't want sympathy, didn't want to open her heart to strangers, didn't want to give attention to anyone other than her husband and daughter, and wouldn't let outsiders intrude on their togetherness, albeit out of concern or kindness. In a few days, perhaps. Now, no.

The counsellors who had been called in knew when to back off. They left their contact details with Magnus and assured him that they were ready to come at any time of day or night. The period ahead would be intense, with sudden